LEPERD

LEPERD

Desperation ❧ Expectation ❧ Restoration

a novel by
Marc Thomas Eckel

TATE PUBLISHING
AND ENTERPRISES, LLC

Published by Tate Publishing & Enterprises, LLC
127 E. Trade Center Terrace | Mustang, Oklahoma 73064 USA
1.888.361.9473 | www.tatepublishing.com

Tate Publishing is committed to excellence in the publishing industry. The company reflects the philosophy established by the founders, based on Psalm 68:11,
"The Lord gave the word and great was the company of those who published it."

Book design copyright © 2013 by Tate Publishing, LLC. All rights reserved.
Cover design by Marc Thomas Eckel
Cover illustration by Terry Julien
Back cover photo by Adam Rollins
Author photo by Kari McGrath
Interior design by Jake Muelle

Published in the United States of America

ISBN: 978-1-62510-762-6
1. Fiction / General
2. Fiction / Christian / Historical
13.01.04

DEDICATION

This novel was inspired by a sermon preached on May 27, 2007, by Pastor Kondo Simfukwe at Christ's Covenant Church in Winona Lake, Indiana. The sermon "A Leper Like Me" started with the following prayer, which I have chosen to use as the dedication for this book:

> Our Lord, this is the cry of our hearts: that we'd be drawn from the perimeter of your presence—that place of mere speculation, intellectual calculations, discussions about you—and that we would be ushered into your very courts. It's you we want to see. It's you we want to encounter. We want to hear about you, Lord. But when it's all said and done, it's you we want to be near. And so we ask that by your Spirit, you would bring us into contact with the risen Savior, Jesus Christ. And do something in our hearts that doesn't allow us to settle for trickles of grace and mere glimpses on occasion. We want to be ushered into the courts of the King and live in proximity to him. Spirit of the Living God, we ask that you would help us to see Christ afresh. You'd help us to be enamored with him anew. Again, do that work in our hearts that won't let us settle for anything less. So draw near to us even as we draw near to you for your name's sake. Amen.

ACKNOWLEDGMENTS

Thank you to my Lord and Savior, my Redeemer—Jesus Christ. As always, without you, there would be no story to tell. Thank you for healing spiritual lepers like me and for giving the creativity to tell this story. May you use this project to reveal to many their need for the healing of spiritual leprosy—and may you get all the glory!

Special thanks to Kondo Simfukwe for your wisdom of the Scriptures. Thanks for a great sermon that initially inspired the writing of this book. I am thankful for your consultation on this project.

Special thanks to Mark Hall for your friendship and for inviting me to come on the ride of my life! I always enjoy doing ministry with you, my friend. May God continue to grant you favor as you cast all your crowns at the feet of Jesus.

And to the rest of the Crowns: Hector Cervantes, Juan DeVevo, Melodee DeVevo, Megan Garrett, Chris Huffman, and Andy Williams, "the Bald Wonder." Thanks for allowing me to throw paint around your stage and for letting me become a part of what you do. What an amazing experience! I cannot thank you enough, my friends.

Thanks to my wife, Juli, and our sons, Beau and Tyler, who sacrificed so much and allowed me to go out on the road during the tour. Your constant support and encouragement amazes me. You are such a vital part of our ministry. I love you so much.

Thanks to Larry DeVincent and Michael Boze for your part in making this story come to life.

Thanks to those with whom I shared a dressing room with on tour: John Waller, Chris Forslund, and Bobby McGraw. Especially to John, thank you for being the man of God that you are and for your wisdom and constant encouragement in life and in the ministry. May God continue to bless you as you minister to the "House of God." My friend, you are a blessing for life!

Thanks to all the members of *The Altar and the Door Tour* family:

1. Casting Crowns and family: Mark and Melanie Hall, John Michael Hall, Reagan Hall, Zoe Hall, Hector and Christy Cervantes, Juan and Melodee DeVevo, Jesse DeVevo, Megan and Ryan Garrett, Lillie Garrett, Chris and Amanda Huffman, Bailey Huffman, Tom and Gail Lynn, Andy "the Bald Wonder" and Kelly Williams, Aden Williams, Mary Catherine Williams, Cindy and Bubba Bryant, and Rebekah Allen
2. Leeland and family: Leeland and Mandy Mooring, Jack and Whitney Mooring, Matt and Erin Campbell, Jake and Aprelle Holtz, Mike and Hannah Smith, Daryl LeCompte, Marcus and Meghan Gibson, Todd and Cyndy Mooring, Shelly Mooring and Rachel Woodward.
3. John Waller band and family: John and Josee Waller, Baylee Waller, Hadlee Waller, Sophee Waller, Chris and Angie Forslund, and John Forslund
4. Casting Crowns crew: Denny Keitzman, Valdy and Fran Borchgrevink, Eugene Brown, Jesse Chastain, Bill Compton, Jeff Culmer, Jack Cummings, Carl Deese, Ben Darby, Susan Dose, Dale Dudley, Chris Farnsworth, Michael France, David Harrison, Carter Hassebroek, Charlie Howell, Darren Hughes, Sarah Hughes, Curly Jones, Chris "Snooch" Lighthall, Tim Lighthall (my main man and the official tour crowd "enthusi-izer"), David Longobardo, Dale Manning, Randy Meyer, Josh Mockerman, Jason Morales, Bob Morton, Adam Rollins, John Sapp, Kenny Sellers, Harry Shaub, Corey Smith, Kristi Vanoy, Shane Waldsmith, and Greg Yeager

5. Mezz Merch: Ed Bunton, Chris Byers, Scott Davidson, Brett Ferencz, Zach Harrison, Collin Peterson, and Walt Smith
6. World Vision: Jeffrey Barfield, Chris Henning, Scott Phillips, and Kevin Stevens
7. Global Youth Ministry: Bobby McGraw and Kristy Reed
8. Aquasis LIFE H2O: Chris Dunn, Andres Ruiz, and Phil Young
9. Proper Management: Norman Miller, Mike Jay, and Jill Hickman
10. 33 Miles: Jason Barton, Chris Lockwood, and Collin Stoddard

And to all the promoters, behind-the-scenes volunteers, caterers and food service personnel, World Vision volunteers, runners and friends we met along the way—thank you.

Thank you to everyone at Tate Publishing who worked on the production of this book.

FOREWORD

During the fall of 2007 through the spring of 2008, our friend Marc Eckel joined us on tour to perform the painting presentation *Truth* during the songs "The Voice of Truth" and "The Word Is Alive." While on tour, Marc worked on a book project that you now hold in your hands. It is just another creative way Marc has found to share the gospel—the good news—of Jesus Christ. In fact, our presentation of the gospel, which I shared from the stage during all the concerts on *The Altar and the Door Tour*, has been incorporated in this book.

Leperd is based on three verses in Luke 5. This book is a fictional account of a man we know little about. In fact, the biblical text doesn't even give us his name. All we really know is that he was in need. He was desperate. He was helpless to find fulfillment and restoration through his own efforts. In distress and anguish, he broke all cultural norms to enter the city to see the Master—an unthinkable act. When there was nowhere else to turn, his unclean journey culminated in peace, restoration, reconciliation, and salvation at the feet of Jesus.

It is my prayer that you would be drawn closer to Jesus through this tale of one leper. May you rejoice in the joy of your salvation, or perhaps, for the first time, may you see your need for forgiveness and healing for your soul at the feet of the Savior—the only place where cleansing for the "spiritual leper" can be found.

Enjoy this book that proclaims the good news, the life-altering news of the love of our Lord Jesus Christ!

Until the whole world hears,
Mark Hall
Casting Crowns

While Jesus was in one of the towns, a man came along who was covered with leprosy. When he saw Jesus, he fell with his face to the ground and begged him, "Lord, if you are willing, you can make me clean." Jesus reached out his hand and touched the man. "I am willing," he said. "Be clean!" And immediately the leprosy left him. Then Jesus ordered him, "Don't tell anyone, but go, show yourself to the priest and offer the sacrifices that Moses commanded for your cleansing, as a testimony to them."

—*Luke 5:12–14*, NIV

—— INTRODUCTION ——

As a Christian performance artist with Splat Experience, I was given the great privilege and honor to perform during Casting Crowns' *The Altar and the Door Tour*. I performed our *Truth* painting on stage with the band during the songs "The Voice of Truth" and "The Word Is Alive" in eighty-two cities across the United Sates during the fall of 2007 and the spring of 2008. This novel was written during that tour on the tour bus, in dressing rooms, in basketball stadiums, in hockey arenas, in airports, in hotel rooms, and during off tour breaks at home in Claypool, Indiana. This novel, originally completed in 2008, was expanded and revised in 2010–2011.

Congratulations to Casting Crowns for garnering an American Music Award and three Dove Awards during *The Altar and the Door Tour*: Group of the Year, Album of the Year (*The Altar and the Door*), and Song of the Year ("East to West").

CHAPTER 1

The early-morning sun glistened in the city of Tiberias, on the western coast of the Sea of Galilee. As I looked around, the courtyard vendors were setting up their carts for a new day. How I especially loved the fresh fruits and the flowers. They symbolized the vibrancy of life, which brought joy to my spirit. I looked forward to another day to see what God had in store, and I was willing to be used, whatever that entailed. I longed for another opportunity to reach out to a hurting soul with hope and peace as I started to pray, "Lord, use me this day to help someone in need. Allow me to bring hope to the hopeless as you brought hope to me."

As I finished my prayer, I noticed a white butterfly fluttering my way. I raised my hand as it came near. It softly landed on my outstretched finger. It made me smile as I thought, *Oh, the faithfulness of God.* I reflected on another day when a butterfly fluttered by. "Sweet release!" I exclaimed with a chuckle.

A commotion behind me interrupted this delightful moment. The butterfly flew away as I turned around, facing the city gate, where I saw a man stumble to his knees. A loud cry of anguish accompanied his fall, disrupting the morning calm. I could tell from the expression on this man's face that his vexation came from inner turmoil—something more than a physical ailment. He fought the urge to remain in the dirt, climbing back to his feet. With each belabored step, he panted like a thirsty dog.

Though this man's struggle brought sadness to my heart, I also felt an overwhelming joy, realizing how suddenly my prayer had been answered as this pitiful sight unfolded before my eyes. I did not recognize this man who grimaced with every step. I recognized his desperation, and my willingness to be of help had never been greater. I clenched my cane tightly with determination as I headed toward him.

The weary traveler stopped as he looked up, focusing on the city before him. He had finally completed this segment of his long journey. Tiberias, "the City of Water," must have been a welcome respite for a man so parched. How fitting that this one who appeared so low would arrive at the lowest city in Israel, nearly six hundred feet below sea level. He barely noticed the peaceful, picturesque view that had been before him, rarely looking upward. Even the majestic, snowcapped peak of Mount Hermon to the north failed to hold his attention.

Afar off, he saw the outline of the temple. A series of gold spikes adorned the pinnacle, and a band of gold leaf surrounded the large, white block building in grand ornamentation. Many white columns, embellished with gold Corinthian caps, stood majestically among ferns leading to the temple steps. Just beyond these steps were two, large golden ornamental doors: the entrance to the temple. With confidence, he pushed on with determination toward those steps and those doors; then surely some measure of hope might be found.

His pace slowed as he looked ahead. With each belabored step, he drew nearer his destination. In fact, the temple steps were nearly in sight. They were so close yet so far away. Nearing total exhaustion, each difficult step stole more of the little energy he had left as he fell face-first down to the ground. As much as he wanted to, he could not take one more step. He had to rest, just for a moment.

Between his sobs, I heard him cried out, "What more can I do? Who can possibly help me? Who can understand all I've been through? Will my search for assistance end in vain? Please, won't someone help me? Please!"

I watched as he wallowed in self-pity, as did many others who stepped back. Alone, I decided to show compassion for this troubled soul. I approached him quietly and bent down beside him. I placed a strong hand upon his shoulder and grasped him firmly.

He cowered as he looked downward, throwing both arms over his head, afraid to face whoever might be touching him. Unintentionally, I had startled him.

"Who's there? Who are you? What do you want from me?" he asked nervously as his voice quivered. Cowardly he slowly lowered his arms and slowly raised his head, peering toward me.

"I mean you no harm," I said with reassurance. "I'm here to help."

He wiped his eyes with the sleeve of his cloak, attempting to focus on me through his tears. Obviously he had expected someone who might attack him, though he found a simple old man who posed no threat at all.

He exhaled with relief, wiping the dirt from his brow. He took a few deep breaths before looking directly into my eyes. "You have a strong, firm grip for an old man."

I chuckled as he had anticipated someone fierce, someone that commanded fear. He expected a person who might certainly bring bodily harm to him momentarily. I didn't understand who he thought I might have been, but I hoped to find out. He surely found my appearance unalarming. I had a full head of short, white hair, and my light-bronze skin had become slightly weathered, though incredibly smooth. It often made me laugh when my wife told me how she felt envious when she looked at my skin. She also said I had a face that looked as if a master artisan had sculpted it. You might say that she found me to be handsome. If this were indeed true, it could only be credited to God's hand of favor.

"Working many years with my hands has given me a strong grip, I suppose." The stranger sat still for a moment as I lessened my hold on him. With a gentle but powerful voice, I asked, "Can I help you?"

After he rubbed his eyes again, he looked back into my face. When he peered into my eyes, he became still. His whole demeanor changed as an unfamiliar calmness came over him. His grief halted momentarily for the first time since I noticed him faltering through the city gates. He looked hopeful, expectant. Silently, to myself, I prayed once more, *Lord, allow me to bring hope to the hopeless.*

He raised his eyebrows with a timid eagerness. "Who are you? Are you one of the temple priests? Are you here to help me? Can you help me?"

He looked into my eyes with such hope. How he longed for help!

Before I could answer, he elaborated, "I'm heading to the temple. That's where I'm heading. I'm desperate and didn't know where else to turn. I thought I might find someone there who could lead me to a place of peace—a place of rest for my tormented soul. I longed to find someone there who can help me. I must reach the temple!" He spoke in a hurried voice, with a slight notion of panic.

As he stared at me intently, I knelt down before him, just a simple old man with a cane. I did not look anything like a priest— no fancy robes or headpiece. Perhaps, my earnest willingness to help a downcast stranger could not be understood.

He continued his thought as he muttered, "And if no man can help me there, perhaps God will." Hopefulness left his face. I heard an apathetic tone as if he longed for something so far from reach. I could immediately tell he had decided to bypass my offer for assistance. He reaffirmed my suspicion as he continued, "Please, move aside, old man. I must go to the temple."

Once more, I firmly gripped his shoulder. He stopped, feeling the strength in my hand again. "I am not a priest. I'm just a minister and servant of the Lord. But I will help in any way that I can. I am willing."

"But I need a priest. What could you do for me? You're just an old man. I don't even know who you are. And you could never understand all I have been through. Just look at you. Have you ever faced any kind of adversity? There's not a scar or any kind of indication that you've ever faced the trials that ravage my soul. How could *you* help *me*?" His eyes were filled with despair as the optimism he displayed just moments earlier had completely vanished like a vapor. With determination, he resolved to move ahead without me. I had to stop him.

"Please don't go quite yet. You can call me Simon," I said with a smile. "What is your name, my friend?"

Reluctantly he responded, "My name is Archippus."

"I can see you are not from Tiberias. Where did you start your long journey?"

"Our caravan left about a week ago, from Cairo."

"Oh, you are from the land of the pharaohs? We have been told much about the pharaohs of Egypt and of the mighty pyramids. You are indeed quite a way from home. Tell me, what brings you to our city?"

Archippus gave me another look, which again expressed his disinterest in me.

"Would you like to tell me what burdens you?"

As a result of my prayer, I believed God had sent this traveler to me so I could be of assistance. In my opinion, to let him move on without offering help would be irresponsible, bordering on disobedience.

"I may appear to be just a foolish old man with nothing but time to squander. But you just might be surprised at my insight. You may not believe it, but I too have lived through difficult days. Though you may not see them, I have scars from my past that bear witness to my own trials and tribulations. Many, I trust, you will never have to experience. I just might be able to offer you the help you seek."

Archippus looked at me sternly. "But you are not a priest. What do you know?"

"Well, young man, I've known many priests from this very temple. Some, I am sure, may be helpful in your quest. And, yes, some are indeed righteous men of God. But I have heard that some are simply evil men in long robes. How will you distinguish between the two?"

Archippus looked instantly bewildered. "What are you saying? How could that be? Are you suggesting some priests are evil? Men of God who are agents of the devil?" Even the consideration of such a statement presented a strange paradox indeed!

"You need to find someone you can trust. Someone who can lead you in the right direction."

"And you are that someone, old man? Are you some kind of wise old sage?"

I couldn't help but smile. "I am just a minister and servant of the Lord. If you would allow me, I would be more than delighted to offer my help."

Archippus pushed away from me as the tone in his voice turned toward irritated hesitation. "But how can *you* help *me*? How could *you* understand what *I've* gone through? I've lost *everything*! Do you know what that feels like? How could *you* know how *that* feels? A man of your stature and position could never—"

"Archippus, tell me what burdens you," I interrupted in a calm voice. "Then we'll see if I can be of any help. If I cannot be of assistance, I will personally take you to the temple and introduce you to one of the priests." I made an honest proposal. I waited for his response. After a few moments, I added, "Let me help you. I am willing."

Archippus reluctantly consented to my offer. At this moment, as he sat in the dirt, tired and distraught, where else could he turn? And if I could not help him, he could surely expect me to keep my promise, which would lead him to a temple priest. What did he have to lose?

I helped Archippus stand to his feet. He stumbled as he took his first few steps.

"You are still weak. Here, take my cane."

"No, thank you, old man," he insisted. "I can make it on my own."

"None of us can make it on our own. We all need each other's help."

Archippus looked at me with frustration. "Are you a philosopher now?"

I chuckled softly. "Let's walk to the temple. On the way you can tell me what you've experienced in the past few days. Tell me what troubles you."

I looked toward one of the flower carts where I saw a pretty young girl. I called out to her, "Zoe, please fetch me a basin of water from the well. And also, bring me a towel. We will be on the temple steps."

She smiled back and then headed off joyfully.

"Now tell me, what concerns you?"

I listened intently as Archippus started relaying his story.

I joined a group of men who were to accompany a caravan of goods, a common assignment. We started in Egypt as we set our sights toward Damascus, the capital of Syria, and a major cultural and religious center of the Levant, the crossroads of western Asia. We each had our own horse, except for two men, Helam and Jecoliah. They each held the reins of two horses that pulled their respective carts, filled with our cargo and provisions. Alexander, who had been assigned to lead this caravan, would ride up front on a white horse, symbolic of his dominant position among us.

Although he had been a friend of my father, he never thought very highly of me. He considered me to be more like my fragile mother than my brave father. His constant demeaning remarks emphasized the fact that he disliked me and disapproved of my assignment on his detail.

"Archippus, why aren't you on your horse? Let's go! Now!" he impatiently yelled toward me, singling me out, inferring a lack of readiness on my part. He sought to plant a discouraging seed in everyone's mind so they understood my inferiority, as well as his superiority. He looked at me with disparagement as he walked away toward his horse.

My friend Stephanus simply said, "Do what he says and fall in line. Don't give him any reason to mistreat you. Though it would have been a better argument if he had been in his own saddle, everyone understands what he is doing." Stephanus hadn't mounted up yet either. He eluded rebuke as he had somehow earned Alexander's favor, receiving the treatment a son might expect.

I mounted my horse and rode up to the wagons as several finished securing our cargo—the finest linen Egypt had to offer. Soon we were ready to begin our journey.

"Do you understand what we have here?" Alexander asked me as if talking to someone totally unaware of his surroundings. Before I could answer, he continued with a haughty speech, which had become all too common to anyone who knew him. "Today, we carry the cloth of the gods: the very same linen the pharaohs of Egypt used for burial. These self-exalted men rest as their souls enter the afterlife while their bodies start to decay into dust. This fine linen, *Linum usitatissimum*, is the most expensive fabric the world has ever known! And we are its guardian!"

He spoke mockingly as if he had to reinforce our cargo's worth. We all knew what our cargo consisted of. We were all quite aware of the valuable treasure we were carrying.

He started moving around the wagons as he continued his rant. "The rich love this fabric's exceptional coolness and freshness during the hot days of summer. Quite a useful commodity indeed." He paused from his glorious statement as he chuckled. "Rich fools. They only think of themselves and the folly of their own personal comfort! I can think of much better uses for this cargo than allowing selfish, self-indulgent wealthy snobs to rot in it."

"Be careful what you say, Alexander, and to whom you say it," Olympas remarked sternly as he walked up behind him. Alexander looked over his shoulder. He didn't have much respect for Olympas either.

"This is my detail. Everything is under control."

The tension between the two could have been cut with a sword as long as it had been recently sharpened. It would be difficult to find friction much thicker.

Olympas spoke sternly, with authority. "Don't betray the 'rich fools,' or you may never side with the rich, but with the fools."

I had much respect for Olympas, who had the same ranking as Alexander. He had gained a solid reputation as a trusted commander, a true leader, and a man of honor. He had much to teach Alexander, if only he would listen. No one expected such courtesy, especially Olympas. Though no words were ever verbalized, all of us would have surely preferred to be under the command of Olympas.

Alexander turned his head from Olympas. "Let's go!" he commanded out of anger. "We have a long journey ahead of us." He headed out on his white horse as Helam and Jecoliah cracked the reins from the wagons. We were finally on our way. We understood the road would be hard and long, but we were up for the task. This seven-day journey to Damascus would indeed be a tiring assignment. We traveled that first day until nightfall, where we stopped outside of Ismailia for some needed rest.

Early the next morning, I awoke to the demands of Alexander once again. "Get up you lazy swine! It's time to get back on the road! It's a full day to Bir Quatia." Everyone else took this as a cue to get into line though I alone had been singled out. We continued our steadfast journey.

"So do you miss your father?" Stephanus asked as we rode side by side behind the second wagon.

"I do. Since Mother passed away from a high fever several years ago, life has changed for us. It had been just the two of us, and her death had a strong effect on him. He never recovered from that loss. No one could ever take her place. How he loved her! How he missed her! Then, he died on his last journey, just one year ago."

"Your father was a brave man. I admired him," Stephanus said.

As I had been so often over the last year, I became consumed with regret.

"I should have been beside him," I said with little feeling.

"How could you have known what destiny would bring? To this day, no one really knows what happened. Surely you could have done nothing to alter the events of that day. How can you blame yourself?"

Stephanus sought to encourage, though I still experienced guilt. I appreciated his kindness, but he did not understand the constant thoughts that lingered in my brain. "I might have been able to save him. I should have been there."

After an awkward moment of silence, Stephanus followed with the question I expected but did not want to hear. "Where were you, Archippus? Why weren't you along for that detail?"

"We had a fight just before we were set to head out. It was nothing really, but I allowed something rather insignificant to come between us. I will always regret that." I could still see my father's face. That last look of frustration and anger had been ingrained in my mind for the last year. I did recall happy times with him. How I longed to change those last few moments we shared!

Overall, I found it difficult to talk about my father's death. Not only because of the pain it brought, but also because it had been so mysterious, and I knew I could have been by his side. I should have been there. He had been traveling with a caravan, similar to this one, when they were attacked. Everyone met their demise that day. No one really knows the details of what really happened.

What good would it do to talk about such a haunting tragedy? I always wondered if I could have done something to save his life if I were there. That would prove to be the one question that I would revisit over and over and the one that would never garner a satisfying response.

We continued our journey as the discussion about my father never resurfaced. Instead, the air filled with the cadence of horse hooves and the noisy wheels of our wagons. After several days, we labored through Masyada and found ourselves closing in on Hebron, about the halfway point of our journey.

"Helam! Jecoliah!" Alexander called out from the front of the caravan. "Let's proceed to Jerusalem tonight."

I remember the puzzled tone in Helam's voice. "There are far too many miles between Hebron and Jerusalem. We will never be able to cover that distance before nightfall."

"I agree," stated the older Jecoliah without hesitation. "We should stop in Hebron. I think the horses are getting weary as am I."

Alexander's demeanor changed instantly. He did not like someone questioning his judgment or his authority, especially two old men who were merely coachmen. How dare they dispute their commander's order. "We started early this morning. I am sure we can make it to Jerusalem. We will proceed. This will shorten the next leg to Tiberias." He arrogantly turned and galloped ahead.

It became tense among all the riders, even more so than it had already been. I believe we all disagreed with Alexander's decision, but we understood his authority as our commander, and knew we were subject to him even if he led in error. We obeyed his order and continued on, not even stopping to eat that evening.

As night started to fall, we found we were still quite a distance from Jerusalem, and we were all very tired.

"Let's make camp here," Alexander commanded arrogantly, giving no hint that he had made an error in judgment. Darkness had fallen over us, and we could not continue on. The wagons pulled off the road, and one by one our horses were tied to them. A rather quiet night quickly engulfed us. Several men built a small fire as others unpacked some of our provisions. Being self-centered, I still focused on my own personal dilemma. As it had been doing for some time, it consumed my every thought. I wandered from the camp to get away to think and to rehash the same issues that I had been dealing with again during the course of the last few days. I walked a safe distance away as I sat down on a large rock and gazed up into the heavens. I moved just beyond the light of the fire as I sought to separate myself from everyone's view. Perhaps the darkness would help hide my pain. Whatever the case, I wanted to be alone. I surely did not want to face any undue criticism from Alexander, not right now. The night had turned rather quiet as I barely heard the crackling of the fire in the distance. I could faintly hear the rustling of our men as they moved about in the camp.

A moment of peace, I thought. How refreshing, and how needed! I looked up toward the heavens. The stars were twinkling in the night sky. They were mesmerizing. I couldn't help but remember sitting outside with my mother. She loved looking at the stars. I remembered the warmth as she held me in her arms. I remember her love. I never wanted to leave that place of comfort. How I still missed her!

Suddenly something startled me as I turned back to look toward the fire. A group of men had rushed into the camp on horseback, accompanied by yelling and screaming. Immediately I could tell these men were hostile. Before I could even react, fighting broke out in the camp. We were under attack! Many loud cries accompanied by the panicked sounds of our horses filled the quiet night. My moment of peace was over.

I knew my duty. I had been trained for just such a moment. I needed to defend those in our company, but before I could even react, I found myself cowering close to the ground as I hid behind the rock I had been sitting on. I heard the undeniable sound of clashing swords as I watched our men fight back. *Cling. Clang.* The sound of metal against metal could not be mistaken for anything else. And the sound rang through the quiet night sky as I understood the strong force of each clash. This would be a fight to the death. From the rather dim light of the fire, I tried to identify our men among the silhouettes before me to no avail. Sheer mayhem broke loose as I heard bloodcurdling cries. Men were obviously being wounded and killed. I could not tell who was who. Did they need my help? Were they being overpowered? I drew my dagger from my belt as I lay there. My hand trembled in fear. What should I do? Be part of the slaughter or part of the victory? I knew my place—fighting beside my fellow guards. But I sat still, hesitant.

A scene flashed into my mind as I imagined this same scenario with my father in the midst of the battle. Could it be that this same scenario was what happened to him? What if I had been there? What would I have done? Could I have done something to save his life? That opportunity had been lost, but now I faced a situation where I knew I should fight. But fear paralyzed me as I crouched down even lower. I did nothing. I simply cowered as I watched.

I recognized Alexander close to the fire as several men jumped on his back. Another man wrestled the commander's sword from his hand. Still another knocked him down to the ground before grabbing his hair, pulling his head back. Alexander grimaced. Surely he had been identified as the commander of this expedition. He would be considered the most important, most influential man in our camp. Everything happened so fast. The assailants had launched a quick and calculated attack. Within a matter of seconds, they had a knife to his throat.

"Tell your men to drop their weapons!" one man yelled. Without a chance to react, the man screamed, "Tell them to drop them now, or I will cut off your head!" Though I could not clearly see this man's face, I could hear an assertive anger in his voice. I believed in the coming moments I might possibly witness a cold-blooded murder.

Everyone stopped as they understood the commander's life swayed in the balance. The night that had been so starry and peaceful just a few moments before had become as dark as a sudden eclipse. Some of our attackers had been hurt, but as everyone stopped, I could tell they far outnumbered us. Surely many of our men were either seriously injured or killed. I could see the silhouettes of many lying still in the dirt.

Alexander remained silent.

"Tell them now!" the man demanded again as he once again pulled his hair.

Along with the moaning of several men, I could hear horses that were still restless beside the wagons.

"I am not going to say it again!"

Alexander spoke up, "Drop your weapons. Do it now." He seemed far too calm for someone who quite possibly faced death in a matter of seconds. He did not appear to be afraid, but more disturbed, as he had been when Helam had questioned his orders earlier on the road.

It became silent. Then I heard the thumping of daggers hitting the dirt. The first one dropped, then another, and another. Then the sound of metal against metal clanged as swords landed on fallen daggers.

Suddenly a man standing behind Stephanus leaped forward with a shout. "He said drop *all* your weapons!" Apparently he had not been satisfied with our men's pace or full surrender of their arms. He did not hesitate, thrusting his sword into Stephanus's back. It protruded through the front of his chest as he finally released his dagger. The sound of his dagger hitting the ground below him seemed to overtake all else. I witnessed this evil act of senseless murder, though I had anticipated this would likely be Alexander's fate. Even at this point, Stephanus sought to be courageous, not intending to release a weapon he longed to use against Alexander's captor.

Stephanus gasped as he clutched his chest. His eyed widened in shock. Slowly he dropped to his knees as the sword pulled back through him. Blood flowed down his torso and onto his legs, forming a pool of blood beneath him.

"Drop your weapons!" the barbaric murderer shouted again.

"Lay down your swords!" Alexander also commanded with authority. "Lay them down—*now!*" he ordered once again.

The remaining daggers and swords fell to the ground as several of the attackers gathered them up. Our men were forced to their knees as several men guarded each one. What had just happened? Were these men going to kill us all? What could possibly be their motive—fine linen?

The attackers stood over each of our men, holding either a knife or a sword to their necks. Every one of our men had been detained. What threat would they bring now? They were helpless.

Alexander casually pushed the man who had been holding a knife to his throat aside as other men simply stepped back. Our men, who were on their knees, glanced toward him. What was this? Alexander stood to his feet and pushed away the man who had been holding him by the hair. I watched amazed as the attackers did not fight with him. What had just happened and why?

Alexander walked over to Stephanus, looking down at him, before addressing the one who had aggressively attacked him with the sword. "What were you thinking?" he asked as he knocked the bloody sword from his hand. He pushed him down to the ground as both hands forcibly hit him in the upper chest. The sound of his body hitting the ground broke the sound of silent disbelief, which filled the camp.

Alexander knelt down beside Stephanus as they looked at each other face-to-face. Stephanus gasped for his last few breaths as he struggled to say one last statement. "Have you lost your honor? I would have died to protect you..." He took one last long breath and fell to the ground.

Alexander, seeing Stephanus's body before him, responded like a furious demon. "What are you waiting for?" Alexander yelled in anger. "Kill them! *Kill them all!*"

I heard a collective gasp as the remaining men from our detail understood they were in the presence of a traitor. As the bandits stood ready with swords drawn, Alexander's orders were given to them—*about us!*

Every man reacted in the same manner as they immediately attempted to fight. What other choice did they have? They displayed a valiant but pitiful effort, though they were no match for the men who loomed over them. In a matter of seconds, all of our men fell to the ground. Other than Alexander, I would be the sole survivor of our mission. My cowardice had saved my life, and I knew at that moment that Alexander's assessment, though harsh, had been accurate. I had proved to be more like my weak mother than my strong father. I didn't know whether to ponder what had been done, or what I hadn't done. I knew I had failed as more regret and disappointment heaped high on my shoulders. The burden was great, and I wondered if I would be able to stand. I continued watching the horrific scene before me.

Alexander brushed the dirt off his garment as he walked over to the man who had pulled his hair. "How dare you treat me that way! The plan did not call for such action!" He stepped right up into his face. "Don't you ever cross me again!" His spit sprayed into the man's face. Before he could respond, the man gasped as his eyes grew wide. He slowly started to bend over as Alexander withdrew a dagger from his stomach. The commander pushed him away, and the once-zealous man fell to the ground with a moan and a thud. The commander had murdered one of his fellow villains with little thought.

Alexander continued his tirade, walking over to the man who had held the knife to his throat. "And if you ever do that to me again, I will cut off *your* head!" He turned to walk away. With a smug arrogance, he ordered, "Now get me something to eat. I'm famished."

How could Alexander be so cold? He had planned the deaths of everyone under his command and then added another man to the number with no consideration for him. I wondered what Olympas would say if he knew what had happened. I also wondered if Alexander had noticed that not every man in his detail lay dead at his feet. The firelight was not that bright. I wondered how soon he would realize I had left the camp. Or would he not even notice? He seemed more concerned with his stomach at the moment. What a perfect time to escape!

Before I could make a run for it, my plans were interrupted as I heard a command from behind me. "Get up!" The cold blade of a dagger now rested on my neck. "Get up, *or you'll never get up!*" I did not want to die there on the spot, so I slowly stood to my feet. "Head toward the camp," he said as he pushed me.

I was well aware that my best chance of escape would come if I overpowered this one man. But I considered that he had a sword. I knew it would be difficult running away from anyone into the darkness. This man would surely overtake me before I would get too far. This would lead to a sure sword in the back. A quick move might startle this man, but upon his call, there would be many more chasing me. Surely one of them would catch him, and again there would be a sword that would pierce him. I quickly weighed all the options, realizing there wasn't one that held any promise. Besides, the sight of seeing my friends being slain still remained fresh in my mind. I was afraid as I started to walk toward the fire.

As we neared the wagons, I heard some of the men talking. "We'll go on to Madaba after a quick stop outside Jerusalem. Those rich fools will surely pay us the same as they did for the delivery we made last year. Maybe even more!" I could sense their greed. Their attack was nothing more than an act of thievery.

The bandit forced me through the remains of my fallen comrades as the other assailants started to understand I had also been a member of this detail. I looked around in the moonlight. I could see many men lying on the ground, many whom I knew. Though some of the fallen stirred slightly, they would surely join the other lifeless bodies strewn around the fire. What a tragedy!

He pushed me just once as I fell on the ground in front of Alexander. "What shall I do with this one? Found a coward hiding behind a rock in the dark."

Alexander turned around and looked down as I looked up. As our eyes met, he stopped chewing. Soon a typical look of disgust crossed his face. "You were hiding? I thought you were one of my men? You are such a coward!" He chuckled though he did not find humor in this moment. "What irony! You're the biggest coward of them all, and *you* are the one that survives tonight's festivities?"

Festivities? I thought. Did he consider the murder of good men some form of perverse celebration? My fear turned to anger. "At least I'm not a traitor," I boldly said as I stood to my feet. These words crossed my lips before I could stop them. I couldn't believe I had spoken to him in this manner, especially since I had been identified as the coward I had become. Everyone became instantly quiet as they watched intently. They had already witnessed what had happened to someone who crossed their leader.

Alexander took a quick step toward me, pushing me as I awkwardly fell over one of the dead bodies. With a thud, I landed hard on my back, which knocked the wind out of me. He yelled with a loud scream of revulsion, like a demonic assault. Then he kicked dirt at me. I covered my eyes with my arms as I curled up into a ball, trying to catch my breath. I had been rendered helpless—I couldn't even breathe. Then I heard him give his final command. "Kill him!" He paused before looking down at me with evil in his eyes. "Kill him—*like I killed his father!*"

I stared at him. I couldn't speak, and that had nothing to do with the fact that I struggled to breathe. I finally gasped as air finally filled my lungs. Before I could say a word, Alexander became oddly and instantly quiet. His mouth opened wide as did his eyes. His look of anger was replaced with shock. He himself now gasped for breath as he flung his hands over his chest. I could see blood seeping through his fingers. One man threw his arm around Alexander's throat. He squeezed without mercy. I watched as the commander's eyes rolled into the back of his head. He stood motionless before me. His eyes were hollow as he looked nowhere. The man behind Alexander released him as he dropped to the ground beside me. The commander was dead.

The large man who had killed him held a bloody dagger in his hand. He had to be the biggest man there, perhaps the strongest. His grip remained strong as I could see his fingers straining. He looked down at the man who had pulled Alexander's hair during their charade. The man's body had not yet become cold, though his soul had surely departed. For a few moments, he just stared at the body. The whole camp remained still. I didn't know what to do.

After a while, he turned his empty eyes toward me. He looked directly at me, though it did not appear that he saw me. His mind had drifted elsewhere. Still on the ground, I wondered if he were going to slay me as well. I believed this would be inevitable but didn't know what to do.

He mumbled something unintelligible. Then he focused on me. I knew he saw me now. Again he spoke, this time with more clarity. "He killed my brother," he said with sadness in his rough voice.

After a moment, I responded, "He killed my father."

His eyes became empty once more as he stared in my direction. After some time, he simply mumbled, "Let him go."

Did I hear him correctly? Would he show mercy as a result of our mutual suffering at the hands of the commander?

Again, he spoke up, "Let him go!"

I started to move slowly. No one approached me. Each of the men standing around actually took a step back from me. I stood to my feet and backed away from the men who were standing before me. I took one slow step at a time.

Then he spoke to some of the other men in an angry voice as he turned away, "The white horse is mine." He walked into the darkness away from the fire.

I didn't hesitate any further as I turned and ran the other direction into the darkness. I ran until I could not run any farther. Only then did I peer over my shoulder. No one had pursued me, but I knew I had not escaped. They had simply released me. I didn't know if my heart beat wildly from fear or from exhaustion. Surely both were contributing factors. I fell to the ground there in the darkness and wept uncontrollably for some time.

For the next few days, I walked without food or water. I constantly looked behind me to see if the men who had attacked our caravan had reconsidered and come after me. My ever-present sorrow and deep regret has been my only companion. What have I done? And who can bring peace to my weary soul? I've lost my family, my friends, my dignity, and my reputation. *I've lost everything!* That brings me here, to Tiberias. I'm looking for help, for someone who can lift this burden of guilt and shame from my weary shoulders.

Archippus had told his tale. His desperation had totally overtaken him, and I could tell. The fact that I responded to his story with a smile surely puzzled him. I must have appeared to be insane or uncompassionate. I wondered if he thought I had found his tragic story to be amusing. To the contrary, now, more than ever, I knew I could be of help to him.

I gestured toward the temple steps. "Please sit here, young man."

Archippus sat down slowly. "Tell me, old man, can you help me?"

"You are not the first one the Lord has sent my way. And now that I understand your predicament, I must admit, I have seen your look of desperation before. I believe God would have me offer you a measure of hope."

I sat down beside him, and as sincerely as I could, I said, "Please now, just listen and allow me to tell you a story about someone who might possibly understand what you're going through. You see, *he truly lost everything.*"

"But how can a story help me?" Archippus grumbled.

The old man simply chuckled. "Just rest, my friend. You have nothing more to lose and, perhaps, much to gain. Besides, when I finish my tale, I will take you to the temple priest, if you so desire."

Though I understood Archippus listened reluctantly, I looked off into the distance and began my story.

Many years ago, in this very Judean region, a young man walked toward the city gates of Tiberias on his way out of town. His name was Tychicus. He led the way as his wife, Rebekah, sat on the back of their donkey. They expected the journey north of Magdala to take several hours of this late afternoon.

Their five-year-old son, Justus, couldn't wait to see his grandfather and grandmother up north in Magdala. He hadn't been this excited since they had visited the natural hot springs south of the city a few months earlier.

Justus ran ahead as Tychicus called to him, "Son, we have a long journey ahead of us. Let's not use all your energy before we even leave the city." He knew the more his son ran now, the sooner he would be asking to ride with his mother down the road.

Tychicus smiled as he glanced toward Rebekah. She was pretty in form and feature and highly favored. Though many knew her for her physical beauty, he loved her more for her heart. She had been such a kind and loving wife and mother. After seven years of marriage, he still saw her as the most beautiful woman he'd ever laid eyes on.

She smiled and placed both of her hands on her heart—their private symbol that meant "I love you." He repeated the gesture back to her.

His smile faded as he turned to see a familiar figure standing several paces inside the city gate.

"Greetings, Tychicus," Jotham said with a devious look in his eyes—a look Tychicus had learned to despise. Though Jotham held the position of the temple's chief priest, there were many reasons Tychicus had an unfavorable opinion of him. He gave him a mild look of disgust and then turned away, walking past the supposed "man of God" without saying a word. Jotham's look cast one of silent judgment, and Tychicus knew it.

As they headed toward the gate, the priest looked at Rebekah with unwavering eyes. Rebekah had learned to notice and avoid them. Jotham whispered, "Keep praying for him." Though he sounded outwardly religious, his inner intentions were far from righteous.

Rebekah half-smiled politely at Jotham and then softly said, "I'll say a prayer for you too."

"Justus, come here!" Tychicus called as they approached the gate. His son ran ahead and had been talking to a beggar named Josech, who sat just outside the gate, where he'd been sitting for years. "Justus!"

His son ran up to him with a big smile on his face. "Father, he's blind!"

Tychicus couldn't help but snicker as his inquisitive son discovered the obvious. His blunt declaration caused Rebekah to be visibly embarrassed. Over the years, they'd traveled in and out of the gates more times than they could count, but they had never stopped even once to speak to or offer help to this blind beggar. Tychicus and Rebekah avoided him, as did most everyone else who ignored his pleas for money, food, or drink. He had become an eyesore, a continual annoyance to everyone who passed through the gates. Before this, Justus had not shown any signs of curiosity about the beggar. But now his inquisitive, little mind could be compared to an empty well longing to be filled to overflowing with fresh water.

Faintly they heard Josech's cry: "Please, help a poor beggar. Please have mercy on me. Please…" His constant cry could be heard though most ignored it.

"Let's go, son. We have a long journey ahead of us." Justus ran up to his father's side as he led the donkey through the city gate and down the road toward the neighboring city of Magdala, which also sat along the western coast of the Sea of Galilee. The nearly six-mile journey to the north would be a long one for a five-year-old boy. There they would spend several days with Rebekah's family during the celebration of Pesach, the Feast of Passover. The actual celebration would last seven days, starting on the fifteenth day of Nisan, though Tychicus had only agreed to stay for three. Rebekah appreciated the three days she would be able to spend with her brothers and her parents, which she cherished.

She especially loved spending time with her father, Zibeon. He had the reputation of being a good man, a righteous man. All who knew him would declare this to be true. In recent days, he had become vocal that he disliked that his daughter lived in what he called a "Gentile city." He didn't want the Greek customs to defile her. The natural hot springs to the south, with their so-called medicinal powers, also made him uncomfortable. He never really elaborated on that, but for some reason, they troubled him. He didn't want his daughter near something he considered pagan. He longed for her to be closer, where he could spend more time with her. So he too looked forward to the time they would spend together at the festival.

He'd offered Tychicus work in his fields. The need for reliable workers abounded, and he knew his son-in-law would be a capable worker. How he prayed that they'd consent to take the trek several miles north of Magdala and settle there with them. Tamar, Rebekah's mother, dreamed of having her grandson close by all the time. But Tychicus decided to go to Tiberias with his young bride to pursue the fishing trade on the Sea of Galilee. This also did not make sense to Zibeon, as Magdala had a thriving fishing industry, which would be so much closer. Through a series of events, Tychicus became a carpenter's apprentice, not a fisherman. He felt as if he had found his place.

As they left the city, Rebekah looked forward to going home. She loved spending time with her brothers, especially Bukkiah. Only two years older than her, they formed a close bond. She also longed to see the rest of her family. She started reminiscing about her childhood. "I remember one man, one of my father's workers. I think they used to be best friends. I used to call him JJ. I don't even know if I ever knew his real name. What a nice man! Then one day he just left. He just disappeared. It seemed that way to me. They never talked to him as if they had forgotten about him. I wonder what happened to him. I wonder if he is still alive." She stopped and looked off into the distance as pleasant memories filled her mind. "I don't know why I thought of that," she said with a chuckle.

Rebekah continued to reflect silently about her youth, being the youngest of four children and Zibeon and Tamar's only daughter. Her three older brothers—Mattaniah, Shubael, and Bukkiah—had all earned a reputation for being hard workers and men of integrity like their father. And how they loved their little sister!

All in all, Zibeon set a godly example for his sons and daughter, being a man of prayer. Tamar also lived out her faith, displaying a rare yet genuine passion for God. Rebekah had followed in the footsteps of her parents, becoming known as a woman of prayer. She only wished Tychicus shared her desires for spiritual matters as he once had. After all, they first met in the temple. She prayed daily that God would intervene in his life and bring her husband back to himself. Zibeon wondered if Tiberias, with its Greek influences, had caused his son-in-law to turn from God. Rebekah knew better.

Tychicus looked back at his wife and smiled as they continued down the road. Justus chattered by his side. "Father, what will the festival be like? How much farther do we have to go? Are we close? Will I ever be as tall as you? How tall are you, Father?"

Tychicus knew the excitement of this trip had not yet become stale to his young son. He still viewed the adventure ahead with enthusiasm. Tychicus placed his hand on the top of his own head and said, "I'm this tall. How tall are you?"

Justus placed his hand on the top of his own head, giggling. "I'm this tall!"

Rebekah laughed as Justus ran ahead, while an unexpected stranger stepped toward the road. She gasped as she recognized who this man might be. His long hair covered his face, and his clothes were dirty and tattered. His form and posture were irregular as he bent over. Several fingers were missing from his hands, and several toes were missing from his feet.

Tychicus called out to his son. "Justus! Justus! Come here now! *Now!*"

As Justus ran back to his father, Tychicus called out, "Unclean! Unclean! Unclean!" Rebekah left her place on the donkey, jumping down to the ground, receiving her son into her open arms where she held him tight. The uncertainty of the moment caused Justus to cry. What was happening? Who was this? He did not understand.

"Get back! Don't come near! You are unclean! You need to call out, 'Unclean! Unclean! Unclean!'" Tychicus shouted angrily.

"Please," pleaded the diseased man in a tired and raspy voice. He stretched forth a malformed and grotesque hand. "Please help me. Please, just speak to me. Please..."

Tychicus barked back without giving this man an ounce of consideration. "Get back! Unclean! Unclean! Unclean!" he continued to shout, looking around to warn anyone else who might be in the vicinity. He only wanted to protect his family from this sickly, unclean man—a leper. This incident ended almost as quickly as it had occurred. The leper turned and slowly walked away, mumbling, "I'm so thirsty. So thirsty. So thirsty."

Tychicus ran to his son, still engulfed in Rebekah's arms. "You're safe now, son. I sent him away. He will not harm you."

He understood his son had no way of knowing the potential danger this man represented. Justus had never seen such an odd, ugly-looking man as this before.

"What's wrong with that man?" Justus asked timidly as he sniveled.

Rebekah lovingly brushed back Justus's hair. "Did you see the spots on his skin? That man is a leper."

Justus looked over his shoulder toward the road where the stranger had confronted them. He wanted another chance to examine the man who now slowly walked farther and farther from them. Though he looked back at his mother, his eyes appeared distant. "Mother, that man, is a… *leopard*?"

As Tychicus knelt down beside his son, looking him in the eyes, he couldn't help but snicker at his cute response. "That man is not a *leopard*. He's a *leper*."

Justus lowered his eyebrows, trying to make sense of this mystery as he wiped his nose with his forearm. Though Justus had heard his words, Tychicus knew they were not fully understood.

He took hold of his son and faced him as they looked eye to eye. "The law tells us we are not allowed to talk to people like that. We are clean, and they are unclean. We cannot touch them or talk to them or anything, or we could get sick ourselves. Do you understand?"

Justus nodded his head up and down slowly. Then, acting like a leopard, he turned and roared in the direction of the unclean man who had walked some distance away from them. "Stay away, leopard," he said in his little voice before growling like a large cat.

Tychicus and Rebekah hugged their son as the leper eventually disappeared from sight.

"Thank God," Rebekah proclaimed, looking at her son, "that you didn't touch that man."

"God be with the one he does touch," Tychicus said as he helped Rebekah back onto the donkey. Soon they headed back down the road toward Magdala and the house of Zibeon.

CHAPTER 2

Tychicus held the reigns of their donkey as Rebekah rode quietly, enjoying the occasional breeze off the Sea of Galilee to her right. Justus loved watching the fishing ships as they sailed near the coast of the large freshwater lake. Other than the short encounter on the road with the leper, the trip to Magdala had been fairly common. Justus grew tired of throwing rocks as they walked, so he decided to pass some time talking to his father about the days of festival ahead of them.

"Father, what will the festival be like?" He had asked this question earlier on this trip, yet he was not given an answer.

Tychicus looked over to his son, who walked beside him. He looked back at Rebekah, whose attention had been fully directed toward him. He knew exactly what she was thinking. She wondered how he would answer this question in light of his lack of enthusiasm concerning the days of celebration before them. She simply smiled at him as she looked down toward the ground, enjoying the predicament her son had placed him in.

"Are we going to eat at the festival, Father?"

"Yes, my son, there will be plenty of food for everyone. Surely we will not leave hungry." Tychicus chuckled.

"Is that what the festival is all about? Eating?"

Rebekah smirked at her son's inquiry. She knew he had a healthy appetite.

"My son, you've been to the Pesach feast before. Do you not remember the food? Do you not remember the big feast, the Seder meal?"

As Justus fondly recalled the previous year, a look of excitement grew across his face. "I liked the meat!" he exclaimed with delight.

"The roasted meat we eat reminds us of the lambs that were used as the Paschal sacrifice the night before the Jewish people were led out of Egypt. Do you remember that story?"

Justus nodded in affirmation.

"Son, who was that story about? Do you remember?" Rebekah asked.

"It was about the man who was a baby with the bullfrogs in Egypt, wasn't it?"

Again Rebekah smiled. "That man is known to us as Moses, though he did not receive that name from his mother. When he was just a small baby, she placed him in a papyrus basket, then set him among the reeds along the Nile River, in the *bulrushes*."

"Why did she do that? Did he like playing in the water?"

"Oh no. She put him in the basket to save his life. You see, the pharaoh gave an order to all his people: every baby boy must be thrown into the Nile after their birth, but let every girl live."

"So he didn't like little boys?"

Tychicus looked at his son, who did not completely grasp the severe nature of the story. "Son, the pharaoh feared the Israelites because they were growing in number. He thought they might someday fight against him and take over the land. So he thought, if he killed all the baby boys, it would stop them from having so many soldiers."

"He killed them?" he asked in disbelief. Who could be so cruel? Such an act did not make sense to his little mind. "That's mean!" Justus stated with fervor.

"Yes. The pharaoh showed himself to be a mean man, a wicked man."

"So she had to hide the baby Moses in the basket, in the river, to save his life?"

Rebekah smiled as she enjoyed this stage of life. This history lesson had been communicated to him, and he understood.

She continued, "Then one day, the pharaoh's daughter went down to the Nile to take a bath. She heard something in the bulrushes, and when she went to see what it could be, she discovered the basket. She opened it up and found a crying baby. What a surprise! She said, 'This must be a Hebrew baby.' She felt sorry for him."

"Then what did she do?" Justus asked, fully attentive with wide eyes.

"Well, the baby's sister approached the pharaoh's daughter and asked if she should find a Hebrew mother for her, one who could feed the baby. To her delight, she agreed. Can you guess who she brought back to take care of the baby?"

"I don't know. Who?" he asked after shrugging his shoulders with a puzzled look crossing his face.

"Well, she brought her the baby's mother. So the baby stayed with his own mother, and she took care of him. And the whole time he had protection from the pharaoh and his law to kill all the baby boys. And to make it even better, the pharaoh actually paid Moses's mother to take care of her own baby!"

Justus couldn't believe it. A broad smile stretched across his face.

"Isn't God amazing?" Rebekah asked, eyeing her husband, who now walked ahead. She had taken over retelling this story. As a mother, she could not help but be excited about the way God had saved this baby.

"She called him Moses, saying, 'I drew him out of the water.' That's what the Scriptures tell us in the book of the Exodus."

"Were there any frogs in the river?" Justus asked with excitement, changing the course of the story.

"I am sure there were many frogs," Rebekah replied, "but this story is not about the frogs."

She knew Justus loved frogs.

"There's more to this story. Your father can tell you the rest if you like," she said, more than hinting that she wanted Tychicus to continue from there. She wanted Justus to hear this history lesson from his father.

"Please, Father, tell me the rest of the story!" he said with enthusiasm.

Tychicus peered back at Rebekah with a look of hesitation.

"Please, Father, please?"

Tychicus started reluctantly, though deep inside he wanted to tell the story. "Well, the baby's mother took care of him until he grew older. Then she took the baby Moses back to the pharaoh's daughter, who took him in as her own son. He grew big and strong in the house of the pharaoh. One day he watched as the Hebrews were working as slaves for the Egyptians. He saw a poor Hebrew worker being beaten. When he came to the man's help, he ended up fighting with the Egyptian, and during the fight, Moses killed him. Eventually the pharaoh heard about this and came after Moses. In fear, he ran away, far from Egypt."

"Why did he run away from his mother?" Justus could never imagine leaving his mother or his father.

"He was afraid," Rebekah said.

Tychicus glanced over toward her with a scolding eye. He did not want her to interrupt him again. She glanced back as if apologizing. She lowered her head with a hidden grin.

"He was afraid of the pharaoh," Tychicus reinforced. "He fled to Midian where he married a girl named Zipporah. He became a shepherd, and they had a baby boy named Gershom. Moses thought he would always stay there, but God had different plans for him. One day he saw a burning bush that did not burn up."

"How could that happen, Father?" Justus had never heard of such a thing.

"God can do whatever he wants," Tychicus said. Rebekah enjoyed hearing these words spoken from the tongue of her husband. She prayed that the words he spoke would pierce his own heart. God could do whatever he wanted, even mend his wounded heart. She smiled at him, though he did not notice.

"Well, God spoke to Moses from the bush."

"What did he sound like, Father?"

"We don't really know, but I am sure his voice was very powerful, very strong."

"Like this?" Justus asked. He then added, "I am God." He tried to use the lowest voice he could muster, though it turned out to be more humorous than authoritative.

Tychicus and Rebekah both broke out in laughter. Justus joined them, giggling uncontrollably.

"You are close, my son. God did call himself I AM. When Moses asked God for his name, he said he was I AM. It was like God was saying he was God."

"He is God, Father." Justus didn't really understand the depth of this name, or its meaning. He just accepted that God was God as he displayed a simple, childlike faith.

"You are correct, Justus," Rebekah added to reconfirm his statement. She aimed her comment toward him, though she hoped Tychicus would also embrace the truth of the moment as well. God could only be defined by himself—the Almighty Creator and Sustainer of all, self-reliant and self-existent.

"What else did they talk about, Father?" Justus asked curiously.

"God had a mission for Moses. By this time, Moses had discovered his Hebrew heritage. He had really been a Hebrew the whole time, though the pharaoh's daughter raised him as an Egyptian prince. God heard the cries of the hurting people in Egypt, and he wanted Moses to go and rescue them from slavery."

Justus walked as he hung on every word. He wanted to hear more about Moses, someone he had just started to admire—a man about to be a hero.

Tychicus saw how his son had connected with him during this time of relaying history, and he enjoyed it. They both did. He determined they would have to spend more time talking about stories from the Scriptures. Though his heart remained hard toward God, he understood his duty as a father to share these stories with his son. Rebekah's heart beat with excitement hearing her husband talk about God and the Scriptures. She prayed that God might use this time to start the process of softening his heart.

"Did Moses save all the people?" Justus asked. The story had stalled, and he longed for it to continue.

"Moses went to the pharaoh, asking him to let the Hebrews go. But the pharaoh didn't want to lose all his workers. They were busy making bricks, and the pharaoh wanted nothing to stop them from their work. The worst thing to do, in his mind, would be to let them go free."

"So the pharaoh said no?"

"That's right. He wouldn't let them go, and he determined that nothing would change his mind."

Rebekah couldn't help herself as she blurted out, "Then came the frogs!"

"Frogs?" Justus said with excitement in his high-pitched voice.

Tychicus gave Rebekah another look before continuing. "Hold on, the frogs will come in time."

Justus smiled wide. He couldn't wait to hear about the frogs.

"When the pharaoh would not let the people go, God sent plagues on the people of Egypt."

"What's a *plague*?" Justus asked. He'd never heard that word before.

"A *plague* is when God sends trouble that affects many people as part of a punishment from God. And when the pharaoh wouldn't let the people go, he sent plagues. He started by turning the water in the Nile River to blood."

Justus wrinkled his nose up in disgust. "That's gross!" he exclaimed.

"But it sure got the pharaoh's attention. Moses went to the pharaoh again and asked him to let the people go. Once again, Pharaoh said no. So God sent another plague. Guess what jumped out of the Nile River?"

"Bloody frogs!" Justus said, raising his hands above his head as if celebrating.

"Well, I guess they might have been bloody if they came from the river. The frogs came from everywhere it seemed. The Scriptures tell us they filled the royal palaces and filled the people's homes—and could even be found inside their beds, in their ovens, and where they kneaded their bread."

"And maybe they had frogs *in* their bread," Justus said as he giggled again, finding himself humorous. Tychicus and Rebekah joined him in laughter, partly at his cute comment but mostly also because of his contagious giggling. Soon they stopped laughing as Tychicus and Rebekah smiled at each other. How they loved their son, and how they longed to add more to their number.

"Finally, the pharaoh said he would let the people go, so God killed the frogs, and they were piled up in heaps, and the whole place really stunk from all the dead frogs."

"So Moses saved the people!" Justus said with a thrill.

"Well, no. The pharaoh changed his mind and wouldn't let the people go. Again, he said, 'God wants you to let his people go so they may worship him.' But the pharaoh again refused to let them go."

"Did he send another plague with more frogs?"

"No, this time God turned the dust of the ground into gnats. They're like mosquitoes—like pesky, little flies. He sent so many that they couldn't see the ground. The pharaoh kept refusing to let the people go, so he sent swarms of flies. He killed their livestock—"

"What's *livestock*, Father?"

"Livestock are their animals. They had horses, donkeys, cattle, sheep, and goats. The plague killed all their animals."

"Just like the frogs? Were they piled in heaps? I bet they really stunk too."

"I am not sure if they made piles or not, but I am sure it didn't smell very good. The pharaoh still refused to let them go, so God sent boils onto the people and the animals. Boils are sores in their skin. Then He sent a great hailstorm upon them. It was the worst storm they ever saw. But still the pharaoh didn't let them go. Then he sent locusts, which ate all the crops that were left after the hail destroyed most of them. They even ate all the fruit from the trees. So they lost all their food."

"I bet they got hungry."

"Son, I am sure they did."

"Just like I am getting hungry right now," Justus said with a slight frown as his lower lip protruded out.

Rebekah knew all this walking would make him tired and hungry. "We will get there soon, and I am sure there will be food waiting for you." She smiled at him. He smiled back.

"Then what happened, Father?"

"Then God sent a thick darkness across the land. The Scriptures tell us it was so dark you could feel it." Tychicus stopped in his tracks as the donkey slowed to a stop. "Close your eyes, son. Is that dark?"

"Yes," Justus said.

"Now put your hands over your eyes as tight as you can."

Justus stopped and raised his little hands up over his closed eyes. "That's dark, Father."

"God sent darkness much darker than that! The Scriptures tell us the darkness was so thick you could *feel* it!"

"How do you *feel* darkness?" Justus asked, pulling his hands down.

Tychicus looked directly into his son's eyes. "I don't know. But I do know that it became so dark they could not see anything at all—for three days! No one could leave their house or go anywhere because they couldn't see. But God allowed light in the places where the Israelites lived. They could see just fine."

"Did the pharaoh let them go?"

"He said he would let them go, but God hardened his heart again, and he did not let them go."

"What is a hard heart?" Justus asked as he placed his hand on his chest. "Is my heart hard?" Before another word could be said, he asked, "Father, is your heart hard?"

Tychicus looked up toward his wife, who quickly looked down. He knew her thoughts. Did he have a hard heart toward God as the pharaoh did? Rebekah's refusal to look into his eyes at that moment spoke loudly. He knew she believed it to be true. He chose to ignore her judgment as he replied, "Your heart is fine, my son. Can you feel it beating inside you?"

Panic crossed Justus's face. "I can't feel it!"

He nearly started to cry as Tychicus knelt down beside him, taking his hand. "Put your hand inside your garment."

Relief overcame him as he exclaimed, "I can feel it! It's not hard!"

Instantly, he put his hand inside his father's cloak. "I feel yours too! It's not hard either!" He smiled with joy, though Rebekah still looked away, not making eye contact with her husband.

They continued on as Justus found a renewed spring in his step.

"What happened next, Father? What happened next?"

"Well, the Lord had one more plague for Egypt, and this time, the Lord said the pharaoh would let the people go."

Justus smiled as he smelled victory for Moses.

"The Lord sent a plague that would slay the firstborn son of everyone in Egypt. This included the firstborn son of the pharaoh, as well as the firstborn of all the Egyptians' children and livestock. But the Israelites were told to take a lamb for each household. They were instructed to slay the lamb, put its blood on the sides and the top of the doorframes, and then eat the meat of the lamb after it had been roasted over the fire. When the judgment of God came to Egypt that night, the Lord would pass over every house protected by the blood of the lamb. That way their children would be spared."

"So they didn't have to die!" Justus said confidently.

"That's right. So we remember that night when the angel of death passed over the houses that had blood on the doorposts. We celebrate God's mercy through the feast of Pesach, or the feast of the Passover, as one of the most important of all the dates on the Jewish calendar."

"Can we talk more about the celebration?" Rebekah suggested, hoping the gruesomeness of the blood hadn't startled their five-year-old son, which it hadn't.

Tychicus sneered at Rebekah's paranoia. "Son, we celebrate the Jews leaving their slavery from the pharaoh of Egypt. Moses led them out of the land, and for the first time in their life, they were free—just like those oldest sons were free to live. Now that's something to be happy about!"

"And I am the oldest son, and so I can eat the meat!" Justus said, raising his eyebrows in anticipation.

"You'll be able to see your aunts and uncles and all your cousins too!" Rebekah declared.

"Who else will be there?" Justus asked.

"Your grandfather always invites his workers to join him for the Seder meal. There will be many people there. We will have a house filled with family, friends, and workers, all celebrating the Passover."

"And we all get to eat the meat!" Justus declared victoriously.

"And don't forget the songs, Justus. There will be much singing and dancing." Rebekah recalled how he had danced in previous years as a young toddler. His older cousins always loved watching him jump around as only a carefree child would. She always found this precious sight so adorable.

"Are we getting closer? How much farther will it be, Father?" Justus asked after walking for some time. The journey had started to get laborious for his little legs. Before Tychicus could give him an answer, he added, "Can I ride on the donkey?"

Tychicus sought to encourage him as he answered, "If you want to grow up to be a big, strong man, you must walk." The journey had started to exhaust him, though he wanted to be like his father as he continued, throwing rocks on occasion. Tychicus longed for the coming years when he could relate to his son, man to man. He looked forward to the days and years ahead. As his young son plodded onward, he knew his time to join Rebekah on the donkey drew near. They were getting closer.

Rebekah's parents, Zibeon and Tamar, were awaiting their arrival in Magdala.

"How exciting to have the whole family together," Tamar said excitedly. Rebekah's visit from Tiberias would make the family complete as she joined her three brothers and their families.

"Just be patient," Zibeon said. "They will be here soon." He turned and summoned one of his servants. "Abednego, please bring some water from the well. We will need to wash several feet after their long journey."

"Yes, master," Abednego replied, heading off in obedience.

"The rooms have been cleaned, and the linens have all been washed. I'm ready for them to arrive." Tamar especially loved having Justus come to visit. Being the youngest of all her grandchildren and the child of her youngest and only daughter, he held a special place in her heart. The fact that she rarely saw him made each visit even more memorable.

"The one you are waiting for has arrived!" proclaimed a handsome young man who suddenly and dramatically entered the courtyard.

Zibeon laughed as Tamar gave him a scolding look.

"Bukkiah, why aren't you in the fields with the workers?"

"Father, how can I work when my baby sister is coming to visit?" Bukkiah walked over to his mother and gave her a big hug. "Sorry to disappoint you, Mother. I know I am not your youngest, but I'm the second youngest."

"Son, you know I love you as I love your brothers. But it's not every day we get to see your sister."

"Father, the workers are in good hands," Bukkiah said, turning back toward Zibeon. "I just wanted to see if Tychicus and Rebekah had arrived. Surely they will be here soon if they are not here already. Besides, I thought you could use some help here at the house getting prepared for the start of the festival. Tomorrow morning will come soon."

"That it will, my son." Tamar smiled. How she loved the gathering of everyone for the festival celebration!

They all walked toward the front of the house in anticipation of Tychicus, Rebekah, and Justus. Abednego walked into the room, setting a basin of water down near the front door. "Here's the water you requested, master. I also brought several hand towels as well."

"Thank you, Abednego." Zibeon always treated his workers and servants with respect. As a result, they served him well. "Please look out for our guests and tell me when they are in sight."

"Yes, master. I will be looking for them."

"Please let me know when you see them. Someone is very anxious for their arrival. Tamar is almost as restless as our grandchildren in midafternoon!" he stated with a chuckle.

Abednego smiled as he left the room. He understood Tamar's love for her grandchildren. How she longed to be with them!

Tamar gave Zibeon a playful look as her husband looked forward to their arrival as much as she did. "I just hope they will stay for the whole festival."

"I just hope they will stay for more than a few days. You know how Tychicus has been. Do not be surprised if he has work to get back to in Tiberias. Let's be grateful for the time we have and pray that God will work in his heart."

Tamar agreed. "I've already been praying for him."

"As have I," replied Zibeon. "Tychicus is a good man. He has treated our daughter well and given us a fine grandson. God will have to change his heart, and we just need to continue praying for that to come to pass."

From the front of the house, they heard Abednego call out, "Master, they're in sight."

Zibeon responded, "Very well, Abednego. We are on our way. Please also get a pitcher of water for them to drink from." Zibeon and Tamar hurried out to meet Tychicus and Rebekah with open arms as Bukkiah followed close behind them.

Step by step, they drew closer to the house. Tychicus walked out front, holding the reigns of the donkey, as Rebekah rode with Justus.

Zibeon walked out to meet them. "My son! It's good to see you!" he declared with outspread arms before giving his son-in-law a fatherly hug. Tamar set her sights on her grandson, who had fallen asleep in Rebekah's arms. "Let me hold that boy," she said, reaching toward Rebekah, who couldn't wait to get off the donkey. Bukkiah helped Rebekah down, giving her a big brotherly hug. Hugs and kisses were exchanged all around as Abednego led the donkey off for some water and rest. Another servant took their packs into the house.

Tychicus sat on a bench outside the house as Zibeon started to wash his feet with water from the basin Abednego had brought. He dried them before also washing Rebekah's feet as Justus ran into the house, looking for his cousins. Typically servants were the ones who washed the feet of guests, but Zibeon displayed humility, as he desired to serve his daughter and her family in a personal way. Tychicus took note of this. He surely understood his father-in-law to be a great man, worthy of adoration. All the while Tamar gave them drinking water from the pitcher, which quenched their thirst. He also admired her.

Archippus surely imagined Tamar's basin of water as he drank from the cup Zoe brought to him. The refreshing water from the well met his thirst. With a smile, she removed Archippus's sandals and started to wash his feet with the remaining water in the basin before drying his clean feet with a towel. What a refreshing feeling!

"Thank you, young lady," Archippus said gratefully. He smiled, showing appreciation for this young girl's servant attitude.

"You are welcome, sir," she said quietly as she bowed her head toward the ground in a gesture of courtesy.

"Thank you, dear," I said with pride. She smiled and then ran off playfully.

Archippus's thirst had been quenched, and he now sat comfortably on the temple steps with clean feet, ready for me to continue.

"Thank you, Zibeon," Tychicus said. "We are glad to be at your home again for the festival." Rebekah echoed his sentiments as Justus ran back to the front of the house and again into Zibeon's arms.

"And we are ready to eat meat, Grandfather!"

Zibeon and Tamar both laughed. Mattaniah and Shubael, along with their wives and children, came from the house to meet them. What a wonderful moment of reunion as more hugs were exchanged. Tamar could not have been happier!

"Let the boy eat meat to his heart's content!" Zibeon proclaimed joyfully. Everyone laughed. The festival would not begin until the following morning, though the celebration had already begun.

Tamar took Justus's hand as they disappeared into the house, followed by the rest of the children. Rebekah, accompanied by her three brothers, followed her father inside as Tychicus looked back over his shoulder, noticing Abednego leaving on the back of a donkey. He paused for a second. Another donkey rode beside them, carrying several sacks draped over its back. He watched for just a moment as they slowly walked toward the road.

"Come on, brother," Bukkiah said as he called back to Tychicus. "Come in and rest awhile. You've had a long journey today. It's time to sit down." Soon the whole scene left Tychicus's mind as he walked into the house.

They entered the courtyard as Justus made a dramatic statement. "Oh, Grandfather," he said, "we saw a leopard on the road!"

"You saw a leopard?" Zibeon asked. This statement surprised him, and the look on his face indicated such as his eyes grew wide. Tamar also reacted strongly, instantly worried. Everyone else also showed similar reactions of concern.

Calmly yet firmly, Tychicus said, "Son, we did *not* see a *leopard*. We saw a *leper*."

Their demeanor did not change much with this revelation. Crossing a leopard, or a leper, brought thoughts of potential danger to mind.

Tychicus snickered as he set the record straight. "A leper came to the road in front of us just outside of Tiberias. But I sent him away."

"Did he touch the boy?" asked Tamar with concern.

"Mother, he didn't come near. We really didn't come close to him at all. Everything is fine," Rebekah added to put her parents' mind at ease. "Other than that, we enjoyed an uneventful trip. We're just so glad to be here for the festival."

"We talked about frogs! And Moses!" Justus said enthusiastically.

Tamar, relieved, gave Rebekah another hug. "We're so glad you're all here as well," she said. Bukkiah agreed.

Zibeon responded, "May God be praised!"

Tychicus looked at Rebekah with a look that spoke volumes. She didn't hear any words from his mouth but heard his silent statement loud and clear. Though he expressed his delight in being at the festival, the truth be told, he'd fallen away from God in recent years and understood everyone knew of it. He hoped he wouldn't be confronted with the fact in Zibeon's home. Rebekah longed for her husband to come back to God and be the man he had been. Again, at that moment, she prayed a silent prayer she'd been praying for so long. In the quietness of her heart, she cried out, *O God, please do whatever it takes to bring Tychicus back to you.* Tychicus, however, hoped the whole situation would be avoided.

The seven days of festival would start in the morning, so Tamar suggested they get some rest as much work awaited them the following day. Zibeon had Justus in his arms as they walked toward their room.

"Rebekah," Tamar said, "will you help me with something, dear?"

Tychicus smiled before turning to follow Zibeon and Justus. After a long walk in the heat of the day, he looked forward to getting some rest.

"What do you need, Mother?" Rebekah knew her mother had servants she could call upon at any time. Why did she need her help with anything? Surely something concerned her.

"How's Isaac? We so hoped he could've made this journey with you."

Rebekah could read her mother's body language. She knew her mother so well. She understood something other than Uncle Isaac filled her thoughts. "Mother, what troubles you?" she asked.

"How's Tychicus? We've been praying for him."

"Mother, please don't say anything. Tell Father not to say anything either. I don't want to start this visit having to deal with this. We actually had a very nice conversation with Justus about the festival on the road. Tychicus actually seemed excited about coming. I know his heart has wandered far from God, and though I don't agree with him, he has his reasons. I trust God will work a miracle in his life, and I'm praying for that as you have been. But right now, please do not say anything to him. Please. During the next few days, he just needs to see the joy of the Lord in this place, in our lives. And I trust God will use that to start Tychicus on a journey back to God." She understood her parents' concern but knew she would hear the backlash of anything that might be perceived as judgment from Tychicus. The journey home would provide far too much time to squabble, and how she would rather talk than face that argument.

"I'll talk to your father. But it will be hard. You know he really loves Tychicus. He just wants him to return to his faith and be the man he used to be. He wants the best for you and Justus too. At the center of your father's heart, he longs for your home to be led by a godly man."

"I know, Mother. That's what I want as well. That's what we need! But Tychicus has to come to that place on his own. He's heard it all from me, so many times. I don't think he wants to hear it from anyone else, not now. All we can do is pray for him." Rebekah became emotional. Tears did not come, though her voice quivered ever so slightly. How she loved her husband! She longed for him to once again place his full trust in the God she loved and served so faithfully. She prayed for restoration.

Tamar gave her daughter a loving hug. "We'll keep praying, dear. We will trust God to do something miraculous in his life. You'll see. We serve a great and mighty God." She smiled at her daughter, squeezing her ever so tightly. "Now you must get some rest as well."

"Yes, Mother. I love you," Rebekah said.

"And I love you too."

Rebekah agreed and headed off to her quarters, where Tychicus would surely be waiting for her. As she walked through the house, she paused in the courtyard. How she loved this place. It held so many fond memories of her childhood. She could imagine Bukkiah chasing her and her older brothers scolding him. She smiled as she appreciated the good family she had. She had been fortunate to live in a close-knit relationship with her mother, her father, and her brothers. She relished in the carefree time of her youth in this place.

The fond thoughts did not last long, however, as she reflected on her mother's concerns. Her mind went back to one incident that had become significant in her life. She had been praying at the temple one day when an incident with Jotham, the chief priest, changed her life. She understood it became the cause for her husband's struggle with the temple and his relationship with God. Jotham's actions had built a foundation where much damage had been built. He didn't care, which made the whole scenario even sadder. She had relived that moment so many times in her thoughts, and though she tried to repress them, they kept resurfacing. Tychicus had become a constant reminder of the fact.

Jotham's wickedness repulsed her to the core, especially considering his position at the temple. How could someone who claimed to be a man of God live with such disparity? He would surely face God's judgment some day, which brought little comfort at the present time seeing the effect it had on her husband, her family, and her own existence. For now she would continue to pray, hoping that the time in her parents' home might start to chip away at the wall Tychicus had set up between himself and God. As she stood still in the courtyard, she prayed.

CHAPTER 3

The early-morning sun rose on Magdala as the first day of the festival had arrived. Soon joy and celebration filled the home of Zibeon as praise lifted heavenward to God for his goodness in the year gone by. The household had truly experienced God's favor with much prosperity and blessing. In response, they stopped to give praise to God.

Many family members and workers joined together around Zibeon's tables. Unlike any other time of the year, the sound of rejoicing filled the courtyard during this time. While everyone enjoyed the Seder meal, Zibeon stood up. "Listen to me, everyone. Please stop for a moment to listen to my words." The rustling of the crowd came to a halt as everyone directed their attention toward their kind host. "Family, friends, laborers, and servants alike, our God has once again been merciful to us and placed his hand of favor over our home and over the work of our hands. He's chosen to smile upon us and bless us. Let us praise God for his loving kindness. We give him praise. Join with me as I proclaim, 'Blessed be the name of the Lord!'" Enthusiastic cheers arose in the house from nearly everyone. The appreciation of so many voices lifted to heaven in one accord, though one voice remained silent.

Tychicus grinned. He would put up with Rebekah's family as they celebrated; he would not stand in their way. Though, at the same time, the harness of his heart refused to allow his participation.

With a wide smile, Zibeon continued. "We praise our God Jehovah for our whole family. I thank the Almighty One for my sons, Mattaniah, Shubael, and Bukkiah, and their wives and our grandchildren. I thank the Almighty for Tychicus and our daughter, Rebekah, and their son—and all the children that are to come!" Zibeon's desire for his only daughter to have more children, shared by Tamar, had become a common topic of discussion during recent visits. "May God increase our number, and may we continue to find favor in his sight!" Again, with enthusiasm, he shouted, "Blessed be the name of the Lord!"

As more cheers arose, Justus jumped onto Tychicus's lap. He looked at his son with a loving smile. Besides Rebekah, this would be the only thing that would bring joy from his heart this day. Surrounded by many who were praising God, he simply enjoyed sitting with his son.

"We praise our God for increasing our flocks and our crops, for increasing our territory, and blessing us with his favor. Let's celebrate this day and give praise to Adonai, our God and King!" Zibeon started singing a song loudly, giving further praise to God with his hands raised toward heaven. Most of the family sitting around the table joined in celebrating the goodness and blessing of their God as they clapped and sang along. Many stood up and started dancing with joy.

Tychicus simply snuggled up to his son because he loved him. This also served as a convenient escape from following the crowd, doing something he did not have the heart to do. How awkward he would feel having to act as if he were praising God, though his lack of enthusiasm would have surely singled him out as a hypocrite.

As Rebekah lifted hands of praise up to God, she glanced over at her husband, noticing his lack of participation. Quickly he placed both hands over his heart. She smiled and winked at him as she placed her hands over her heart. Then silently she cried, *O God, please do whatever it takes to bring Tychicus back to you.*

Her prayer was nearly cut short as Zibeon made his last official declaration: "Let us eat and drink and be merry, for God has chosen to bless us. Praise be to our God!" The feast continued following Zibeon's final cheer.

Tychicus enjoyed spending time with Rebekah's brothers, even though they all shared their father's zeal for "religious matters." Nonetheless, they accepted him, and he appreciated that. They all knew about the struggle he had in the temple and with the chief priest Jotham. They didn't agree with his decision to distance himself from God as a result, but they chose to love him just the same. Justus longed to play with his cousins, and all in all, the festival was a time of rejoicing.

The day went by slow for Tychicus. As the sun started to set, he stood out by the road deep in thought. If all the people gathered in Zibeon's home could see and delight in the greatness and goodness of God, why did he have such trouble embracing it? He really started to wonder. There were no priests in the family. Many gathered there were servants and common laborers—just ordinary men like himself. If they could have such confidence in God, why couldn't he?

He recalled the day when it all started to decline for him: Rebekah had been in the temple praying. Justus, three years old, had fallen asleep in her tender arms as she knelt beside the altar. Tychicus usually went to the temple with his wife, but this day he had been delayed, so she went on ahead.

When he finally walked into the temple, he saw his wife kneeling in prayer. How he enjoyed this sight! But then he noticed Jotham, the chief priest, who, unaware of Tychicus's presence, had positioned himself off to one side where he stared at her. He continued gazing at Rebekah with lust in his eyes. He had a devilish look in his eyes, and Tychicus could sense his dark heart. This wasn't right. Though it could not be more obvious, he wondered how this behavior could be found in a chief priest. Rebekah felt his eyes before and had talked with her husband about it. Tychicus instinctively had doubts. After all, he considered initially Jotham to be a man of God. But now, how could he explain what he just witnessed with his very own eyes?

At that moment, Tychicus remembered the old story of King David and Bathsheba. He was well taught in the Scriptures, and this story instantly became tangible to him. While King David's men were off to battle, he stayed behind, taking a walk on the roof of his palace one night. He saw a very beautiful woman bathing and made a conscious decision to continue watching her. He could have chosen to look away. He could have simply gone back to one of his wives, back into his palace, away from temptation. But he allowed lust to fill his heart. He actively set out to identify her, discovering she belonged to another man. He learned her name was Bathsheba, the daughter of Eliam and the wife of one of his soldiers, Uriah the Hittite. Then as soon as he knew who she was, despite who she was, he sent for her and slept with her. Lust had overtaken him—and it was sinful.

If the king had gone off to war with his men, he would not have been home to walk on his palace roof. If he had stayed in his own bed, he would have never seen Bathsheba and would have never been tempted by her beauty. If he had turned away after seeing her, he wouldn't have been filled with lust that led to his iniquitous actions. But the "man of God" turned to the beauty of a woman and away from God, becoming obsessed with obtaining forbidden fruit.

How could this have happened to David, one so close to God? And how could God permit such a thing? He wondered if Jotham, the priest, had become like David, turning his affections away from God toward a woman—*his woman!* He had truly been tempted and had acted on the temptation as far as he could. What was next? He wouldn't stand for it! Rebekah would not be subjected to this evil man's indiscretion! Everything inside him sought to protect his beautiful wife.

He continued watching the chief priest for just a moment to reaffirm his suspicion. Jotham continued staring as Tychicus saw his actions as not only obvious and unusual but also exceedingly wicked and wrong. Many men had been kind to Rebekah, surely as a result of her beauty, but respectful kindness and this act of lust were like night and day.

Instantly so many thoughts came back to him about the times he'd seen Jotham around his wife and some of the subtle words he had spoken to her. He also remembered his wife's suspicions, which he had dismissed. He now saw the chief priest in a different light. He'd been exposed. Tychicus knew he must put a stop to this.

He ran up to the altar and grabbed Rebekah by the arm, abruptly telling her they had to leave. She had been in deep prayer, and such a sudden command surprised her as she sat up. Almost instantaneously, Tychicus could not believe that someone had grabbed *his* arm. As he turned around, he stood face-to-face with Jotham.

Before Tychicus could say one word, Jotham rebuked him, saying, "Do not hinder a woman in prayer. It is a holy matter between God and—"

The chief priest didn't get another syllable out as Tychicus grabbed him by his cloak with both hands, lifting him up. He forcefully pushed him back as righteous anger took over. "You keep your evil eyes off my wife! You walk around the temple like a saint, a chief priest, but you're the chief of sinners! You may act like a man of God, but I know you're just an actor—*a hypocrite!*"

"Guards!" Jotham cried.

Rebekah, unaware of what prompted this, watched in amazement as her husband threw the priest to the ground. Everyone in the temple stared in utter shock, becoming reluctant spectators to this most unusual event.

Jotham looked up at Tychicus from where he lay. "Leave the temple! Leave this place *now!* You do not treat a man of God in this manner!"

Tychicus fired back. "You are *not* a man of God! *You should be more concerned with your sin than the fact that I call you a sinner!*"

"Where are the guards? Guards!" Jotham cried again.

Justus woke up and started crying as Tychicus forcefully led Rebekah out of the temple. Tychicus determined that would be the last time he would set foot in this temple. What kind of God would have such a representative? If Jotham embodied the semblance of a man of God, Tychicus wanted no part of it. As long as Jotham continue to "serve" in that temple, he would have nothing to do with it. In his eyes, this evil priest had made it an unholy place.

By his response to my story I could tell Archippus had never considered a chief priest who could be so devious. He could not even comprehend what he considered to be such a strong contradiction. After all, he'd headed to the temple to seek help from a priest. Surely he must have wondered how he could trust any of them if some were so secretly unholy?

"How could a chief priest, a supposed man of God, be so ungodly?" he asked.

I responded with a smile. Archippus had not anticipated such a response. "Well, that's what Tychicus had to learn the hard way. If he'd only taken his father-in-law's advice…"

The story continued.

Zibeon told Tychicus many times that he should look to God, not to man. But his pride would not allow him to let go of his bitterness in this matter. He couldn't get past this. And as a result, he now stood near the road, pondering the relationship his wife and her family had with God. It had been a relationship he once embraced but recently walked away from. He just couldn't look past the actions of this evil chief priest.

Just then he heard the sound of donkey hooves coming toward the road from the house. He turned to see Abednego, leading another donkey behind his own as he had the day before. This day the packs looked fuller. He wondered what his destination might be with such a load. Out of curiosity, he asked, "My servant, what have you in your packs, and where are you going?"

Immediately he acted apprehensive. "I'm sorry. The master told me not to say. I'm so sorry. Please forgive me." Abednego didn't know what else to say. He looked a little anxious, hoping he'd done the right thing.

This was not the response Tychicus anticipated. To him, he had asked a rather harmless question. "Very well, go on," he said. His curiosity wasn't that strong.

The donkeys walked down the road as Tychicus turned and walked back toward the house. Another day of festival would soon arrive.

Later that evening, he lay down but could not fall sleep. He revisited so many thoughts that had been awakened in his mind during the day. He thought about the discussion with his son on the road and its spiritual implications. He thought about Rebekah's family and their strong devotion to God. He pondered his inner turmoil in contrast to their outer peace. He thought about Jotham, which, once again, angered him. He pondered his wife and her quiet spirit. He had married such a lovely and beautiful woman. Did she deserve more from him as her husband? He wrestled with all these issues though any form of resolution eluded him.

Two hours later, he heard the sound of donkey hooves approaching the house. He walked over to the window as quietly as he could. He didn't want to wake Rebekah, and he didn't want to be seen by whoever might be coming up to the house. He peered through the window, seeing a single man riding a donkey, with another donkey being led behind them. Abednego had returned from his evening trip. Tychicus noticed the donkey's packs appeared empty. He wondered what goods he had in his pack and to whom he made a delivery. It would be just another question that would remain unanswered this night. He lay back down and stared at the ceiling for some time, finally falling asleep.

CHAPTER 4

The days of the festival had been wonderful, but now the trip back to Tiberias, and the return to the routine of every day life, had come.

"Are you sure you cannot stay longer? The festival will continue for four more days," Tamar begged.

Rebekah wanted nothing more than to stay for the length of the celebration, but she respected her husband, and his decision to leave early had been made.

"Mother, you know we would love to stay, but Tychicus has work to do. You know…"

Tamar knew exactly what she meant and understood she could not express the true feelings in her heart at the moment. Their return trip had little to do with the workload waiting for Tychicus in Tiberias, and it had much to do with his disinterest in participating in the festival. Everyone could see how he had struggled with it.

"Well, be sure to make plans to come back soon."

"We sure will," Tychicus said as he walked up.

"We really wish you would consider making your home here with us in Magdala. Your father-in-law could really use your help here, and…"

Tamar's words had been heard before, and Tychicus did not want to discuss this matter again. He considered her words as another rebuke concerning the decision he had made to move to Tiberias, away from the family. Though this was never her intent, this was how he saw it. Instead of talking through it again, he simply turned away from her to check the donkey. Tamar and Rebekah viewed his response as rude, an accurate perception. He had enough of anyone trying to tell him how to live his life. He had made the decisions he had made, and no one was going to tell him what to do, especially his in-laws.

"Mother, I'm sorry."

"Don't say another word, dear."

"Another word about what?" Zibeon asked as he joined the conversation.

"Nothing, Father. Tychicus is just a little…" She tried to find the right words though nothing rolled off her tongue.

"We will continue to pray for Tychicus and for you, dear." Zibeon gave his daughter a loving hug. Rebekah wrapped her arms around her father. How she loved him!

"Rebekah, we must be going. Where's Justus?" Tychicus asked.

"He's playing with his cousins in the courtyard. I will fetch him."

"Master, would you like me to get the boy?" Abednego offered as he approached them.

"That would be much appreciated, Abednego." Zibeon smiled. He understood the festival continued inside the house, and Justus loved the rare treat of playing with his cousins.

Before Abednego could return to the house, Bukkiah ran out with Justus beside him. They had been racing, and Bukkiah allowed Justus to outrun him as they approached everyone. Soon Mattaniah and Shubael followed with their wives. As a band of brothers, they all embraced Rebekah and adorned her with kisses. How they loved their little sister and wished she would stay for the remainder of the festival. Before long, everyone came from the house to bid them farewell.

"Sure you cannot stay for a few more days?" Bukkiah asked.

Timidly Rebekah responded, "We have to get back. Tychicus has some work he has to attend to." They also understood why Tychicus and Rebekah were leaving the festival early and understood how difficult it had been for her.

"Well, little man, you take care of your mommy and daddy," Mattaniah said.

"I'm not little," Justus insisted. "I'm this tall!" He stood up as straight as he could, placing his hand on his head. Everyone laughed as Tychicus smiled. His son really made him proud.

"Hurry back, our brother," Shubael said to Tychicus as he gave him a brotherly hug. Mattaniah and Bukkiah shared similar statements, also giving him a brotherly embrace. The three brothers' wives and Tamar also embraced Tychicus, Rebekah, and Justus, followed by all the children. Finally Zibeon stepped forward. The family patriarch was ready to give them his blessing for their trip. "Son, may the God of our fathers draw you near to him. Go in peace and with the blessing of our God. May the Lord grant you safety as you travel home. And may he bring you back to us soon, and often, and we will give him praise!"

"Yes! Yes! Praise the Lord," everyone gathered shouted in agreement.

Zibeon gave Rebekah a tender hug and whispered into her ear, "We will be praying." He kissed her on the cheek and then helped her onto the donkey as Tychicus grabbed the reins.

Tamar just couldn't get enough hugs from her grandson, and then their time together came to an end.

"We'll see you soon!" Tychicus declared as he started walking toward the road.

Justus held up his hands, filled with rocks he had just picked up from the road. "See you soon!" he echoed before turning around, throwing his first rock of the journey home. Many would follow as they headed on their way back to Tiberias.

Tychicus and Rebekah started talking on the road as Justus turned to wave good-bye again, now barely able to see the house. Tychicus looked at his wife and smiled as she sat on the back of their donkey.

"I enjoyed the festival," he said. "Your father didn't say anything to me about the temple. Not even one word," he said with surprise and relief.

Rebekah just smiled. He had enjoyed the festival? She didn't get that impression from watching him and assumed this to be an attempt at being respectful to her and her family's tradition. "You know my family loves you. They want what's best for you." She wanted to say more, but something stopped her, and probably for good reason. Silently she prayed for him as she always did. *If only Jotham would leave the temple*, she thought, *perhaps that stumbling block would be removed.* She just prayed and trusted God to work in his own way, in his own time.

Justus followed along, throwing rocks as he walked. Rebekah sat on the donkey enjoying her ride, which hadn't yet become cumbersome. Even more so, she enjoyed being together as a family. She pondered her parents' urging to have more children, and her motherly instincts were strong. Perhaps during the evening ahead, when all became quiet, she might discuss the idea of another child with her husband. Perhaps this night would be special as they might work together toward that end. She smiled at Tychicus, thinking of the potential romance before them, though he did not know her intimate thoughts.

Tychicus, however, thought about the work he had back home. After being away for several days, he knew there would be much to do. As a woodworker, he'd enjoyed his days of apprenticeship, but in the last few years, he had established himself as a skilled carpenter. He loved working with his hands and with wood. He didn't miss dealing with fish on a daily basis. He often joked that the wood smelled better than the fish.

Sometimes, he enjoyed it too much, and his work took him away from his family. At times, it had also become a convenient excuse to keep him away from the temple. He always thought he'd slow down at some point, or so he said on several occasions. There would always be time for family later, and he believed nothing would ever take him away from the work he loved.

The journey neared an end, as the city gates were in sight, and what a welcome sight they were. It had been a rather quiet trip. Uneventful really. Rebekah longed to get off the donkey, and Justus anxiously awaited anything other than traveling. As they approached the city gates, they heard Josech, the blind beggar, who remained by the gate sitting on his blanket. He'd heard the clomping of the donkey, and his voice now welcomed them with his common plea. "Please, help a poor beggar. Please have mercy on me. Please…"

Tychicus and Rebekah had heard this plea so many times, and as usual, they found it easy to block it out. It had become far too common, like meaningless, intrusive, background noise. The beggar pleaded over and over again as they neared the gate.

Then, unexpectedly, he addressed them personally. "Are you thirsty from your journey, sir?" Josech used this term to show respect for someone in a higher position, which was obviously an easy task for him. You couldn't get much lower than being a blind beggar.

"I'm thirsty too. Please help me," the beggar said.

For the first time, for some unknown reason, Tychicus stopped to interact with the man he'd passed countless times. "Don't you have anyone to bring you food or water?"

"No, sir. Just an occasional gesture of kindness from unseen angels. But even they've forgotten me lately. Please, will you help me?" Josech made a plea he'd made so many times before. But his plea fell on deaf ears as Tychicus continued on his way, turning his head.

Rebekah felt compassion for this poor man as she looked at him. Unlike other passes through the gates, perhaps due to her husband's momentary stop, she found herself drawn to his plight. She watched him, not saying a word. His dilemma touched her for the first time, though she offered no help. Her heart swelled with empathy as they continued to move farther away from this man in deep need. What a sad sight. Why didn't someone help this poor man? How she hoped someone would, but who? She started to pray, "Lord, please send someone—"

Her earnest words were interrupted as someone jumped on her husband's back. This unexpected event shocked her as she sat up in horror. She never anticipated such an act. No one did. The assailant had entered the courtyard without notice, without warning, and his attack was both swift and direct. Who would mount such an attack—and in broad daylight?

Tychicus nearly fell down as he let go of the donkey's reins, wondering who had jumped onto him and now held him tight. He desperately fought to throw the man from his back without success as the man held on with all his might. Startled, the donkey jumped up as Rebekah fell to the ground with a hard thud, landing on her shoulder. Justus started crying loudly in the confusion. Everyone in the vicinity scattered, as several started pointing to the man as they frantically called out in terror, "Unclean! Unclean! Unclean!"

Rebekah's natural reaction was to grab Justus and run to a safe place. She reached for him, wincing from the pain in her shoulder. Nonetheless, she reached out to him and drew him near before rushing him away. She looked over her shoulder, wondering who might come to her husband's aid, though no one dared. Everyone ran from the incident that instantly garnered everyone's attention.

Unknown to anyone, the leper they'd seen on the road a few days earlier had entered the town. What an unthinkable act for an unclean man! Didn't he know he wasn't allowed in the town? How dare he enter the city gates, much less attack an innocent bystander in this way! Didn't he know he wasn't allowed to have any contact with anyone? He had appeared out of thin air.

The leper's hoarse voice filled the courtyard in an awkwardly strange manner as he continued to wrap his bony arms around Tychicus. He cried, "Help me! I'm a man! Touch me! Talk to me!" He repeated this over and over, proclaiming his humanity, something he had been deprived of for so long. Now in a frantic effort, he longed for human acceptance and social contact.

The whole time Tychicus yelled, "Get off! Get off! Get off!"

The more he struggled and yelled at the leper, the more the leper screamed in return, holding on for dear life: "I'm a man!"

Tychicus repeatedly punched the man in the head, which rested on the back of his neck. He knew he hurt the leper as blood drained down the back of his neck. He threw his elbows into the man's chest as hard as he could, hearing the crunching of cracking ribs. The harder Tychicus fought, the harder the man held on as he continued to lament as best he could.

Rebekah watched in horror. The man on her husband's back was taking such a beating and doing nothing to protect himself. He did not lash out or do anything aggressive in defense. He simply held on and yelled his desire for acceptance.

The struggle between the two continued frantically as Tychicus threw both of them to the ground. The man gasped as he landed on his back with Tychicus's full weight crashing down on him. They wrestled as they rolled in the dirt as blood stained both of their garments. Tychicus was fighting to be released from this man who fought to hang on.

Tychicus tried desperately to free himself from his attacker, but the desperate man had sunk his clawlike fingers into his flesh. He'd locked on. In his desperation, it appeared that he had manifested a supernatural human strength. The leper had latched on and didn't intend to let go as Tychicus's flesh started to tear. He held on to his innocent victim with all he had—and more.

Tychicus screamed in agony. What a horrible sight! What a horrible sound!

Rebekah felt helpless. What could she do? She could see this man did not want to harm her husband, and the more Tychicus fought, the more severe his injuries became. She started to yell, "Stop! Stop! Stop!"

As she yelled, the leper continued screaming, "I'm a man! I'm a man! I'm a man!"

Tychicus also screamed with even more passion, "Get off! Let go! Get off me!"

It was total chaos as the three screamed while Justus cried even louder, though everyone else watched in stunned silence as the scuffle continued.

The leper hadn't felt the touch of another human being in so many years. He hadn't been spoken to, other than to be sent away over and over again. The only words he'd spoken regularly, other than the moanings of self-pity and utter despair, were the familiar repetition of that one word: "Unclean. Unclean. Unclean." Every time he came anywhere near another person, these words were required to be given as a warning. He decided he'd spoken that word for the last time. He'd been rejected far too long. Now in hopelessness, and perhaps borderline insanity, he tried one last time to be recognized as something more than a hideous creature cursed by God and rejected by men—a walking dead man.

Why did he choose Tychicus? Had the rejection just a few days before remained fresh in his mind? Could this be some form of revenge? Perhaps he had been chosen randomly. No one could ever say. But now he clung on as Tychicus fought to free himself from his grasp. The struggle continued as the two rolled around on the ground.

Finally, one last long, loud deafening cry erupted from the leper before he became eerily still. Years of suffering had been released with one haunting, hellish expression of agony. Then his will to survive ceased to exist. He'd finally given up as he stopped struggling. He was dead. The courtyard had never been so still.

Tychicus pried the remains of the man from his body as each heaving breath filled the ears of a stunned and quiet audience. He slowly made it to his feet. The clawlike fingers had torn into his skin, and his torso now oozed with blood. It looked like a merciless, ravenous, wild animal had attacked him. And even now as he stood as the victor, his body showed the wounds of an intense fight while the remains of his attacker lay at his feet. He stared down at him, wondering why this ordeal had just taken place. The leper had gotten a bloody nose during the scuffle, and his blood had stained his tattered cloak. His long, greasy hair still covered his face. Even now in death, he remained a faceless, unknown man. No one would mourn him. No one would care. But one thing was certain: this man's agonizing existence had finally come to an end.

With every ounce of his being, Tychicus wished this attack had been made by a wild animal. But he'd been attacked and mauled by an unclean and diseased outcast whose contact in any form had been forbidden. He felt like he'd just wrestled with the devil, and though he was the only one standing, he knew he would be the loser. He was now, most likely, unclean.

Many watched from afar. They were afraid of Tychicus now. Covered with blood and dirt, he appeared gruesome. Even Rebekah stood a ways off, watching in horror as she held her shoulder. Justus clung on to Rebekah's leg. His scared and muffled cry broke the courtyard's stunned silence ever so slightly. The fight had ended, and Tychicus stood alone. No one had come to his aid, and no one would approach him now. The quite murmuring started to rumble as some could be heard, saying, "He's unclean."

Only one man took several steps toward him while keeping his distance. Tychicus made eye contact with him, almost expecting his presence.

Finally, a sly and evil half grin emerged on the man's face as if he found some form of twisted pleasure in witnessing this dreadful attack. Without any close examination, Jotham, the chief priest, made a determination. Finally, he spoke. His words were loudly authoritative and without compassion. Though he spoke directly to several temple guards standing beside him; his words were loud enough for all to hear. "Off to the infirmary!"

The infirmary was a place of isolation. Everyone knew no one wanted to visit this place under any circumstance. Immediately, Tychicus knew he'd be separated from his family for at least seven days, in accordance with the law. Instead of heading off to work the next morning, he'd begin a time of waiting to see if this attack had left him with the earliest signs of leprosy—a determination, he knew, that would be ultimately determined by the chief priest.

Before he could totally grasp this, Jotham spoke the words anyone would shiver to hear. They rolled off his lips like a spell coming from the tongue of an evil wizard. He stared at Tychicus before saying, "You are... *unclean!*" It seemed a premature declaration, though he made it nonetheless. Evidently, he enjoyed the power his position granted him in this situation, especially before a captive audience.

Two temple guards, standing on either side of Tychicus, escorted him as he headed for the infirmary. Under the thumb of the chief priest he hated, his anger boiled. What had just happened? In an instant, life took a radical turn down an uncharted, undesired road that only led to despair.

Rebekah watched in silence. She could not speak. Crouched down to the ground in shock, her body trembled as she held her son in her arms. Together they shared tears of sorrow and sadness.

CHAPTER 5

Rebekah walked toward the temple. She had walked this route nearly every day, though this day would not be a typical visit to pray. She walked up the steps, through the doors, and into the temple. A quiet reverence filled this large room. Inside, however, her heart filled with an awkward uneasiness. The tension and anxiety that had built up in her soul along the journey to this commonly peaceful place was unfamiliar. With each step along the dirt path, her heart beat harder and harder in her chest.

She walked up to the temple altar where she knelt down quickly. She lowered her head and offered a simple, distraught prayer. "Lord, give me strength!"

She stood up and looked around. One older woman knelt down far to her right. As still as a statue, she prayed silently. Far to her left she saw the back of a temple guard standing near a window. She walked directly to him.

"Excuse me, sir. I am here to talk with Jotham, the chief priest."

The guard looked at her sternly, without feeling. He possessed an arrogance that looked down on her, a simple, lowly female. His lack of compassion and interest mirrored Jotham's smug demeanor.

"Do you know where he might be?" she asked after a short pause.

He looked at her with indifference before saying, "Come with me."

The guard marched off in front of her as she followed him through several hallways. They walked up to a door where the guard turned, giving a command to her. "Stay here."

He walked into the room, shutting the door behind him. Several minutes later, he opened the door. "This way." His words were short. His abrupt, unkind attitude seemed inappropriate for someone stationed at the temple—the house of God. Nonetheless, she walked into the room.

Jotham sat in a chair as she entered the room. He did not say a word. His lack of speech silently declared a lack of empathy. Surely Jotham knew the reason for her visit this day.

Rebekah wanted to waste no more time. "When can I see my husband?" she asked. The night had been long, and Justus had already asked far too many times when his father would be coming home. His young mind couldn't comprehend what had happened, and Rebekah didn't have any calming answers. One thought kept running through her mind: "How could this be happening?"

The chief priest remained silent. His lack of response was torture, as intended.

"Please, let me see my husband. Please!"

Jotham looked down at Rebekah, whose pleading had now caused her to drop to her knees. Not one ounce of compassion could be found in him. He rather enjoyed the whole scene playing out before him.

Finally, he spoke with a tone of arrogance. "I told you to pray for him. He has chosen to defy the temple, and he will finally face God's judgment. God will not stand for such behavior! Do not forget the sin of King Uzziah, who defiled the holy of holies by offering a sacrifice when he had no right to do it. Even when eighty priests approached him, the sons of Aaron, he responded with unholy anger! And do not forget Miriam, who was racist against Moses's wife then refused to follow his leadership. They were *both* struck with leprosy! *When you sin against God, there will be a reckoning!* Your husband has refused to repent of his sin. He has responded in an unholy manner, and now he must pay the price!"

Rebekah looked directly into the face of the chief priest whose unbridled anger now turned to an evil joy. She couldn't believe the words he spewed toward her. She couldn't believe a priest could have such a cruel and hateful heart. She thought this man should be the one who should repent for his lack of compassion, for his unmistakable evil intentions. But even now as she looked into his eyes, she saw straight into his heart—and its wickedness was evident.

"You have forgotten the end of Miriam's story! Moses pleaded with the Lord for her to be healed from her leprosy—and that is my prayer as well!" Rebekah waited for a response, but once again, Jotham did not respond other than to grin.

How she wanted to put an end to this foolishness! His whole attitude was inappropriate for someone who claimed to be a servant of God.

"When can I see my husband?" Her question became direct and demanding though tears streamed down her face. She had enough of this man's self-righteousness. He had taken her husband, and she vowed he wouldn't have any control over her. He would never manipulate her.

She stared at the priest, waiting for an answer.

Jotham could no longer look into Rebekah's eyes as he started to pace back and forth.

"The initial time of isolation has been determined to be seven days, according to the law. At that time, I will reexamine him to see if his condition has worsened or not. He will then be isolated for an additional seven days. After that time, if his condition has not worsened, I will consider his condition harmless, and then he will be allowed to be brought back into the general population. But I wouldn't plan on that."

Rebekah understood it would be some time, at best, before she saw her husband. She did see the blood, which covered his cloak. She saw his wounds. What a hideous sight! Again, she couldn't believe this had happened. It didn't make any sense.

"What if his condition doesn't get better?" she asked reluctantly.

Jotham smiled an evil smile. "What do *you* think?" he asked.

Rebekah couldn't accept the alternative: banishment. Why would God do such a thing to her husband? To her? To their son? To their family?

"I will continue to plead with the Lord for his healing!" she stated with a zealous determination.

Jotham simply responded with laughter as he mocked Rebekah's faith to her face. Rebekah saw this conduct as mockery, not only to her but also toward God.

She stood up looking at Jotham one last time. The sneer she'd learned to loathe still crossed his face. A feeling of nausea filled her stomach as she turned to walk away. She thought, *This just can't be happening.* But, indeed, it was.

She marched out of the room, down the hallways, and ran out the front doors. She headed toward her house feeling sicker than she had in such a long time. She stopped along the road to vomit. Her body had become weak, and her spirit was uncharacteristically forlorn. Her joyous heart had been wounded.

Jotham walked to the infirmary, where he stood beside the door leading into Tychicus's room. He quickly peered through the small window in the door from the back of the hallway, hoping his presence would not be detected. Tychicus sat on a bench with his head in his hands. Jotham quietly took several steps toward the door to listen.

Tychicus jumped to his feet and paced back and forth in the small room where he'd been confined. This sudden movement startled Jotham as he struggled to keep from making an audible sound.

Tychicus, like Rebekah and Justus, didn't understand what had happened. His mind's eye still saw the look on Jotham's face—and that grin. He kept thinking, *Surely he isn't... smiling...* Tychicus just faced the most traumatic event of his young life, one that could possibly alter the course of his entire destiny toward incredible devastation—and this priest responded with a smile? He mumbled to himself, loud enough for Jotham to hear, "What an evil man. *He* deserves to be penned up."

Jotham knew this statement had been made concerning him, which caused him to step back quietly to guarantee his presence would not be detected.

As each moment passed, Tychicus's anger grew with renewed vitality like a caged animal eager to escape. His rage bottled up inside until it could not be contained any longer. Finally, he screamed at the top of his lungs with a horrifying scream, which scared Jotham even more as he jumped away even farther from the door. His cry echoed through the hallways of the infirmary from the depths of his soul, though Tychicus felt like no one heard him. The pain in his chest and back throbbed as his unattended wounds started to bleed again.

He raised his fist toward the ceiling as he began to curse God. "Why would you allow this to happen to me? What have I done? What did I do to deserve this? You can do whatever you want, and you choose this? What's wrong with you? I didn't do anything wrong! Why don't you strike down that evil priest? Why me? Why?"

He continued to yell, as his words seemed to bounce off the ceiling. As much as he doubted it, God heard him, as did Jotham. After hearing this display of extreme frustration, the chief priest stood silently in the hallway, motionless.

Just then Jotham heard some faint footsteps far down the hallway. He spun around as someone walked toward him. Laban, one of the priests, approached, carrying a tray of food.

Instantly Jotham hurried to meet him.

"What have we here?" Jotham asked in a quiet whisper.

"I have the evening meal for—" Laban began to say as the chief priest stopped him.

"Let me take that. I will deal with it myself. Tychicus is... praying. We should allow him to finish." Jotham snatched the tray from Laban's able hands with a quick jerk, nearly spilling a small jar of water. Only one man had been detained in the infirmary at this time. There could not be any doubt this food was intended for Tychicus.

"Send him my greetings. Tell him we are praying for his recovery."

Laban's words barely left his mouth as Jotham responded, "Yes, now go! Be off with you."

Laban did not understand the chief priest's anxiousness and his quietness. He found it rather curious, suspicious. Even so, the tray now rested in Jotham's hands as he turned to go.

After several steps, Jotham spoke again in a hushed tone, "Wait!" Laban turned back around, facing the chief priest. "Please allow me to take his evening meal to him from this time on. It will give me a chance to encourage him as you have done." Jotham glared at Laban with an uncomfortable grin.

"As you desire," Laban replied with a tinge of uncertainty in his tone. By the way he had handled this whole situation up to this point, he didn't anticipate Jotham's desire to be an encouragement. Perhaps he had misjudged him. He decided to accept Jotham's spoken offer. After all, an attitude of encouragement should be one coming from a man in Jotham's position. This might give him a chance to prove himself.

Jotham watched until Laban walked through the door out of sight. He looked down at the tray. He held a plate of fish, along with some bread and grapes. It did smell delicious, and Jotham wondered if the aroma of the fish had reached Tychicus's nostrils yet. He turned back around and took several steps toward the door. He hurried past, ducking down under the window as he passed by. He scurried down the hallway toward the far door as quietly as he could.

"Laban?" Tychicus called out. "Laban, are you there?"

Jotham was relieved that Tychicus had not heard them talking in the hallway.

He walked toward the small window and inhaled. He smelled a hint of fish, and he was hungry. He peered through the window as best he could. "Laban?" he called out, now in frustration. He pulled on the locked door handle, shaking it furiously before screaming once again at the top of his lungs. "Laban!"

Jotham stood near the door, just out of sight, with an evil grin on his face. He had already slipped several of the grapes into his mouth. As he bit down on them, he found they were juicy and full of flavor. They tasted so good!

Tychicus slammed both of his fists on the door several times, which disguised the sound of the chief priest's steps as he scampered away. All Tychicus heard was the shutting of a door as it slammed behind Jotham at the end of the hallway.

He wondered who had been in the hallway. Again, he called for Laban, but no response could be heard.

Tychicus sat back down on the bench. He was tired, weary, and very hungry. He just wanted answers. He just wanted understanding. And at this moment, he just wanted food. But all he would receive would be a heart of bitterness that overshadowed him. It would churn during the coming days of isolation, and the harsh treatment from Jotham would only add to his rage. He cursed God and Jotham at the top of his lungs.

Meanwhile, the chief priest found a side door where he set the tray down on the ground for some alley dogs to discover. He took the rest of the grapes and the pitcher of water with him as he laughed to himself with undue delight. This scenario would become common during the days that followed.

CHAPTER 6

Josech sat near the city gate. Another day had passed, and he found himself still sitting there. His begging for this day had come to an end. He knew further begging would be unheard.

It had been a typical day. Hunger and loneliness remained his close companions. He once again sat alone as he listened to the sounds of the night, his only friends. There were faint voices in the background of people inside the city. They seemed another world away. There were always the noises from a random donkey or some kind of domestic animal. Soon, he understood, the city would become totally silent. He would be left with the subtle noises of the countryside that would fade into the quietness of the night, as he would eventually fall unconscious. It would prove to be a short period of deliverance as he would wake to another day he'd relived so many times. The lack of respect would return. Begging for daily provision would resume. Disappointment would surely follow. Now he just wanted to sleep—his only reprieve from the existence he endured.

As he started to drift off, he heard an unfamiliar sound. Quiet footsteps were coming toward him on the outside of the wall. They were soft and slow. He'd heard unwelcome footsteps before during the night. His mind filled with the remembrance of one night in particular when a beating followed such footsteps from a drunken man who wanted to take his anger out on an easy, defenseless target. He had become a target for a coward. But these steps were different. He did not hear the mumblings of a drunken man. In fact, he didn't hear any human voice at all. With each new step, the stranger came closer.

He had experienced fear before. This night all fear had been depleted as calmness surrounded him. He hoped for some form of pleasant encounter. He had prayed for an angel to minister to him so many times. Perhaps his many prayers were about to be answered.

Josech listened with anticipation. The quietness still filled the air. He took an inward, silent, deep breath. He could smell something, and it smelled good. It had been such a long time since this aroma filled his nostrils. Could that be *fresh* bread? Whenever he had been offered a morsel to eat, someone most likely had already discarded it. But this was *fresh* bread—he could tell. And it smelled so good.

Had he already fallen asleep? What a cruel dream that would be. Before he could even check to see if he slept, he heard a sweet voice.

"Greetings," a quiet voice whispered. The voice sounded tender and sweet, unlike anything he associated with fear. It definitely sounded like a woman—a kind, loving woman.

"Who's there?" asked Josech with a quiet anxiousness. He waited for a reply. Surely a kind soul would be willing to identify themselves, wouldn't they?

It became silent for just a few moments. Josech waited patiently.

"I brought you some bread. I hope you enjoy it. I also brought you some dates and some grapes, and something for you to drink. It's not much, but…" The voice became silent. He noticed a tinge of shyness in her sweet voice accompanied by a touch of timid apprehension. Nonetheless, Josech was glad she had followed through with this generous offering. After a pause, the steps quietly started to fade away.

Josech called out, "Who are you? Will you tell me your name?"

With his keen sense of hearing, he could tell this kind-hearted being was a young woman, if not an angel sent from heaven, perhaps on her first mission of kindness. He sensed compassion. Regardless of who she might be, she had been an answer to his many prayers.

The footsteps stopped at his query. From several feet away, the voice whispered just loud enough to hear, "I'm an angel…from the Lord." Then the footsteps faintly disappeared. He listened more intently than ever. He wondered if he'd hear the sound of angel's wings flapping ever so gently. He did not.

It became still once more. He reached out and felt a basket beside him. Inside he touched the small loaf of bread. His fingers explored farther as he felt the roundness of grapes. He could smell the dates and soon found them. He carefully felt around, finding a jar of water nearby.

He took the bread and put it up to his nose. He inhaled. Oh, the bread smelled so good! He took a small bite and chewed it slowly, cherishing every moment of this very rare treat. He swallowed as he leaned back against the wall. He pulled one of the grapes off the stem and placed it into his mouth, between his teeth. As he bit down, the juice filled his mouth. Oh, the sweet taste of heaven!

What an unexpected feast for a beggar, he thought. *Fresh bread, dates, and grapes.* For a brief moment, he enjoyed the food as he forgot his sad predicament. This act of kindness had given him a few seconds of happiness, for which he was grateful.

He couldn't contain himself. He shouted, "Bless you, my angel! Bless you!"

From a distance, ears heard as a smile covered the face of the unknown messenger.

He would never forget this expression of selfless kindness as he muttered, "What might your name be, my unseen angel?"

He listened once again, but she had gone.

He raised his head up toward the hidden starry sky and said, "Thank you, Lord, for this feast. You have heard my cry. I have prayed so long for you to send an angel to minister to me. I think I will continue to pray that you will send her back again!" He chuckled to himself. "Yes, Lord, send my unseen angel back to me."

He smiled as he feasted. Afterward, he leaned against the wall with a smile before falling asleep with a satisfied stomach.

CHAPTER 7

Rebekah and Justus walked through the market. *It should've been just another day,* she thought. But this day would be uncomfortably different, and she knew why. One set of glaring eyes after another silently gazed upon her as she made her way past many merchants with their carts in the marketplace. Some eyes were filled with sympathy; some, with empathy. Others were full of pity. By now everyone had heard about the details of the horrid event between Tychicus and the leper.

Timotheus, who stood by his fruit cart, offered a gift to Rebekah. "How are you doing today?" he asked. Justus stood by her side, holding her hand and wondering what he meant. Rebekah had sheltered his eyes from seeing his father's wounds. He had been saved from having those awful images in his head. From his perspective, he knew his father would be gone for several days. But other than that, nothing had changed at home. Though his mother had been crying, she still went to the temple to pray every day. Uncle Isaac lived with them, as he had for some time. Besides the awkwardness of their presence now, the normal routines of each day continued. That's how his young mind viewed it all.

"Have you heard from Tychicus? Will they let you talk to him?"

Timotheus had been originally an old family friend from the area north of Magdala. He had been an acquaintance of Zibeon and Tamar and had known Tychicus since his youth. He watched him grow up as a boy. Rebekah understood his concern but also knew he longed for the details of the day's juiciest gossip. Everyone would be talking about this as his patrons visited him to buy his produce. He wanted to know all the details. She treaded carefully. Besides, Rebekah had faced this question already this morning several times.

"No, they won't let us see him or talk to him. He's at the infirmary, for now."

"Well, we'll be praying for you, Rebekah," Timotheus said, a bit frustrated that he would not have exclusive news to pass on. He turned back to attend to his cart without another word.

Rebekah thought, *Why don't you pray for Tychicus?* She knew her husband's mental state and how he'd become bitter toward God. She feared this chapter in his life would surely push him even further from him. She could only imagine the hatred he had now for Jotham. In her heart, she prayed even more fervently than ever—*O God, please do whatever it takes to bring Tychicus back to you.*

Even amid her prayers, she heard some who talked behind her back. Some said, "Poor dear." Others voiced their pity on a woman who'd forever lost her husband, as they saw it, considering her to be a hopeless widow.

The outlook for someone locked in the infirmary would be grim at best, and most would not wish the fate of leprosy upon their worst enemy. Some of the older women had seen this same scenario played out several times before, and they focused on the worst possible outcome. Although they believed their hushed voices went unheard, Rebekah *and Justus* heard each word.

Rebekah gathered what she needed as she headed toward home. The walk seemed so much longer this day as people stared, and unknown thoughts concerning her husband's fate abounded. Justus did not understand the full weight of what turned everyone's eyes toward his mother. How could he fully understand what his father's fate might entail? How could anyone? She still prayed for a miracle. She hoped the waiting period would pass quickly and he would come home, and it would soon become a distant and forgotten memory.

Uncle Isaac greeted them as they walked into their home. "Rebekah, my dear. I'm leaving to go to the house of Zibeon."

"When are you leaving, Uncle?"

"At once. Epaphras, my dear friend, has agreed to accompany me. I think Zibeon needs to know what's happened to Tychicus."

"How long will you be gone? You know the festival is still going on."

"We'll be back sometime tomorrow." Isaac knew that Zibeon and Tamar needed to know the valley their daughter had been forced to walk through, even though the festival celebration continued. Obviously Rebekah wanted to stay close to home, hoping she could see her husband, even for a few moments.

"Mother, can I go with them? Please?" Justus begged. How he wanted to see his grandparents again.

Rebekah just gave him a loving smile and a look that said she needed him at home. She knew Isaac and Epaphras were older, and having a young boy along would perhaps be more than their patience could muster. Somehow Justus understood.

She threw her arms around her uncle, whom she loved so dearly. "I love you," she said. "On your way, please pray for Tychicus, that he would rely on God."

"I've already been praying, my dear," he said softly and lovingly.

"And pray for healing!" she added.

"We will, my dear." Isaac loved seeing Rebekah's faith and trust in the Lord.

He gave her a hug, then walked outside where Epaphras waited for him. "Demas will look in on you while we're gone. Please don't hesitate to ask him if you need anything," he insisted.

"Thank you," she said. "You're so kind. Please hurry back." She gave Epaphras a tight hug and also encouraged him to pray for Tychicus. They said their farewells once more as Justus waved enthusiastically. They headed for the city gates and soon were on their journey northward along the sea.

Rebekah and Justus returned to their home, where it became strangely quiet.

— CHAPTER 8 —

Early the next morning, as Demas watched Justus, Rebekah went to the temple.

"Good morning," Laban said as she walked through the doors.

"Good morning," she responded. "How are you today?"

"I am doing well, but how are you doing? We have all heard about Tychicus. This must be very difficult for you and for Justus. How is he taking this?"

Laban had always been kind to her. What a stark contrast to the attitude she saw in Jotham, the chief priest. Though he had only been a priest at this temple a short time, due to Rebekah's many visits to pray, he had come to admire her diligence as a woman of prayer.

"It's hard on all of us. I don't think Justus really understands all of it, and that is just as well. We are praying for God to heal Tychicus's body and allow him to come home."

"We will pray likewise," he said with a reassuring smile. Laban had proven himself to be a compassionate and caring priest. "Is there any way I can encourage you today?" he asked.

"I wanted to speak with Jotham. Can you tell him I am here?"

"I will see if I can find him. You know he seems to be hiding these days, especially from you and your uncle. If I can locate him, I will let him know you are waiting to speak with him."

"Thank you," Rebekah said in appreciation.

As Laban walked away, she did what she had grown accustomed to. She turned and headed toward the altar. By the time Jotham entered the room, he found her kneeling there in prayer. He quietly walked up behind her and ran his hand along her back.

Startled, she rose to her feet. "What are you doing? Where's my husband? It's been seven days, and the trial period has come to an end. I want to see him," she demanded. She knew he wouldn't respond to her request.

Jotham enjoyed this. She was out of place as a woman making such demands. But he knew he had agitated her, and it brought him an odd satisfaction.

"Be quiet in this holy place," he demanded in a hushed tone. "Follow me," he demanded.

They walked past a guard, through a door, and down a hallway. Finally, they walked into a room. Rebekah felt very uncomfortable finding herself in a room alone with this evil man. She hoped he would not make any advances toward her.

Jotham continued, "My evaluation will come later this afternoon. At the proper time, I will send a temple guard to get you. Then you can see your husband. But remember, there are strict limitations we must adhere to. We have to follow the laws as they are written. Do not ask me to do otherwise!"

He tried to sound righteous, though it came across more as a scolding. By the way he gazed at her, his dark heart became more evident than ever. She understood Jotham's actions had caused her husband to turn from the temple in the first place. Now, she was convinced that his actions were hurting the matter even more. How she longed to put some distance between herself and this evil man, but she had one more task before her.

"I've brought clean clothes for him. I beg you to let him have them. I know you've instructed the temple guards to deny this request these last few days, but I beg you to hear me today." She could only imagine what her husband had been going through in isolation. Her many requests on his behalf had fallen to Jotham's deaf ear, as had her uncle Isaac's. The other priests always deferred to him, as he'd instructed. She only hoped her husband would sense her efforts to help. She laid the folded garment on a bench, determined not to leave again with it in her possession.

"Go home, Rebekah," Jotham instructed her. It had become a common order she had heard too many times during the last few days.

"Why won't you allow me to see him? How can you be so cruel? I cannot believe this is how God would have you treat us. Let me see Tychicus!"

Jotham just looked at Rebekah with glaring eyes. He refused to answer her pleas. Her requests were dismissed without consideration, which frustrated her all the more, to his delight.

Again Jotham spoke to her, "Did you hear me? At the proper time, Rebekah, I will send someone to get you." She had become accustomed to his empty words, and she didn't believe this promise would be fulfilled as any form of credibility had been lost long ago.

Once more, he added, "In the proper time, Rebekah." His words were cold and impersonal. How she hated the way he said her name. She walked out anticipating, but not expecting, the invitation to come back to see her husband.

Jotham followed her, watching her as she walked out of the temple. Several minutes later, he walked back into the room where he sat down on a chair. He sat there for several more minutes as a grin emerged on his face. He nearly chuckled aloud. Surely he did inside. How he enjoyed tormenting Rebekah and her family.

"Massa," Jotham called, summoning the priest.

"Yes, sir. What may I do for you?"

"Has Tychicus arrived for his evaluation yet?" he asked.

"Yes, he's been waiting to see you. I brought him earlier as you requested. Shall I bring him in?"

Jotham scratched his chin for a moment. "Have Laban bring him to me, with several of the temple guards. That should take a few minutes."

"Excuse me?" This was a rather strange request. Tychicus had been waiting for some time. Why would Jotham want them to stall? "I could bring him in right away if you want, sir."

"Did you hear what I said?" Jotham shouted angrily. "Are you questioning my authority? I told you to have Laban bring him in with several of the temple guards!"

Massa did not understand this. This did not make sense. The request Jotham had made was strange enough, but this reaction was even stranger. Before he could respond, Jotham rose to his feet. "Do it! Do it now!" he demanded.

Massa took a step back as he looked into Jotham's eyes. There was something devious lurking there. He paused for a brief moment before turning to go. He walked back into the temple area with a look of bewilderment on his face.

"Greetings in the name of the Lord," Laban said quietly as he walked toward Massa, who did not respond. "Massa?" he said a little louder.

"Yes?" he responded, looking up as if suddenly waking from a trance.

"What's wrong? You look dazed."

"Did you hear Jotham? He was screaming for no reason as if possessed by a demon."

"What was that all about?"

"It had to do with Tychicus," Massa said.

"I just spoke with Rebekah a little while ago. She looked distressed, upset. I don't think Jotham will let her see Tychicus."

"That doesn't make any sense. Why?" asked Massa.

"Isn't this the seventh day of the first quarantine period?" asked Laban.

"Today is the seventh day. I brought Tychicus to the temple from the infirmary earlier, as Jotham instructed, and he's been waiting here ever since."

"That's strange. I wonder why Jotham did that. Have you talked to the high priest about this? It seems rather cruel to treat Rebekah and Tychicus this way."

"Amon's not here. He's still in Gadara."

"Well, Jotham wanted you to gather several temple guards to help you bring Tychicus in to see him."

"Why do we need the guards?" Laban asked.

"I'm not sure. I brought him here from the infirmary without their help. I think he's stalling so he'd be sure Rebekah had left."

"That's odd. I think we need to speak with Amon when he returns. Jotham has been acting rather strangely."

They both agreed as they parted ways.

Soon Laban and two temple guards escorted Tychicus into the room.

"Is there anything else you need?" Laban asked.

"That will be all, Laban. You are dismissed." Jotham spoke with his head aimed toward the floor. "Guards, stand ready outside the door in case I need you." It had been seven days since the attack, and time for the priest's first evaluation had finally come.

Tychicus knew Jotham would be waiting. He could only hope another priest would be waiting to meet with him. But deep inside, he knew Jotham's cruel mind and that he relished in his pain. He would not give anyone else the opportunity.

Jotham had anticipated this day. No matter what might seem apparent, he'd already made up his mind concerning the evaluation before him. Although he knew Tychicus's wounds might be healing and the possible absence of infection might exist, he'd already made his determination. No matter what he saw, he knew Tychicus would have another seven days to spend in the infirmary, in accordance with the law.

Tychicus stood before the chief priest without speaking a word. How he longed to reach out and grab this evil man and beat him senseless. Having to wait without seeing Rebekah had caused his anger to grow, as Jotham hoped. Slowly Jotham stood to his feet and walked toward him.

"Have they been feeding you well?" he asked after a moment of silence. He took pride in the fact that he had successfully diverted Tychicus's evening meals to the dogs in the streets for days without anyone seeming to notice.

"I want to see Rebekah," he replied. "Why haven't you allowed me to talk with her? It's been a week! I want to see Amon!"

Jotham did not reply. "Looks like you haven't been eating." He began looking at the sores and cuts on Tychicus's neck and arms. An unseen smile emerged inside him, and soon an evil grin crossed his face. Visible wounds did indeed show the promise of infection—at least that's how Jotham saw it. Had leprosy taken hold? He could only hope.

"I want to see Rebekah! Bring her to me!" he said angrily, this time more determined to get an answer. Both of the temple guards stepped into the room, ready to accept orders from the chief priest if their prisoner became too volatile.

Jotham stopped pacing. He looked into Tychicus's eyes without feeling. "I presume she's in town. She has not come to see you." Tychicus did not accept this subtle lie. It was inconceivable that his wife hadn't tried to see him, especially today.

He looked off to his right where he saw a set of clothing resting on a bench against the wall. It had been folded neatly as Rebekah would have folded it. Tychicus recognized his garment. Jotham perceived his discovery. Quickly he commented, "Isaac brought you a set of clean clothes this morning as we requested." It was another lie—another seed of discouragement Jotham sought to sew. He handed the clothes to him once again, looking over his wounds.

"I see your wounds have not fully healed. I have no choice but to send you back to the infirmary once again for another seven days as prescribed by the law. At that time, I will evaluate you once again. If I see evidence that your body has not recovered from the consequence of your rebellious heart, we will proceed with what the law demands."

Jotham stood face-to-face with the one whose life he held in his hands, or so he presumed. A troubled grin emerged on his face as he looked past Tychicus with evil thoughts of Rebekah in his heart.

Tychicus wanted to strike again, seeing his pious self-righteousness—an evil facade. But he knew that would not be in his best interest. Again, he spoke, "I want to see my wife. Bring her to me!"

"I cannot do that. She is not here. Perhaps that should indicate something to you." Jotham looked at Tychicus now with a blank look on his face. His head turned down slightly as he looked up at him with his eyes. Tychicus knew what the priest insinuated, but he knew his wife hadn't given up on him. He knew she loved him. But he stood under the authority of the temple and of this priest.

"Let me speak with Amon," he demanded. He had enough of this evil man. He wanted nothing more to do with him and his mistreatment.

Jotham just looked at him without saying a word. His request would not be honored, and he knew it.

"You call yourself a man of God?" Tychicus asked sternly.

"Guards!" Jotham called. They both took several steps farther into the room. "Take him back to the infirmary," he ordered.

As the guards each grabbed hold of one of Tychicus's arms, Jotham spoke his final word. "As far as you are concerned"—he paused for a brief moment before whispering—"I am god."

An odd silence filled the room.

"Off with him!" Jotham commanded again loudly. Tychicus looked back toward him as the guards forcibly pushed him out of the room. Did he hear what he thought he just heard? Didn't the guards hear it as well? Had he claimed to be a god? How absurd!

Tychicus held onto one hope: perhaps the next waiting period would pass, and his wounds would be healed. He hoped he could endure another seven days, and then this nightmare would end. He just hoped Rebekah could hang on.

Jotham sat back down, now alone to ponder what had just transpired. He broke the silence with a sinister chuckle. He couldn't believe everything was falling into place just as he had hoped. He knew Tychicus headed off to spend his last week in town. Jotham believed indications of leprosy were evident, and he rejoiced as laughter filled the room.

At that very moment, Laban stood outside the door, just out of sight, listening.

CHAPTER 9

The door creaked open as a smile emerged from Justus's face. "They're here!" he cried as he ran into Zibeon's arms. Tamar wrapped her arms around her grandson, kissing him on the cheek over and over. In response, he squeezed her tight. How he loved his grandparents. And how he loved their embraces.

"Greetings. My name is Demas. I'm watching Justus. Rebekah has gone to the temple, hoping to see Tychicus."

Zibeon embraced Demas with a brotherly hug. "It is good to meet you. And the beautiful woman wrapped around Justus is my wife, Tamar." She looked up with a smile.

"I see where Rebekah gets her beauty," Demas said.

Just then, the door opened once again. "And this is our son, Bukkiah."

"Just had to come support my little sister," he said with a grin.

"Uncle Bukkiah," Justus cried as he ran into his arms.

"I was tying up the donkey outside. Where's Rebekah?" he asked, looking around the room.

Demas walked over and shook Bukkiah's hand. "It's nice to meet you. Rebekah talks fondly about you and quite often. She is at the temple, hoping to see Tychicus."

"Hoping?" Tamar asked. "What do you mean?"

"This has been quite a strange predicament, but we have not been allowed to see Tychicus. I cannot recall how many times Rebekah has gone to the temple to see him, but we've been denied. Today is the end of the seven-day waiting period. She hoped they would let her see him—"

Just then the door creaked open again as Rebekah walked in. She looked dejected, unsatisfied. A common smile could not be seen, and a barrage of hugs for the visitors was absent. "Hello," she said in an uncharacteristically unenthusiastic manner. Typically she would have been full of life when greeting her family, whom she did not see nearly as much as she would have liked to. She appeared more deflated than ever.

"Rebekah, did you see Tychicus?" Zibeon asked, greeting his daughter with a hug.

"How is he doing, dear?" Tamar added as she also enveloped Rebekah in her arms. Isaac and Epaphras greeted her as well, noticing the look of discouragement on her face. Bukkiah, who stood with Justus off to one side, waited his turn to embrace Rebekah, who actually feigned a smile when she realized he had made the trip. It wasn't overly apparent by her actions, but her brother's visit meant more than the world to her. The sweet smell of a family reunion should have resonated in the air. What would commonly be a time of joyous celebration had been replaced with a dark cloud of apathy. Everyone understood, more now than ever, any family gathering would be incomplete without Tychicus.

"So how's Tychicus?" Zibeon asked again. "We want to see him."

If there was even a tinge of joy in the house, it quickly dissipated as Rebekah's face turned to sorrow. "They won't let me see him or talk to him or have any communication with him at all. They promised to come get me today for the first examination. It's been seven days!"

"You didn't even get to see him?" Bukkiah barked, stepping forward. "Why not? This is unacceptable!"

Although Rebekah tried to hold back her tears, she could hold them back no longer. The emotions she endeavored to hide from her son could no longer be bottled up as her emotional dam broke wide open. She fell into her brother's arms and sobbed in deep grief. Bukkiah loved his sister. How his heart ached seeing her in such unmerited torment. Though everyone in the room shared these sentiments, her sorrow possibly affected her closest sibling the most. What injustice!

"I have not been able to see him either," commented Isaac, hoping to show what others had shared in Rebekah's frustration. "We've been given absolutely no access at all. They treat him like some kind of criminal."

"They treat us that way too," Rebekah added.

"I don't understand. What reasons have you been given? Have you spoken to the high priest?" Bukkiah asked, with conviction, looking into his sister's teary eyes.

"I believe he is celebrating the feast of Pesach elsewhere. We're not sure when he'll be back in Tiberias," Rebekah said softly. "He is a good man, and his absence couldn't have come at a more inopportune time." She sounded so defeated as she vented her disappointment.

Bukkiah was particularly puzzled by all of this. He understood there were restrictions, limitations, but what he just heard sounded out of the ordinary. It seemed cruel and beyond the law.

"Did you talk to the chief priest?" Zibeon asked, understanding he would be the next in authority in the absence of the high priest.

"We've tried, but Jotham, the chief priest, is the one who's built the wall between us." Rebekah could've said much more but chose to hold her tongue. There would be time to discuss more details later, far away from Justus's attentive ears. She decided to wait for someone from the temple to come for her, which, of course, did not happen.

"Well, we'll stay as long as you need us to," Zibeon promised as he hugged his daughter again, kissing her on the forehead. Bukkiah agreed, though he would not sit and take this mistreatment.

He looked off to the far corner of the room. His focus once again returned to his sister. She looked into his eyes, seeing a look of determination, though it was tainted with a hint of treachery. He gave Rebekah a tight hug and then walked out of the house in a huff. Rebekah had experienced this before. Her brother would protect her, no matter what it would take and no matter what he would have to endure personally. He only thought of her in that moment, and she knew it. She believed his intentions were to go after the chief priest and perhaps cause him some bodily harm if he resisted again. She had already seen Tychicus mistreat Jotham in a malicious way. She didn't want to involve her brother in all this nonsense.

"Where are you going, Bukkiah?" Tamar asked.

"This is ridiculous! I'm heading to the temple to talk to the priest—and then to Tychicus!" Bukkiah's voice boomed back with his response. If Rebekah ever had a protector within the family, it was surely her brother Bukkiah. His actions in this heated moment once again confirmed this to be true. Though she wanted to speak, she was speechless. She didn't think any words would stop Bukkiah from storming the temple.

"You better go with him," Tamar quickly said to Zibeon. She had also seen this behavior from her youngest son and knew he might need to be bridled.

Zibeon headed out after his youngest son. "Bukkiah, slow down." Determined to catch up with him, he hurried along, though Bukkiah quickly started to pull away. "Bukkiah!" he said again with a little more fatherly authority.

He stopped, turned around, and waited for his father to catch up. "This is unacceptable!" he barked again. "How can they detain him and not give anyone in the family any kind of consideration, especially his wife?" Bukkiah's anger was justified. The family had indeed been unjustly mistreated.

"I agree with you, but what do you intend to do when you're faced with the same response they've already seen? You cannot overrun the priests or the temple guards."

"Father, I cannot bear to see Rebekah suffer this way. I will do whatever it takes to talk to Tychicus!"

They continued on at a slower pace as Bukkiah fumed. Soon they marched up the temple steps and through the door.

"Jotham!" Bukkiah demanded. "Where is Jotham?"

"He is not here at this time. My name is Laban. I am one of the temple priests. How can I be of assistance?" Laban did not recognize Zibeon, who stood several steps behind this strange man who caused such a provocation.

"I want to see Jotham, and I want to see him now!"

Laban once again tried to talk with Bukkiah. "I am sorry, but I really do not know where he is at this time. If he were here, I would try to get him for you. Please, can I help you?"

"I know he is here. I want to see him now! And I want to know why he has not allowed us to see Tychicus!"

"You are a member of the family?" Laban asked calmly.

"He's my brother! And I want to speak with him now!"

Bukkiah's declaration spoke volumes, especially to Zibeon. Tychicus was not a physical brother; he was a brother through marriage. By calling him his brother, he considered Tychicus to be a member of his immediate family—as if he were a flesh and blood relation.

"Rebekah is my daughter, and Bukkiah is my son," Zibeon added.

Laban understood who they were now, and though he had been sympathetic to Rebekah's plight, he had to follow the orders of his superior. "I am so sorry. Jotham has given direct orders that no one is to see him. I am not aware of—"

Before he could say another word, Bukkiah exploded with anger. "I want to see the high priest! I need to see *someone* who can help me!"

"He is not here either, I am afraid. He is—"

"Is anyone here? Are you here?" Bukkiah continued to rant. Zibeon reached out, grabbing his cloak, trying to settle him down to no avail. "It doesn't seem like you are going to help!" Bukkiah said, insulting the priest.

"I am not sure what we can do," Laban said apologetically.

"We have come before though we have been turned away. We just want to hear how he is doing," Zibeon added, trying to bring even a smidgen of calm to the conversation, at least from their side.

Bukkiah stormed toward a side door, where one of the temple guards stood at attention. He had been watching Bukkiah, though he had not reacted to his outrage yet. Another temple guard stepped into the room, waiting to see if his services would be needed.

The first guard took a step forward, fully blocking the door, though Bukkiah determined this would not deter him from searching for the priest he believed could be found hiding somewhere in the temple just behind that door.

"Stand back!" the temple guard warned as the other guard approached.

"I will not stand back! Let me through!" Bukkiah demanded.

"Son, let's head back to the house," Zibeon pleaded. They had tried, and he saw no reason to bring any more confrontation into this quandary. Bukkiah typically heeded his father's words, but such action would not be associated with his father's words this day.

Again the guard gave a verbal warning. "Stand back! Now!"

Bukkiah forcibly pushed the guard toward the wall. The other guard immediately jumped on Bukkiah's back, throwing him to the ground. Zibeon could not believe what his son had done—especially in the temple. Though he had not been an eyewitness, this reminded him of the tussle Tychicus had with Jotham and what had come from that. But before he could do anything to help, the two guards had subdued his son, who continued his verbal rant.

"Throw him out," one of the guards said as they pushed him through the door. "Throw him back into the street."

"You cannot take me to the infirmary!" Bukkiah cried, looking back toward Laban. "You cannot take me there."

Laban's eye locked into Bukkiah's. They were pleading eyes, calling out for assistance.

Laban rushed up to Bukkiah and the guards. "Take him to the infirmary!" he ordered.

The guards heard the command of the priest and were too proud to take any kind of order from a commoner who challenged their authority. One of the guards responded, "Take him to the infirmary! Now!"

The guards pushed Tychicus through the door as he continued to scream. The door slammed behind them as Zibeon and Laban stood side by side, listening until the temple became quiet and reverent once again.

Zibeon remembered the words of his son, spoken just moments before as they walked toward the temple: "I will do whatever it takes to talk to Tychicus!" Although his actions were unexpected, they were calculated and planned.

Zibeon looked at Laban. "Thank you for your help."

Laban smiled innocently. "I hope he is able to see him, and I hope the guards don't hurt him too badly." Laban understood the treatment Bukkiah might face on the way to his cell, especially if his masquerade continued behind closed doors.

"He will accept what he is given gladly for the sake of his sister," Zibeon said proudly.

"Your daughter is a wonderful woman, a woman who loves our God," Laban said with a smile. "Would you like me to pray for you and your family?"

Zibeon smiled back as they met on common ground. "Let us pray and give thanks to our God!"

As Laban and Zibeon knelt at the temple altar to pray, Bukkiah took steps toward accomplishing his goal as he headed toward the infirmary.

CHAPTER 10

The door opened with authority. It led into a long hallway filled with doors on either side. One temple guard pushed Bukkiah through the door and down to his knees. He looked up, feeling like he had been taken to some form of prison. What a dingy, unwelcoming place.

"Move!" the guard demanded as he struck Bukkiah with the blunt end of his spear in the back as he had done several times already.

"He said *move*," cried the other guard as he kicked him in the ribs.

Bukkiah gasped for air, falling down on his side in pain.

The two guards continued this mistreatment until they opened a door down the hallway, throwing him into a dark cell.

Bukkiah again gasped for air as he coughed over and over. He had made it to the infirmary. The walls were cold, which matched the whole atmosphere of the cell. He noticed a bench on the far wall nearly unseen in the darkness, which overshadowed this lonely place. He listened as he lay on his back. He had received several blows, which now caused him to ache. He had anticipated such treatment, which now led to his groaning. He had expected no less from these men, who had lorded over him. Even though they stood inside the walls of the temple each day, they were so far away from God, he thought.

A slight grin finally made its way to his face. He remembered why he had done this and decided he would do all this again for his sister if he had to. He had fooled the guards, and he found satisfaction that his scheme had succeeded thus far.

He slowly stood to his feet and made his way to the door. He pushed on it. It moved slightly, though it was surely locked tight. He put his ear to the small window, which had several bars dissecting the opening. He listened for some form of sound from down the hall, but it was still—quiet.

"Tychicus," he whispered. He waited in the silence. "Tychicus," he whispered just a little louder. After a moment, he heard some rustling from several cells farther down the hall. "Tychicus," he said again even louder.

"Yes," he heard a voice reply. "Who is it?"

"It's your brother."

"Bukkiah?" he asked with a tinge of surprise. He listened again as Bukkiah chuckled slightly as if to acknowledge his own craftiness. "My brother! What are you doing here?" Tychicus asked.

"The only way I could think to talk to you was to get thrown in here."

"You are quite the sly fox, aren't you?"

"Rebekah has been so worried about you. How are they treating you?"

"Well, time passes slowly here. There are times when I get lost in my thoughts, and I forget whether they have fed me or not. Sometimes my stomach aches. Perhaps from hunger, perhaps from boredom. Personally, I don't think they remember to feed me in the evenings. How is Rebekah? I have thought so much about her."

"She has come to the temple every day to see you, but they have not been kind here. At least that is what I've gathered concerning Jotham. He has stopped everyone from visiting you."

"I would expect nothing else from that snake," Tychicus said in a tone of revulsion. "I will never forgive him for what he has done to me, my family, my wife! Never! If I could just get my hands on him…" His tone had changed from dislike to intense hatred, something that had grown more and more fierce during his days of confinement.

Just then the door opened with a loud crash as it banged against the wall. Hurried footsteps approached from down the hall as Bukkiah's door was unlocked before it flung open.

"Out!" cried Jotham. "Out of your cell. Now!"

Bukkiah stood a few steps back into his cell. His clever plan had not fooled everyone.

"No one is to talk to Tychicus. We don't allow visitors to come into this place to talk with those who defy this holy place! If you wanted to fool me, you should not have brought Zibeon with you. You fool!"

The guards took a few steps into Bukkiah's cell, grabbing him before throwing him back into the hallway. They realized now they had been tricked, and they weren't happy about it.

"Get him out of here! And teach him what happens to those who try to deceive the priests and guards of this holy place! When I said 'no one sees him,' I meant no one!" Jotham cried out in anger. "Let him feel the wrath of God before you throw him out with the dogs!"

One of the guards immediately punched Bukkiah in the face. The blow had been unexpected, taking Bukkiah off guard. His nose started bleeding profusely as he fell toward the floor. Jotham turned and walked out, unconcerned with this further mistreatment. The other guard kicked him again while the first guard started punching him mercilessly. A word of rebuke from Jotham would never be heard.

Tychicus yelled through the window of his cell door, "I thought this was a *holy* place—yet you are treating my brother like a dog! He has done nothing wrong! You are the fools that act in sin—you should all be flogged!"

The temple guards simply disregarded his comments. "Get him out of here!" one of them shouted, pointing toward the end of the hallway. He did not point back toward the temple area, but toward the back exits, which led toward the streets. "Let's throw him out like the dog he is! Let's get him out of our sight!"

Tychicus continued to yell, this time toward Bukkiah. "Tell Rebekah to remain strong! Tell her I love her! Tell her!"

Bukkiah was dragged down the hallway and eventually thrown out into the street. The guards pushed him through the door and slammed the door behind him. He fell to the ground, where he lay in pain. Blood covered his cloak from the blow to his nose. He moaned from the beating the guards had just given him. He hadn't recovered from the beating he received earlier when he entered the infirmary. But he had accomplished his goal for even a short period of time, though at a costly price.

As he lay in the street, several footsteps were heard as they approached him. Several dogs that had started to come near him turned and ran. Bukkiah recoiled as someone touched him. Convinced that more guards would pick up where the previous ones left off, he cowered to protect himself from another attack.

"Bukkiah?" a soft, kind voice addressed him.

He looked up, trying to focus on the man who stood over him. He wore robes, unlike the uniforms of the temple guards.

"Bukkiah. I am Massa, one of the temple priests. Let me help you. Are you hurt?"

Bukkiah tried to get up, relieved that further blows from temple guards would not rain down on him. His only answer was summed up through his groans of pain.

"Can you stand up?" Massa asked.

Bukkiah struggled to get up to his knees. With every movement, he winced in pain. His ribs, especially, were very sore. Bukkiah had taken quite a beating, unlike anything Massa had ever seen before. He understood the temple guards were to blame, and his suspicions of Jotham were starting to be confirmed more and more.

"Please sit back down," Massa said as he held his arm carefully. "I will go get Isaac and Demas. They can help put you on their donkey and carry you home, where you can rest."

Bukkiah lay back down. He strained to smile as he said, "Thank you, Massa."

The kind priest ran off toward Rebekah's house to get help.

At that same time, Zibeon sat down in the house, lifting Justus up onto his knee. "My little man. Do you miss your father?"

Justus said, "Yes, I do. But I'm not little." He jumped down to the floor, placing his hand on top of his head. "I'm this tall!" he proudly proclaimed. Zibeon chuckled, as did Tamar, who also witnessed his proud display from across the room.

Justus's demeanor seemed to change instantly. "Grandfather, is Uncle Bukkiah going to be coming back?" Without waiting for an answer, he added, "And when's my father coming home?"

"Well, those are good questions," he replied, knowing he didn't have very good answers for either question. "As for your uncle, I do not know. As for your father, according to the law, someone who has blemishes or sores on their skin that might be—or could be—leprous has to spend time by themselves to see if they'll get better or not."

"Seven days," Justus said.

"That's right," Zibeon confirmed. "After those seven days, the priest will decide if they're getting better or not. Then they have to spend seven more days to see if they're really better or not. So the total waiting period will last for two weeks."

"How long has it been so far?" To Justus, it seemed like a few months had gone by since they walked into the city gates. He'd been walking just a few steps beside his father when the attack in the courtyard occurred. He recalled what happened right before that terrible moment. His father glanced over at him. They made eye contact. Then his father smiled. He smiled back. It seemed like it all happened so slowly, like a moment that would never end, a solitary moment to cherish forever. He'd never forget that look, which would soon be taken from him.

Zibeon looked into the eyes of his five-year-old grandson, who looked to him for one thing: reassuring words that would guarantee his father's imminent return. Zibeon knew such words wouldn't come this day.

"He's starting that second waiting period now."

"So he'll be home soon?" Justus still sought hope. His eyes started welling up with tears. Unsuccessfully, he fought hard not to cry. As the floodgates opened, his grandfather wrapped his strong arms around him and squeezed him tight. He too found tears welling up in his eyes. He could only imagine the pain his grandson felt.

Tamar spoke sternly to Rebekah, "We're going to march down to the temple tomorrow and demand to see Tychicus *and* Bukkiah!"

As she saw her son cry, Rebekah's heart broke once again. She fell to her knees in prayer. In her heart, she cried, *O God! Bring healing to our family! Bring solace to our hearts!* As she prayed, Tamar wrapped her arms around her. They still didn't understand why this had happened to their family. It made no logical sense, though they trusted God as best they could.

Just then they heard a fervent knock. Isaac got up from where he sat and opened the door.

"Isaac. I'm glad you're here. I need your help," pleaded Massa. "Bukkiah has been beaten by the temple guards. They tossed him out on the street behind the temple, and I couldn't carry him by myself. I believe Jotham was behind it all."

"How bad is it?" Rebekah asked. Though her anger burned toward the evil chief priest, her concern for Bukkiah was much stronger.

"He's very sore, but I don't think he has any broken bones… I don't know for sure. His ribs were sore. But he needs our help. Right away. Please come with me!"

Instantly Zibeon and Isaac ran out the door, heading toward Bukkiah. As they released the donkey from its post, Rebekah called back to her mother, "Take care of Justus." Then she ran on ahead. She ran through the streets, not letting anyone slow her down. She came to the front steps of the temple, pausing only for a brief moment to huff in disdain toward the ungodly men who were even at this moment hiding within its walls. Her soul mourned for the injustice Bukkiah had experienced and that Tychicus still endured. She ran around to the right side of the temple toward the back, where she saw the silhouette of a battered man lying against the wall. Several dogs had started to surround him.

"Bukkiah!" she cried, running toward him faster than ever.

The dogs looked up in unison before turning to run away again.

He looked up as she approached him. What a wonderful sight!

She fell down beside him. "Oh no!" she cried. "The blood from his nose still stained his face and his cloak. It looked very bad—worse than it actually was. She didn't want to touch him for fear that she might cause him more pain.

"Rebekah," he said as their eyes met. "I did this for you."

Tenderly she held his face to her chest and kissed his head. "I love you, Bukkiah. I love you!"

"I love you too, little sis. I'd do anything for you." His voice strained as he tried to mask his pain.

She was overwhelmed at her brother's selfless act.

"So did you get to talk to Tychicus?" She did not know what had transpired; he hadn't been gone that long. Perhaps, he had just been beaten and left in the alley.

"I did talk with Tychicus," Bukkiah said. "He is very frustrated, and I am afraid he's been overtaken with anger, which is understandable. I don't think they are treating him very well. The chief priest is not a very nice man. But I don't want you to worry about him. He is still strong. He is a fighter. And he loves you so! He told me he hasn't stopped thinking about you. He wanted me to tell you to be strong, and he wanted you to know that he loves you very much."

Rebekah cherished these words. How she had longed to hear them straight from her husband's own lips. But for now, this relayed message would suffice.

Bukkiah knew that Tychicus had fallen away from God, and he hadn't been a strong spiritual leader in their home, but he did treat his sister with honor and deep love. He had been a good man.

"And I love him too," she said. The emotion of her love for her husband and the concern she had for her brother were nearly too much. How much more could she bear?

"I know you love him. He is a good man. I just wish I had more time to talk with him. Jotham ran in and had me thrown out." Bukkiah ached with every breath as he stopped to moan.

"Zibeon and Isaac are coming to get you with the donkey. They will be here soon." She did not understand why their family had to suffer this way. Wasn't it enough that Tychicus faced suffering and she and Justus lived in despair? Why did her brother have to go to such lengths to assist them? As they waited for Zibeon and Isaac, Rebekah prayed to the Lord. She prayed for her brother, and she prayed for guidance and help during this time of trial.

CHAPTER 11

The days passed slowly as the fourteen-day waiting period finally came to an end. Jotham had treated Tychicus as if he had already been declared unclean. In the priest's mind, he'd made his determination the moment he saw Tychicus standing in the courtyard with the dead leper at his feet.

His treatment had been harsh and cruel, as Tychicus had been given absolutely no time with his family, other than the few moments Bukkiah had stolen. Expect for his brief words, they had been totally deprived of any information of his condition despite constant objections from Rebekah, Isaac, and Zibeon. Bukkiah had started to heal, and their hopes were the same for Tychicus.

When Rebekah and Zibeon confronted Jotham concerning the harsh treatment he dealt to Bukkiah, through the abuses of the temple guards, he denied it all. Even though Bukkiah himself stood before him, he did not accept any responsibility as he refused to look at him. This infuriated the family and caused Massa and Laban to take notice of their chief priest.

The constant lies Jotham fed Tychicus had slowly started to wear him down. He didn't believe any of them, but the priest's insistence sowed dishonorable seeds of doubt. Jotham's deliberate attempts to unnerve him had been somewhat successful, as any form of compassion or sympathy could not be found.

Most of all, Tychicus missed Rebekah and Justus. He realized during his confinement that they comprised everything of value in his life. His separation from them continued to become immensely hard to deal with each passing day. He could only wonder how this might have affected his wife and son. It seemed so unfair, an accurate assessment.

Finally, the second week came to an end as Laban led Tychicus into Jotham's presence. The atmosphere in the room turned extremely tense, quiet. Judgment day had arrived, and they both knew it. Tychicus faced the man who held his destiny in his hands, and he faced him alone. Jotham dismissed Laban, who left as instructed. The same two temple guards who had beaten Bukkiah stood near Jotham in the room. They were even more prepared this day in case Tychicus tried to attack the chief priest, which he had threatened from his cell. And with the situation before them, they expected some form of response, which they were ready to control.

Jotham continued looking toward the floor, refusing to make eye contact. He feigned concern for the situation before him. He really wanted to make the most of the moment, leaving a false impression while euphoria filled his inner being. He'd seen Tychicus's wounds over the last two weeks and knew the possibility of contamination could become reality. He knew he shouldn't show his true emotions, at least not in front of any of the other priests. But now they were gone. He didn't care what the guards thought. He knew they were as crooked as he.

Slowly Jotham looked up at Tychicus. He scanned up and down, looking for visible wounds. He walked around, examining him further. "Take off your garment," he said coldly.

Tychicus knew the moment of truth had come. As he took off his garment, the cuts across his chest were revealed. The cuts across his back and on his arms were uncovered. As Jotham examined him, his beliefs were confirmed. He now felt he had justification for what he had longed to do for some time.

"You can put your garment back on," Jotham said without feeling.

Tychicus stood in front of the priest, awaiting his next word.

Jotham slowly circled around him several times, not saying a word. He just walked around him. Tychicus waited. The longer he waited, the more anxious he became, just as Jotham planned.

"Guards!" Jotham commanded. They stood at attention beside Tychicus. "One of you, go get Massa and Laban. Bring them to me. The other, guard the prisoner." Jotham sat back down, staring at Tychicus, who questioned the chief priest's words in his head. He had not been a "prisoner." That term was reserved for someone who had done something criminal, someone worthy of prison. He had been mercilessly attacked. He was a victim. He was not a prisoner.

As he pondered this, he also realized he stood closer to this evil man than he had in two weeks. If he was going to make his move, to bring on his own revenge, the time was at hand. If the guard were not standing beside Jotham, protecting him, he just might have taken action against him. Before he could follow through on his desire, Laban and Massa entered the room. They stood on either side of Tychicus. The temple guards mirrored them standing on each side of Jotham, looking more like the chief priest's personal bodyguards.

Jotham's determination would soon be announced. The verdict was in. The time of waiting had come to an end.

"Take Tychicus... to the courtyard..." Jotham paused. Tychicus wondered if this meant he would be released. Perhaps his wounds weren't as bad as he led himself to believe. Laban and Massa also hoped for a declaration of dismissal.

But before this idea could be fully contemplated, Jotham continued, "Then walk him out the city gates. It has been determined"—Jotham stopped, looking directly into Tychicus's eyes—"he is unclean. Unclean. Unclean!" With each repetition, a grin broadened across his face. Then Laban and Massa noticed this, wondering why he had announced such horrific news with such joyfulness. They wondered why he'd offer a brief moment of hope only to dash those hopes to the ground.

Tychicus stood in shock. Surely this couldn't be happening. He knew infection might be possible, but it was still shocking to realize it had been determined to be a matter of fact. He could not move. He never really imagined this to be the verdict. He would heal, wouldn't he?

"You shall not cut your hair. You shall not touch any person. You shall be banished from the city—do not ever enter the gates. You shall not speak to anyone unless you are giving the warning lepers are required to give when someone comes near."

Tychicus's thoughts of denial were interrupted as he considered the words he had just heard: *Did he just call me a leper?* His mind saw that hideous person who lay dead at his feet in the courtyard just two long weeks ago. Would that be him someday?

Then as if Tychicus had been unaware of the warning, Jotham felt compelled to instruct him. "If anyone comes near, you shall declare in a loud voice, 'Unclean! Unclean! Unclean!'" Mockingly, Jotham loudly made the emphatic declaration.

Jotham and Tychicus stood face-to-face. Tychicus finally spoke, trying to contain his rage. "You don't have to instruct me in the ways of the law! I know the law, just as well as you do, you evil, wicked animal! You're not even a man!"

The other priests were shocked! They'd never heard such language directed toward a priest in the temple.

Just then Tychicus lunged toward the man whom he had grown to hate so intensely. The temple guards quickly grabbed him by the arms, subduing him.

As Jotham cowered backward, he said, "I am a man of God! And you have defiled this holy place once again!" He then reached out, grabbing Tychicus's garment—the same one Rebekah brought to the temple for him. "And your garments shall be torn and tattered," he yelled as he tore a large rip in the garment. Anger and spite consumed Tychicus as the chief priest made his bold statement. This garment was the last tangible item Tychicus and Rebekah had in common. To tear the garment symbolized his desire to tear them apart. He wanted to come between them in order to fulfill his lustful desires.

Tychicus could not grab him with his arms so he held onto the guards tightly, thrusting his legs up, kicking Jotham in the chest. Jotham did not anticipate this blow as it knocked him against the wall. He bounced off the wall and fell to the floor as Tychicus tried to assault him again, though this time unsuccessfully.

Jotham looked up. "You are strong, but not for long. Off with him!" he commanded.

The guards forcibly removed Tychicus from the room as he fought them. Laban and Massa followed close by. They understood that it was their responsibility to escort someone like this to the city gates. Sadly they fulfilled their duty.

Tychicus couldn't accept what had just happened. Surely he'd find justice as soon as someone saw through Jotham's facade, which he believed would come in time. Everyone would understand who he had been—*an evil hypocrite*! He had no way of knowing at that moment that these hopes would never be realized.

As Tychicus was moved toward the courtyard, the priests declared "unclean" as they came near anyone on their way. The law required them to say this. It didn't take long for people to start talking—and to gather around. So many had heard of Tychicus's attack, and his condition had been unknown for the last few weeks, which led to much gossip. Now the truth of what they feared had been revealed, and you could not deny the amount of talk this generated. Though the crowd started to gather for this one-man spectacle, they kept their distance as a hushed murmur filled the outskirts of the courtyard.

All of a sudden, one person emerged from the crowd. "Tychicus!" she cried. Rebekah ran toward her husband with all the strength she could muster. They hadn't seen each other since before his quarantine two weeks earlier. Tychicus turned around as soon as he heard her voice. He took a step toward her as the priests once again stated, "Unclean! Unclean! Unclean!" They intentionally needed to warn Rebekah. Her husband had been declared unclean.

But she would not be deterred by their verbal warnings as she ran into her husband's arms just as Tychicus shook himself loose from the grasp of the temple guards. They embraced as they fell to their knees. Rebekah held on as if she knew they would be taking Tychicus away forever.

"I love you!" Rebekah declared. "They wouldn't let me see you. Jotham wouldn't let me see you—I love you!"

"I love you too," Tychicus said as his emotions overwhelmed him. He knew this might be the last time he'd hold the woman he loved so much. How had this come to be? Could this possibly be a bad dream? He knew it wasn't, and he placed full blame on Jotham and God!

The embrace lasted just a few seconds as the guards pulled Rebekah from her husband. "He's unclean! Unclean! Unclean!" the priests declared to their dismay. As soon as they made their declaration, they pointed toward the gates, looking into Tychicus' eyes. "I am sorry. But you must go! You are unclean!" Laban never hated the duties of the priesthood until that moment.

Unclean. The word entered Tychicus' ears as it echoed in his mind. How amazing and devastating one word could be! As a result of it, he would be deprived of his wife and his son, who was nowhere in sight. He would soon be banished from the city. He would soon lose his life as he knew it. He would soon lose everything he once took for granted. Everything.

He looked around the courtyard. He had walked here countless times without a thought. He would never again be permitted in this place. His whole world had changed in an instance—and he knew it! He stood in a daze, overtaken by shock. How could this be happening to him, to Rebekah, to Justus? Couldn't God have prevented this? Why didn't he?

Tychicus knew he was unclean, and that fact would never be more apparent than it was at that moment—and it seemed so wrong. Again, quite suddenly, anger and rage consumed him.

"Tychicus, the law has dictated that you must leave the city." Massa also disliked his duties at that moment. He and Laban held onto Rebekah's arms as she still fought to free herself and run back to her husband.

She cried long and loud, "No!" And it pierced Tychicus's heart. Though the courtyard hummed with the voices of so many, he blocked them all out. His ears only heard the cry of his beautiful Rebekah. He knew she was in agony, and he knew he could do absolutely nothing to help her, which caused his anger to increase even more. Everyone watched from a distance, and no one came to his aid. The laws and regulations concerning the unclean were well known. No one dared to come close lest they might also be declared unclean.

A loud voice boomed from across the courtyard as everyone turned their gaze in one direction. Tychicus looked at the man standing some distance away from him. He'd placed himself there purposely. Everyone could hear his loud voice as they all became silent.

Jotham spoke loudly, declaring, "You have defiled the temple. When you sin against God, there will be a reckoning. You are unclean! Unclean! Unclean!" His voice had grown louder with each repetition of that dreaded word. Jotham then raised his arm and pointed toward the gates as if banishing him from the city in dramatic fashion. Jotham's arm remained raised as he lowered his head. No one saw his face as a sly grin grew into a wide smile. To the crowd, he appeared to be a righteous priest cleansing the town by banishing the unclean. But he fooled them all.

Tychicus turned in fury as he headed toward the city gates. Timotheus tossed him a few pieces of fruit from his cart. Tychicus caught them and headed through the gates. He turned around one last time, making eye contact with his wife, who still struggled with the priests who held onto her. Then he turned and ran. To stay and grovel would only bring more pleasure to Jotham and more pain to Rebekah.

The blind beggar, Josech, listened intently as he heard the footsteps disappear into the distance as Rebekah wailed. He heard the whole drama from his spot just outside the gates.

Just then, a young boy ran out of the crowd. "Father!" he cried. But it was too late. His father had gone, and he didn't get a chance to say good-bye. He saw his mother, who had fallen to the ground in grief, as she wept. Justus stood alone, sad and confused.

"Justus, come here." The young boy ran into the arms of Zibeon, his grandfather, who'd shown up on the scene. Justus started to cry as his emotions finally overflowed.

Tychicus had gone. Rebekah lay on the ground, wailing as her mourning began. In their hearts, Laban and Massa mourned as well.

Jotham crossed the courtyard dramatically as everyone watched. He walked up to Rebekah and looked down on her with an evil eye. Finally, she looked up at him with a tear-streaked face. Her heart ached more than she ever imagined it could.

Laban and Massa stood silent, wondering what Jotham might say. Hadn't he done enough damage already? To their shock, Jotham raised his head and arrogantly spoke to them, giving them an order, "Take her to the infirmary."

CHAPTER 12

Rebekah sat by herself on a cold, dark bench. She never felt more alone. She sat inside the infirmary, where her husband had spent the last two weeks. She wondered why she had not been permitted to be here during his incarceration.

The events of the early afternoon were still sharply engrained in her brain. She could still see her husband as he looked at her that last time. She couldn't stop thinking about him, running through the gates and out of the city. She prayed and again asked God how this could be happening. Her life had become a bad dream—and how she longed to wake up to a normal day.

Jotham walked in. She remained seated at the far side of the room.

"Rebekah," he said, addressing her in a harsh tone. She knew his heart's intent, and his tone reflected it.

She looked at him without saying a word.

"Rebekah, must I remind you of the law?" he asked arrogantly, scolding her as if she were a child.

Again she sat silent as she looked at him.

"You must know you are not allowed to *talk* to an unclean person. You must know you are not allowed to *touch* an unclean person. You must know you are not allowed to—"

Rebekah had heard enough of his self-righteousness. She wouldn't stand to be belittled any more. "Don't you know a priest should have compassion and love toward his fellow man? Don't you know a priest should act *somewhat* like God?" Her words were strong and forceful.

"Don't speak to me with such a tone!" Jotham barked. "Your husband—or should I say, *your former husband* spoke with such a tone, and look what God has done to him! When you sin against God, there will be a reckoning!" His words were harsh and cruel, without any hint of concern for Tychicus's plight.

Rebekah just sat looking at Jotham as her anger raged inside. Who did this man think he was? He had revealed his true identity, simply a pious sinner hiding behind priestly robes. She'd seen past his facade, and it angered her that *he* had sinned against God!

Jotham continued without regard for her, "Tychicus is no longer in your life. He is dead to you. You will never *see* him again or *talk* to him or *hold* him or have anything more to do with him. He is now a dead man walking. The sooner you come to terms with that, the better you will be." Then unbelievably, he added, "And when you come to terms with that, perhaps you could turn your affections toward another man."

Rebekah couldn't believe her ears. She looked around to see if another priest could've possibly heard him. But Jotham was aware of his surroundings and knew no one had heard him. His blatant flirtation disgusted her to the core.

"Tychicus is my husband, and he always will be! And that is something *you* had better come to terms with!"

Jotham just stared at Rebekah with lust in his heart. She couldn't bear to look at him anymore as she turned away.

"We shall see," he said softly. "You have seven days to think about it." He turned and walked out of the room.

Rebekah did have much time to think. She thought about her husband and wondered what thoughts ran through his mind. Again and again, she prayed the same prayer she'd prayed for so long—that God would draw her husband back to himself. She also thought about her son, now in the good hands of her father and mother. How she longed to hold him and try to explain all that had happened. Why should he have to go through life without his father? And at this moment, without his mother? She knew he must be so confused! Could this really be part of God's plan? She longed for answers, which didn't come.

Zibeon stood in the temple near the altar, demanding answers. "Where's my daughter? Why has she been quarantined?"

Laban didn't know the right words to say. "Zibeon, Jotham has placed her in the infirmary. After being in the arms of someone determined unclean, she might be unclean as well. We need to see—"

"How ridiculous!" Zibeon said loudly in frustration. He struggled to control his anger as he paced. The answers he sought seemed to be kept from him, which he considered unacceptable. "Where's Jotham?" Zibeon had seen Jotham in action and wondered how a priest could be so cruel. Who was this man? And why would God allow such an evil man to preside as one of his representatives?

Laban and Massa were caught in the middle, and they didn't like it. "I'm not sure where he might be at this time," one responded. "I would recommend you talk to Amon, the high priest—"

"Where is he?" Zibeon demanded.

"He is scheduled to return from Gadara any day now. We thought he would be back to the temple by now," Massa said, understanding his answer brought no satisfaction.

The priests really didn't know where Jotham hid, and they were starting to wonder why he acted as he did.

This scenario would play out many times over the next days as Jotham hid from Zibeon and Isaac. Though aware of their many visits, the chief priest wouldn't face them or give them answers to their many questions.

All the while, Rebekah sat alone, wondering about Tychicus. How she wanted to reach out to him, but she felt like she'd been locked in a cage, and she couldn't find a way of escape. She felt utterly helpless, unable to reach out to him. At least she could've left him something to eat. She could've left him clean clothes. She could've tried to talk to him from a distance, even though the law would have surely frowned upon that. She didn't care. She loved him. She couldn't believe life had turned on them in this way. She prayed for a miracle.

Justus remained the most confused. "Where's my father? And where's my mother?" Everything had happened so fast. As much as they tried, Zibeon and Isaac just couldn't explain any of this to the mind of a five-year-old boy. They couldn't make sense of it to themselves either. Logically it didn't make sense.

They just waited for the seven-day waiting period to end.

CHAPTER 13

I could sense Archippus's bewilderment. The puzzled look on his face displayed his effort to try and make sense of what he'd just heard as no reasonable explanation could be found. He asked, "Why would God allow so much to happen to one family? It didn't seem like they deserved any of it."

"Well, my friend, God works in mysterious ways. But be assured: he's in control, and he knows best. Consider what you've gone through. God knows about every aspect—every detail— and it's all part of his plan. Though it may have been hard to understand, God remained in control of Tychicus's situation, even as the most difficult time of his life was still ahead." With a smile I continued.

Tychicus walked. He paced. He walked back and forth, back and forth. He didn't know what else to do. For some time, he paced until his feet hurt. Finally, he succumbed to fatigue as he sat down to rest beneath a tree. His stomach growled, revealing his hunger, but he had no food. He had already eaten the fruit Timotheus had tossed to him, and his hands were now as empty as his stomach. He'd heard that the family of a leper would find a drop-off spot where food would be delivered, at least during the earliest days. But he hadn't heard from Rebekah or anyone—not one word. This puzzled him. She didn't send any kind of message. She hadn't tried to contact him. No one had. Why?

He didn't know where to turn. So he walked once more. He wandered. He hoped someone would try to make contact. He stayed near the city, though keeping his distance as the walls remained in sight from afar. He knew by now everyone knew to stay far from him—he had been declared unclean. The laws forbid anyone to come near him. Still, he wondered why Rebekah had remained completely absent. How could this be?

In some ways, he actually dreaded contact with anyone at first. He couldn't stomach hearing those dreadful words for the first time coming from his own lips: "Unclean! Unclean! Unclean!" He almost expected Jotham to search him out just to relish in hearing those words coming from his mouth, only to reaffirm they were true.

It had been two days. More than ever, hunger followed him like an unwanted companion. Aside from the fruit Timotheus had given him, he hadn't eaten anything else, and he knew he had to find something to meet his need.

Without even a word or attempt to contact him from Rebekah, his mind started to wander. Where had she been? Why didn't she reach out to him? How could this be happening? Of course, he blamed God for most of it, though he reserved some of his bitterness and hatred for Jotham. He didn't know about Rebekah's incarceration. He could only imagine what his son was going through, and it angered him. From his perspective, he had been instantly and totally cut off—abandoned. He didn't realize the pain of separation would come so quickly.

The sun started to set as Tychicus decided to walk closer to the city as the night sky drew dark. Perhaps he could find some food outside the city, he thought. From a distance, he sat beneath a tree and watched as the day finally turned to darkest night. Silence filled the night air, other than the occasional quiet sounds of rustling here and there. What a lonely time this would prove to be. How he missed the giggles of his son and the warm, comforting voice of his beautiful wife. How he longed to hear her say, "I love you," as she enveloped him in her loving arms. He wished he'd been more outspoken of his love for her when he had the opportunity. He longed to give his son a good-night hug and tell him a story before he fell asleep. He could imagine his soft, little face as he dreamed. He missed the occasions when he would stand beside his son's bed, often with Rebekah, and stare at him. Smiles were present during those late-night visits. Such peace existed in those moments. Such comfort and security filled the room. Often, watching him sleep, breathing ever so softly, led to conversations and dreams of having more children someday. Though the night was somewhat peaceful now, it did not compare to those precious moments that were now only treasured memories.

His eyes looked toward the city. The night was filled with an awkward stillness, with the exception of one who sat outside the gate. It was the same blind beggar who had been sitting there for years. Even as the day disappeared into darkness, he remained in his place outside the walls near the gate. From time to time, he'd roll over on his dirty blanket, disturbing the quietness ever so slightly. Quietly, step by step, Tychicus started making his way toward the wall and the beggar. He didn't know why. Something had drawn him to this place. Something had drawn him toward this man. With each step, this blind, forsaken beggar would become the closest person to him than anyone else in the world. He knew this man couldn't see him. As a result, perhaps, if he confronted him, he wouldn't be able to recognize his uncleanness. He just might be impartial to his dilemma, to his unfortunate plight. And even if he would somehow be able to understand whom he dealt with, what would he be able to do? He was in no position to cast him away.

He took one slow step at a time, moving closer and closer to the city and toward the blind beggar. He found himself against the wall, about fifty feet away in the shadows. He knew this man could not see him, but he was concerned someone else might. As he came closer, Josech sat up, waking from his slumber. Tychicus could sense his fear. The beggar's ears were very keen, especially to unfamiliar sounds in the night.

"Who goes there?" he whispered nervously. "Is someone there?"

Tychicus took another step. A stone crunched under his sandal.

"Who goes there?" Josech asked again, clenching to his blanket in fear.

"A friend," Tychicus said for some unknown reason. He had acted far from friendly for many years, walking right past this man in need. Now he considered himself a friend? How absurd this statement seemed, especially to Tychicus, who couldn't believe it had come from his lips. A sense of relief filled Josech as he heard a somewhat-friendly voice. He rested in assurance that this strange noise had not been made by a wild animal coming to take advantage of easy prey.

"What do you want? I have nothing to offer you," Josech muttered, speaking the truth. "All I have is my dirty blanket and the tattered clothes on my back. Please, I beg of you. Don't harm me. Have compassion on me."

"I won't hurt you," Tychicus said calmly.

Instinctively the beggar sought help and asked unashamedly. It had become the very fabric of his life. "Do you have any food?" he asked instinctively.

Tychicus realized at that moment that he'd been reduced to the same level as this beggar. He too longed for food—something he didn't have. It became quiet for a moment as Josech waited for a response.

"I mean you no harm. I'm also a beggar." Tychicus listened to the words that came from his mouth. He could scarcely believe them—though they were true.

Relief came over Josech again. He knew a beating wouldn't meet him this night.

"Are you scared?" he asked. It seemed like a strange question coming from a blind beggar. Tychicus wondered why he'd ask such a thing. But it nonetheless hit a nerve. Tychicus *was* scared.

He had found much to fear, and unbeknown to him, this beggar was smarter than most acknowledged.

"Your voice," Josech said, "you sound scared."

Tychicus didn't say anything. A personal analysis from someone who didn't know him or by someone who couldn't even see him had not been the norm in his experience. What could this blind poor beggar possibly know about him? Tychicus didn't respond. As he stood in the shadows trying to remain invisible to this blind man, he paused to consider this odd scenario.

"What's your name? Where are you from?" Josech asked softly as if to keep his conversation hidden from others who might hear. He had never before had the opportunity to converse with someone during the night, not as far as he could remember. This rare treat, for someone who practically lived his entire existence alone, would be cherished as long as it would last.

Josech's question caused Tychicus to think. He stood still as so many moments instantly flashed before his mind's eye.

He thought of his wife, remembering how they met. He would never forget that day.

It had been raining all morning. The uncommon, brisk air blew across his cloak as he ran into the temple in Magdala. The coldness touched his bones, and the marble floor failed to provide warmth. His elderly mother, who told him to visit the temple, had sent him there. She saw the temple as a haven for prayer, a place to meet with Jehovah. She lay in bed with a fever, and upon her insistence, he headed to the temple to pray for her. It had been a long time since he had visited the temple. He hadn't had much to do with God in recent years, but at this time of sickness, he realized this might be where he could find help. He never anticipated what else he would find that cool morning.

As he walked toward the altar, he noticed a young woman praying. She knelt down with her eyes closed. As she prayed, he looked upon her face. Her beauty at that moment astonished him, and he could not look away. He didn't realize how young she was, though that fact held no concern to him at that moment.

He watched her for some time. He had often wondered what Eve might have looked like—the perfect woman formed by the very hands of God. He always believed that when God created the first woman, she must have possessed an incomparable beauty—until now. He found himself truly infatuated with this young woman he had never seen before.

As he watched her, she opened her eyes and looked at him. He was embarrassed that she had caught him looking at her. She appeared to be at such peace as if sleeping. He never expected her to look at him.

Just then, another man walked hastily down the aisle toward her. He put his hand gently on her shoulder. "There you are," he whispered. "We've been looking for you!"

Her gaze turned from Tychicus to the one who had come for her. "I am praying. Didn't you know I would be here?" she asked softly with a hint of joy in her voice. She had an angelic voice, Tychicus thought. He realized he still watched her as he knelt down to her left near the altar. He closed his eyes, feigning prayer as he listened for her next words.

"Bukkiah, why do you disturb my prayer? Can't you see I am seeking the Lord?"

Tychicus had discovered a rare treasure. This young woman was not only physically beautiful, but she also had a heart for God. This was the kind of woman his mother had been praying he would find.

He listened carefully, identifying the man's name: Bukkiah. Could he be a suitor? If not, who might he be? Had she been spoken for? And what was *her* name? His heart sank at the prospect that the most beautiful woman he had ever seen might be out of his reach. He never imagined this trip to the temple would be filled with such excitement.

"Rebekah, Father sent me to get you…"

Tychicus did not hear another word Bukkiah said as he realized two things. He had spoken her name: Rebekah. What a beautiful name, he thought. He also realized this man was her brother. In his mind, that meant she could possibly be single. He remained hopeful. He glanced over toward her once more. As she rose to her feet, she looked at him again. Their eyes met for just a brief moment. She raised her eyebrows slightly and smiled at him. His heart filled with delight as she turned and walked away.

As she walked out with Bukkiah, Tychicus remained at the altar. He closed his eyes and prayed. "Lord, who is this beautiful young woman? I pray you would allow me to meet her again." He remained quiet for some time, reliving this experience over and over in his mind. After some time, he stood up to walk out of the temple before stopping in his tracks. He turned back around and headed back to the altar where he knelt down again. "And please, Lord, bring healing to my mother."

Though his mother's fever had broken, the next day he went to the temple at the same time, happy to see who might be kneeling at the altar. He watched Rebekah from the back of the temple as he prayed. Finally, she stood up and slowly walked toward the door. Just before she passed him, she looked up. Again their eyes met as Rebekah stopped in her tracks.

"Hello," he said timidly.

"Hello," she responded with a smile.

An awkward quietness surrounded them as they looked at each other.

"Well, the rain stopped," Tychicus said with regret. "I was praying it would stop." Couldn't he have thought of something else to say? He had been dreaming of talking with her since the previous day, and that was what he chose to say?

"Yes, it has," Rebekah responded.

They both waited to see who might say the next word.

"My name is Tychicus. I saw you here yesterday, praying."

"I saw you too. I'm Rebekah, the daughter of Zibeon. I was thanking the Lord for the rain. My father's crops desperately needed it."

"I was praying for my mother. She had a fever."

"Is she well?" Rebekah asked with a look of anticipation. She knew God answered prayer. That reason alone led her to the temple.

"Her fever broke yesterday, by the time I walked into our house."

"God answered your prayer while you were here at the temple?"

Tychicus thought back to the previous day. After he first saw Rebekah, he turned to leave before going back to the altar to pray for his mother's healing. God had answered his prayer at that moment. What an amazing realization!

He looked back at Rebekah with a smile.

"Our God is good," she said. Then she smiled in celebration.

From that day on, Tychicus and Rebekah met frequently at the temple. They prayed and celebrated God's goodness. Eventually they took walks together along the Sea of Galilee. Soon he looked beyond her beautiful exterior as he fell in love with her tender, compassionate heart. There was nothing about her he didn't love. He couldn't believe she fell in love with him as well.

He remembered their first kiss. What a tender and romantic moment they shared standing in the moonlight on the shores of the Sea of Galilee. He thought back to their wedding celebration with so many members from both of their families present. He remembered their wedding night—and the intimacy of the passionate love they shared.

How he missed holding her, kissing her, talking to her, or simply watching her from across a room. How he ever captured the heart of such a perfect woman, he'd never know. God had blessed him far beyond measure. She still intrigued him as she had that first day when he spotted her praying in the temple. There were so many moments he now treasured in his heart that he'd taken for granted. He understood that now, wondering where she was at that very moment. What was she doing? What thoughts filled her mind? Who had come to help her in this time of need, or was she all alone?

How he missed her! If only he could hold her once again, he'd never let her go.

His thoughts turned toward his son. He recalled his sweet, little, high-pitched voice and when he would call for him with unintelligible sounds. Then when he could call him "father," pride elevated him to new heights. He had become someone important in a way that he had never known before. He remembered first steps and many skinned knees. Years later, his little boy ran into his arms with unbridled avidity. But of all the thoughts of his son that crossed his mind, he could not forget that last look they shared in the courtyard. He remembered his exact thoughts at that moment. He didn't voice them, though now he wished he had. Before he could say what pressed on his heart, a leper pounced on his back, stealing that moment from him.

What was his name? Where was he from? Could he really answer these questions without considering his wife and his son? They made up so much of his identity as a father and a husband—as a man. Now he had been reduced to a homeless wanderer with nowhere to call home. He recalled the events of the last few weeks that took him from a place of social norm to the place of utter despair and exile. How did this happen?

"My name's Josech. What's your name?" the beggar asked, disturbing his thoughts. He sounded a little more confident in his questioning. He sensed he had been approached by someone who needed a friend as badly as he did. What did he have to lose?

After some thoughtful consideration, Tychicus slowly said, "My name is… Leperd." Once again, he remembered the leper on the road to the house of Zibeon. He remembered the whole conversation with his son. He could almost hear Justus asking, "That man, is a… *leopard?*"

Now he'd become that shunned person. So from this moment on, he decided, that was how he would be defined. The man Tychicus had died, and this new, cursed man had taken his place. As time passed by, he would become even more of a leper. He would become more and more "lepered," if that even made sense. It sounded like something his son might say.

Again, quietly but confidently, he said it again, "I am Leperd."

"Do you have a family?" Josech asked.

Leperd simply put his head down and faintly said, "No."

He loved his family but didn't want to talk about them. He knew he'd lost them, and talking about them would simply be too painful. He surrendered to hopelessness, and even in the presence of someone else, he never felt more alone. It had been just a matter of days since his banishment, and he already felt as if he had already started to lose his sanity. He wondered how this blind beggar had remained sane living his whole life with loneliness, hunger, hopelessness, and abandonment, an existence he had just started to experience.

His heart sank to depths he didn't know existed. He already felt half-dead, and he wondered how it could get much worse—though he knew it would.

With that, the conversation ended. Leperd turned and walked away from the city, looking for a place to retire for the night.

"Come back again, Leperd," Josech said. "I'll be here."

Leperd decided he'd leave in the morning. He wouldn't stay near the gates. Eventually he'd head toward the hot springs south of the city. He'd heard of their medicinal powers, but he knew they wouldn't bring healing. But what else did he have to do? Where else did he have to go? He had nothing but time. He would become an aimless drifter, a man without a home. And so it would be.

CHAPTER 14

Leperd woke before the sunrise. He grinned as he said the day's first words. "Rebekah, my dear?" As he slept, he'd been taken back to a world he could now only dream of. For a brief moment, he'd forgotten the last few weeks as if it had all been a nightmare. He sat up as reality took hold. He looked off into the distance over the Sea of Galilee. He rubbed the sleep from his eyes. Now, aware of where he found himself, he realized he wasn't at home with his wife but under the open sky in the hills west of Tiberias. From his vantage point, he could see the city, which hadn't yet become busy with the normal routine he once took for granted.

A sick feeling stirred in his stomach. He didn't know if it was a repercussion of sorrow or hunger. Most likely it resulted from a healthy mix of the two. He looked down at his cloak, which had become torn and dirty. The wounds across his chest were a condemning reminder of his uncleanness. He already despised the day, and it had just begun.

He stood to his feet and stretched, which caused pain in several of his cuts. He'd also temporarily forgotten about them. He slowly started walking. This day he'd head toward the hot springs south of the city. He knew he had plenty of time. He had a lifetime ahead of him, though he believed his remaining days would be shorter than he hoped. He had just one task to focus on: getting food in his stomach.

He remembered the hot springs. He and Rebekah had visited them in the days shortly after they took their marriage vows. He remembered them vividly. Her beauty was never more resplendent. As they kissed in the bubbling hot water, they experienced a state of euphoria like never before. Their romance had never been more intimate than during those moments, and they both vowed to return there someday to recapture that loving spark. Somehow life became hectic with the routine of daily life, and once Justus was born, the whole notion slipped from their mind. They did take Justus there on a recent trip, which, of course, led to a totally different experience.

Before he could revisit too many specific details, something distracted him. A grasshopper jumped onto his cloak. He grabbed it before it could hop away. He looked at it. He studied it. It seemed so helpless in his hand. In relation to the plant-eating insect, he stood like a monstrous giant, but in the grand scheme of everything, he really felt quite small.

He put the grasshopper in his mouth and started chewing. Even as it kicked and squirmed with its long hind legs, he swallowed. It wasn't much, but this small nugget of food would help start his day. This short event would become common.

He continued walking.

He thought the warm waters of the hot springs would bring some physical comfort if nothing else. He wondered if they could possibly bring healing as some believed. Though he did not think they would, considering the possibilities of such an event gave him something to think about.

As he walked, he watched the sunrise. He stopped and looked for a while. What a beautiful sight, one he'd never really stopped to appreciate like this before. He wondered how a God who could create such an awesome sight, which brought hope for a new day, hadn't allowed the sunrise to bring him hope. His day would be filled with hopelessness. Once again, he didn't understand his lot. Even in the presence of this amazing handiwork, he became angry as he cursed God. He also sent another curse toward Jotham. Eventually his anger subsided, and he continued on his way.

He started to recognize the terrain as he neared his destination. From a short distance, he saw the road and some travelers coming toward him. He stopped and looked at them as they drew near. Without a thought, he decided to greet them.

"Hello," he said. As he wandered in the hills, he hadn't talked to anyone since he spoke with Josech at the city gates several days before.

The travelers noticed him as they drew near. They kept an eye on him as they moved closer. When Leperd took several steps toward them, one of the men called out, "Are you clean or unclean?" His torn garment, his wounds, and his unkempt look had given them indication of his possible condition.

He had not yet been confronted by someone in this manner. He knew it would come eventually, which he'd dreaded. Instantly he thought back to the road that led to Magdala. He could still see the leper on the side of the road, and he recalled how he had reacted. His words from that day came back to him as if they'd just left his lips: "Get back! Don't come near! You're unclean! You need to shout, 'Unclean! Unclean! Unclean!'"

His thoughts were interrupted as the travelers waited for his response. "Are you clean or unclean?" one of them asked again.

They'd seen him for what he was, and now he had to respond. He took a step backward, then another, and another. He moved slowly as he said, "I'm… unclean."

The travelers looked at him where they'd stopped. They wondered why this unclean man hadn't given them early warning. They did not recognize him or realize what he'd just experienced.

The anger in Leperd started to grow. To hear those dreaded words coming from his own mouth seemed wrong. He shouldn't have to say them. It should've been someone else—someone who deserved this punishment, someone who'd done wrong. The rage inside him swelled until it could not be contained any longer. He began to scream, "Unclean! Unclean! Unclean!"

He'd finally spoken those dreadful words, and his condition never appeared more obvious. He looked at the men as they looked back at him. He must've appeared to be possessed—a madman. He turned and started walking away from the road.

At that moment, he realized he'd never make it to the hot springs. Others would be there, and the law forbid him to be near them. He decided to head back into the hills and look for something to eat and somewhere to stay.

This incident caused his condition to be more real than it had ever had been. Once again, he questioned God, not understanding why his life had taken this unbelievable turn. Though he waited, answers didn't come.

CHAPTER 15

Several days later, Rebekah appeared before Jotham. She'd been submitted to harsh isolation, especially for a woman, and without justification. His intent to discourage Tychicus and Rebekah had been successful. He never stopped to consider the damage he'd caused. She'd been deprived of her last chance to help her husband and to communicate with him, even from a distance.

"I've waited these seven days, and now I demand to be released!" Rebekah said forcefully.

"We must see if you are clean or unclean," Jotham said deviously, looking at Rebekah as if examining her. She knew he looked lustfully, which disgusted her. "I said this to Tychicus, and I must say it to you." He smiled. "Take off your garment."

Rebekah looked at him in disbelief. What? She'd never think of such a thing! And how dare he demand it of her.

Before she could say a word, Jotham spoke. "We must see if there is any sign of contamination."

"I know what you want to see, and your eyes will never see me—*never!*"

Just then Amon, the high priest, entered the room.

Rebekah took advantage of his presence. He had a good reputation and was known to be a highly respected as a man of God. He had to be. Otherwise, he wouldn't be allowed to enter into the holy of holies, where sacrifices on behalf of the people were presented to God. A wicked priest, like Jotham, would surely be struck down in God's holy presence.

Jotham turned around. "So I see you have returned from Gadara." The chief priest's time of unsupervised abuses would end as the high priest regained temple authority.

Rebekah spoke before Jotham could say another word. "Amon, I've been held for seven days in the infirmary for no reason. I demand you release me!"

Amon looked at Rebekah. He recognized her from the many times he'd seen her praying at the temple. Like Amon, she also had a good reputation.

The high priest had compassion on her but understood the law. "I hear you've had direct contact with an unclean person, and proper measures had to be taken to ensure the safety of the community. I hope you understand."

"I do. But my husband was found unclean, but I'm clean. I have not been defiled. Can't you tell that by looking at me?"

Amon looked at Rebekah with decent eyes. He then looked at Jotham. "She looks clean to me," he said solemnly.

Anyone who looked at her with discerning eyes could conclude she was clean. Her momentary touch with her husband hadn't contaminated her.

"I do understand the law, but I actually wondered why you've been detained this long and with such harsh treatment. I have talked with some of the temple priests," Amon said with his eyes still focused toward Jotham. "I believe it was a cruel and heartless act to detain you for the full seven-day period, especially since you have a family to care for. I assure you, if I had not been detained on my journey, this whole debacle would not have happened."

"Yes, sir. I have not been allowed to see my five-year-old son during this unnecessary confinement. And as you know, my husband is no longer with us."

"And who's been taking care of your son these seven days?" he asked sincerely.

"He's been with my father and mother from Magdala and his uncle Isaac."

Amon looked again at Jotham, reflecting on the harsh treatment she'd received under his supervision. The room became filled with thick tension as the evil priest had been placed in a position he hadn't anticipated. In his mind, he'd already decided to send her back to the infirmary for the following seven-day waiting period, just as he'd done to Tychicus. It was, in fact, within the parameters of the law and within his authority to decide. But now with the high priest breathing down his neck from close range, his intended course of action would be altered.

"I think... we can determine... you are clean," he said. Jotham hated to say those words, though not as much as the words he would now have to speak. "You are free to go," he said quickly as his countenance turned from eager anticipation to disturbed reluctance.

Rebekah refused to make eye contact with Jotham as she turned her eyes toward Amon. "Thank you," she said. "It's nice to finally find mercy and compassion at the temple."

Amon glared at Jotham more intently now as Rebekah headed for the door. He had started to get a glimpse of Jotham's hidden side—and he wasn't happy about it.

Before Rebekah left the room, Amon spoke to her. "Rebekah, forgive me for not being here during this time of trial. If you need anything from this day on," he said, "please come see me directly." He caught himself before nearly making a statement, telling her the temple helped widows in need. He knew that wouldn't strike the proper chord, though most would consider her now, for all practical purposes, a widow.

She would indeed take advantage of Amon's generous offer in the days and months to come, seeing it as provision from the hand of God. After all, in her culture, women did not work and someone needed to help provide her needs. She would become grateful for the help she would receive from the temple, her father, and other neighbors and friends.

"Thank you, Amon. You're so kind. God be with you," she said before turning to leave.

Once again, Amon looked at Jotham with a scolding glance before walking away.

As Rebekah walked through the temple doors, Zibeon and Tamar greeted her with hugs. Her brother Bukkiah also hugged her gently, as his wounds still ached from his experience with the temple guards. They had all anticipated her release and were waiting for her.

"Jotham wouldn't allow us to see you," Zibeon said.

"It's so good to see you. How are you, my dear?" Tamar asked with motherly concern.

"I hear the high priest arrived back in town today," Bukkiah added.

"Yes. I finally had a chance to talk with him, and I'm fine."

Rebekah's loving heart could no longer be silenced, displaying her concern for her family. "Where's Justus? Have you heard from Tychicus? Where are they? I must see them."

Before they could even tell her Justus was safe with Uncle Isaac, the question concerning Tychicus confronted them. They hadn't had any contact with him—the law forbid it. They were not allowed to contact or associate with someone determined to be unclean. Surely their daughter understood what the law demanded. They wondered if their daughter hadn't embraced the truth of the matter yet as denial gripped tightly. All of the ramifications of Tychicus's condition were truly hard to accept, and they understood they couldn't see this from her perspective.

Zibeon spoke first. He spoke firmly, yet lovingly. "Dear, we'll not be seeing Tychicus."

Tamar lovingly held her daughter's hand. "He's gone, dear."

"He's been banished," Bukkiah said. Of everyone, Rebekah couldn't believe he had just allowed Tychicus to walk away without helping him.

Rebekah just stood silent for a moment. They hadn't talked to him? They hadn't told him why she hadn't tried to help him? Did he even know she had been in isolation these last seven days? Where had he gone? Did he feel abandoned? The thought that he might have considered she didn't love him was something she couldn't accept. Surely he would never consider such a thought, would he? So many questions filled her mind, and they just seemed to keep coming like water from a broken dam.

She simply stood in a daze. Her eyes were empty as she stared afar off. Finally, overwhelmed with grief, she pushed her mother away and ran toward the city gates.

Zibeon started to run after her, though Tamar stopped him. "She needs to deal with this herself. Let her be." Nonetheless, Zibeon ran behind her toward the gates. Bukkiah wished he could run, though his physical ailments would not permit it as he started walking.

Rebekah ran as fast as she could, leaving everyone far behind. No one would stop her. As she ran, she sobbed, drawing attention from nearly everyone along the way. The people in the city knew her, and they knew what had happened to Tychicus. Many recognized her grief as they watched from a distance.

She ran through the city gates, falling on her knees right in the middle of the road. At the top of her lungs, she cried, "Come back to me, my love! Come back to me! Oh my God, where has he gone? Come back! Come back to me!" She fell facedown into the dirt as she wailed.

Tychicus could not be seen. He'd moved on, and she'd missed him. Unbeknown to her, Josech sat nearby listening to the whole episode. He felt sorry for her. But what could he do? Though his heart went out to her, he felt completely helpless. "Oh, that a kind angel would minister to her," he said to himself, "as one ministered to me." For a brief moment, his own predicament escaped his thoughts.

Finally, Zibeon made his way to the gates, out of breath. He looked at her, his only daughter. Outwardly, he appeared to be a strong pillar. Inside, he was overtaken with emotion. He prayed for her, that God would bring comfort and strength. After the well of her tears had run dry, he held her in his arms. She felt comfort from her father, though she longed to be in the arms of her husband. She knew this desire may never be fulfilled—such a harsh reality would take a long time to truly accept, though she would never fully understand it.

For now, she mourned.

CHAPTER 16

The next morning, Rebekah went to the temple to pray. Zibeon, Tamar, and Bukkiah all went with her. This gave Isaac some time with Justus. He cherished these moments. He only wished Tychicus could still be a part of them. In the last year that he lived with his nephew and Rebekah, since his wife passed away, he especially watched Tychicus interact with his son. They had such a close bond.

He often thought his older brother, Tychicus's father, would've been proud to see his son as a father. He also knew this current scenario would have been one that would have been difficult for his brother to witness.

Justus played on the floor as Isaac watched while sitting at a nearby table. In a moment, it seemed that Justus's little mind turned. He stood up and walked over to the table and sat down next to him. They sat there together, ready for a discussion. Isaac often initiated conversations, but today it would be Justus's turn.

"Uncle Isaac, what did my father do?" He had some ideas but never really understood it all.

He welcomed the conversation, though he knew it would be a difficult one. But he tried his best to bring it down to his level without avoiding the truth.

"Well, what have you heard, my boy?" Isaac asked.

"I heard he did something bad at the temple, and he was kicked out of there, and now he can never come back here." Justus looked sad as he stated what he'd heard from some of the other children who'd heard their parents' version of the situation, which were most likely exaggerated. Surely many different speculations were made.

"Your father didn't do anything wrong like that. He tried to take care of your mother, and the priest didn't like it." Isaac thought that might sum up what happened at the temple, even though his words were somewhat vague. All in all, it wasn't a satisfying answer.

"Why didn't the priest like that?" Justus asked.

"He's not a nice priest."

"But I thought all priests were nice... Don't they work for God?"

Jotham's damage to the priesthood had far-reaching effects, more than he'd ever realize. He didn't even come close to the stereotypical standards even accepted by young children.

"There will always be good people and bad people. Wherever you go, this will be true—even here in Tiberias. Some people are good. They love God, and they do what he wants them to do. Some people do what they want, and it isn't what God wants. They can be bad people. The priest who talked to your father isn't a nice man." It seemed strange talking about a "bad priest," but the truth was the truth, though unfortunate.

Justus stopped as if in deep thought. Isaac could sense his brain churning, contemplating something. He knew another question would come soon, which it did.

"Is my father bad?"

Justus started to get emotional as Isaac picked him up and sat him on his knee. "No, your father isn't bad."

"Then why won't they let him come home?" This made no sense to this young mind, which saw this situation as black and white. If his father was good, then he would be home; if he was bad, then he wouldn't be home—and he wasn't home!

Isaac hugged him as Justus rested his head on his shoulder. Isaac reassured him that though his father had been good, he couldn't come home. These words contradicted his young logic and really confused him. For a few minutes, they sat there. They were both thinking, neither one of them finding any answers to their questions.

Justus seemed to change direction for a moment. "Uncle Isaac, remember at the festival when we were all playing, and I got really dirty in the dirt?"

"Well, I wasn't there, but your mother told me about it. It sounded like a lot of fun!" Isaac could just imagine his nephew's son totally covered with dirt like any typical young boy.

Isaac thought back many years ago, remembering Tychicus as a young child. Like most boys, he'd naturally learned the fine art of playing in the dirt. In his mind's eye, he could imagine Justus with all his cousins—filthy dirty! Like father, like son.

"Is that 'unclean'?" Justus asked with a look of confusion.

"Why do you ask that, my boy?"

"They said my father was 'unclean.' I never saw him play in the dirt." He paused for a moment before adding, "*I* played in the dirt."

Isaac understood the trouble Justus had with understanding all the terminology that had entered his ears. It didn't make sense to him, and at his age, why would it? Isaac understood a "clean" man could be dirty and that an "unclean" man could be clean to some degree—in terms of physical cleanliness. He confused himself just trying to think through it, much less seeing it from Justus's perspective.

"Justus, your father wasn't 'unclean' because he played in dirt. His outside was not dirty." He paused for a moment. This would surely be hard to explain. "Being unclean means...you're sick. He's dirty on the inside."

"He didn't look sick." Justus couldn't understand the unseen nature of his father's disease.

Isaac struggled to help Justus understand. "He's sick inside, and we cannot see it right now. We cannot understand it. He's just sick, and we don't know how to help him get better."

"Am I going to get sick? Is mother going to get sick?" He now looked directly into Isaac's eyes. "Are *you* going to get sick, Uncle

Isaac?" Justus looked worried. Confusion set in, now stronger than ever.

"No. You're going to be fine. But that's why your father had to go away. If he came home now, we could all get sick. Part of the law says if an unclean person even sticks their head into someone's house, the whole house would be declared unclean. Does that make sense? We just can't be near your father right now." Isaac could not have been more frustrated. How he wanted Justus to find some measure of sense in all this. He didn't know how else to help him.

Justus nodded, signifying he understood. However, he did not convince anyone. He stopped and thought for a moment and then said, "If my father came home, we'd have to clean the house?" He looked sad as he added, "I'll help."

Isaac couldn't help but smile. He enjoyed seeing the simplicity of the mind of a child. Justus understood his father would have to stay away, and he would understand more in time. Isaac decided he'd now change direction.

"My boy, our God is a great and mighty God. We must pray and ask him to make your father better. That's what your mother is doing right now. So are your grandparents and your uncle Bukkiah. They're praying at the temple, but we can do it right here or even quietly in our heart."

For the first time during this conversation, Justus smiled. "Will God make my father better?"

"He could if he wanted to. Why don't you pray and ask him?"

Unashamed, Justus folded his hands and started to pray his simple prayer out loud, "God, make my father better right now!"

Isaac smiled again. "My boy, your father would be proud of you." He rubbed his hand through the boy's hair.

Justus smiled. He liked when Uncle Isaac did that. He remembered how his father used to do that too.

"Let's keep praying for your father. Let's ask God to do what he wants. And if God chooses to heal him, we must be ready with the sacrificial lambs. You see, when your father is away, he cannot go to the temple and make the sacrifices he needs to make for his sins. So when he's better, and when he comes back, he has to make up for all those sacrifices. So we better have some lambs ready. We can talk to Demas about helping us with that. He has some lambs. Maybe he'd let you take care of some of them? Then after he becomes well, the community will throw an eight-day celebration for your father to celebrate his cleansing!"

Isaac spoke the truth. A person healed of leprosy needed to make sacrifices for those he could not make during his exile. Then the law required an eight-day cleansing restoration ritual that included a seven-day party thrown in their honor by the community. He mentioned it to Justus to bring him some hope. Though he believed Tychicus's chances of restoration were minimal at best, in his heart he really didn't believe he'd ever see him again. Anything to the contrary would simply be a hopeless dream. And he wondered how long he should give Justus false hope. For now, he offered something he could hold on to.

Just then, Rebekah walked in. Zibeon, Tamar, and Bukkiah followed close behind her.

"Father's coming home!" Justus declared with a wide smile as he ran into her open arms. A strange look crossed her face as she glanced toward Isaac.

Zibeon, Tamar, and Bukkiah looked hopeful. What did they just hear?

"I prayed for Father, that God would heal him. When he comes home, we need to get the lambs and have a party, and everyone is coming!"

This was not what they expected as hope turned toward disappointment.

She half-smiled as she hugged her boy. "I'm praying too." She prayed, believing that God could heal her husband and, more importantly, that his heart would turn back to God.

CHAPTER 17

Another day had passed as Josech listened in the quietness. The moon loomed large in the sky, though the fact was unknown to him. It had been some time since he heard the sound he longed to hear again. The every night sounds of the evening were once again his faithful companion. But he listened for something more. He waited for some time. He nearly dozed off when suddenly his ears perked up. Softly in the distance, he finally heard them—footsteps. These weren't the heavier steps he'd heard before. He'd longed for these softer ones for a long time. He'd been waiting for them.

"Good evening, my unseen angel," he whispered.

A few more footsteps came closer.

"I smelled the bread. I wondered if you'd come back."

Quietness filled the air for a moment as Josech felt a piece of bread placed in his hand. He breathed in, enjoying the freshness he hadn't enjoyed for some time.

"Are you hungry?" the angel asked quietly.

"Yes," he said, taking a first nibble. How he enjoyed that first taste. Hunger had become his closest companion, and he spent every day with it.

"I also brought you some fruit," she said.

"Thank you. You're so kind." Josech didn't know how else to express his gratitude. The only thing he had to reciprocate this act of kindness was the offer of friendship.

"I am Josech. What's your name?" He waited. He listened. It remained silent. "Are you still there? Have you flown back to heaven?"

"I'm still here."

"Why are you so kind to me?" he asked. Kindness had not visited the poor beggar in a long time. For someone to give him *fresh* food was practically unheard-of. He wondered who this angel might be. Who would be so kind to a stranger, especially a blind one?

"I have been sent from the Lord," the quiet voice replied. "He gave me this bread and told me to feed you."

"Please tell me. What's your name?" he asked again.

"I'm just an angel, sent from the Lord," she said after some thought.

Josech waited until he heard the start of footsteps walking away.

"Please don't go," Josech begged. He'd begged for food and drink on a regular basis. Now for a change, he begged for company. "Can you stay just a little longer?"

The footsteps stopped. Then he heard a few steps walk back toward him.

"Do you know about the man who has been banished from the city?"

"Yes. I was there when it happened."

"Does he have a family?"

"Yes, he does."

"How are they doing?"

The air became quiet again, for a long time. Josech didn't hear her anymore. She had become very still or had flown away without a sound.

"Are you still there?" he asked quietly, hoping for an answer. He listened intently.

"I'm still here," the voice said softly, followed by quietness once more.

Finally, she spoke, "Josech, what happened to your family? Do you remember your mother? Your father? Did you have brothers or sisters? Do you remember them at all?"

"I remember my mother holding me as a child. I remember her warmth. My father had strong hands. Other than that, I don't remember much. That was so long ago. Then they left me here. I don't know what happened to them, or why they abandoned me. I don't think I'll ever know." Josech sat still, trying to recall memories that had faded long ago.

"That's how they feel. Like part of their family has left, never to return. How do you think they feel?" Once again, it became silent. "I think you know how they feel. They feel lost, abandoned. A part of them has been stolen away. They wonder what each day will bring and how they will cope on their own."

Josech understood the angel's point. Surely they were empty inside. Surely they mourned their loss. He understood that. How his heart ached for them.

He started to hear soft footsteps walking away from him again.

"Angel?" he called out. "When will you come back?" He waited for her response, but she did not respond. He couldn't get the sick feeling out of his stomach. He recalled the strong loneliness and deep ache he felt when he first started sitting in this spot so long ago. It took so long for him to forget it, and now somehow, it all came back. He didn't even feel like eating his bread. He just sat there listening to the night, wondering what the family pondered at that very moment.

CHAPTER 18

Two beggars started searching for food among the heaps of waste that had been deposited at the city dump earlier that morning. They joined several others who had started earlier, as they rummaged through the previous day's garbage, hoping to find any edible scrap or morsel to start to fill the emptiness of their stomachs. An unwritten code had been understood in this place. All who gathered here to search held a level of respect for each other. They understood they stood on level ground, all hungry and hoping.

It had been a common morning, for the most part, until one person changed all that.

"What is that?" a young man yelled. He forcefully pushed one of the beggars down. A treasure had been found—a partial loaf of bread, which he determined would be his. He revealed he was an arrogant thief as well as a young outcast.

"Well, look here. I found some breakfast."

"You must be new here," another beggar proclaimed. "We do not steal from each other. You find what you find—that's the rule!"

"You little punk, where's your mother?" one of the beggars asked.

"Shut up, old man!" the young man said as he pushed the older beggar down, who stumbled before falling beside the other who already lay on the ground. "I need her as much as I need you!"

Several others stood up to him, remarking, "You do not belong here."

Before much more could be said, he shouted, "This is my place now! You don't belong here anymore!"

Another shouted, "Who do you think you are? We've never seen you before in our lives!"

"My name is Achan. And this is my place now. You better get used to it," he proclaimed as he kicked one of the old beggars on the ground, landing a firm kick in the ribs. The boy growled, attempting to intimidate them all.

For the most part, the men who came to the dump were peaceful, just down on their luck. They were gentle and meek and poor. They just wanted to find something to help them make it through another day. How dare this young pubescent step into their circle with this unacceptable, arrogant attitude. They had never had to deal with such a person here. They helped the older men up and slowly scattered to different areas in the dump.

"Who wants to find me more to eat?" He continued to munch the stolen bread as he laughed arrogantly.

A short distance outside the dump, Leperd rubbed the sleepiness from his eyes. Depending on how he slept, there were times when his arm or hand fell asleep. As he woke, he felt the numbness in his hand. He knew the feeling would come back, for now. He could barely feel his fingers this morning as his hands tingled. He knew a day would come when the feeling would leave and not return. His joints were stiff, and his back ached in several places, which had become part of each morning. The manifestations of his disease seemed more evident each day.

He stood up and looked across the landscape. The Sea of Galilee sat before him off in the distance. He could barely see the city of Tiberias. As he looked around, he found no one in sight. He spent much time on alert, it seemed, making sure no one approached him. This had become a big part of Leperd's life.

Each day became defined by meeting several practical goals.

He focused on staying far from anyone. The laws forbid him to come too close to a clean person. And if he could stay a safe distance from everyone, he'd not have to speak those dreadful words: "Unclean! Unclean! Unclean!" How he hated hearing that declaration coming from his own mouth. Living through a full day without having to speak this warning brought an odd sense of satisfaction and accomplishment.

Finding food became his main goal on a daily basis.

How sad that his life had been reduced to this.

As his day began, he started the process of scavenging for something to eat. He dreamed of eating lamb or fish. How he'd love just one slice of fresh bread. There were so many dishes that came to mind as he tried to remember how they tasted. It had been so long since he'd really eaten a good meal.

He tried fishing along the Sea of Galilee. But many fishermen, who were extremely territorial, had chased him away from the shores. He soon found fishermen weren't friendly to lepers. He didn't have a boat, and he didn't have any nets, which made fishing an unlikely option for him. How he wished some fishermen would come ashore from time to time and toss him a single fish from their catch. But this never happened.

He couldn't own land, so he couldn't plant or harvest.

Finding food became more than a difficult challenge that confronted him every day. He often thought of the festivals he attended in Zibeon's home—and all the food. There was always so much to eat. He'd taken it all for granted. How he longed for just a portion of one of those meals now. Looking back, he wondered how those at the festival could eat all the food he remembered seeing there. Every day he struggled to find something to put in his stomach. Many days—most days—found him falling far short of reaching that goal. He couldn't remember the sensation of a full stomach.

There were several times when he begged for food from travelers, which he totally detested. He always felt so small during those humiliating moments. He had bowed to desperation, and he learned to swallow his pride. He found most shunned him away, as he'd done to the leper on the road to Magdala. He learned to beg from a distance. At least this way he could plead his case before he had to make that awful, required warning he loathed. Most travelers just continued on their way, refusing to acknowledge his presence or his need. Besides, the law forbid them to talk to him or have any contact with him. For them, to help him would be breaking the law.

He thought of Josech during those times. He'd lived with that scenario most of his life. Very rarely would someone dare to leave any portion of food for him at the road. Some did so out of fear, wondering what a shunned leper might do. He lived every day with the reminder that a leper could cause life-altering damage to another's life.

He found one of his best sources for food scraps at the city dump, though he typically didn't find much. After all, someone had discarded everything there. He also had to consider the possibility that a clean person might be in the vicinity, and then he'd have to give that dreaded warning. Some days he avoided the dump just for that reason.

Since there were poor beggars who settled down at the dump, he knew the chance of coming in contact with one of them would be more likely than not. Quite commonly, these beggars recognized a leper from afar and moved away to another part of the dump to maintain safe distance. They understood leprosy and respected the disease. By no means did they welcome the presence of lepers. But when one arrived, they knew to stay far from them.

Most days, Leperd also saw these poor beggars when he arrived. Depending on how hungry he had become, he might look for a while or simply walk away. After all, the law wouldn't allow him to come near a clean person, even if they were beggars. He understood the law and the limitations it placed upon him. The only exception he'd ever made had been with Josech. Otherwise, he abided by the restrictions that governed his life. He was also mindful of certain areas of the dump where these beggars made their home. He respected those areas and stayed away from them.

He'd grown accustomed to the feeling of hunger, finding it to be something he recognized as more common than not. But this day he found the hunger pains to be a little stronger than usual. He decided to head to the dump to look for something—anything. He did not intend to walk away hungry—not today.

It had been nearly a year since his exile began. His hair had grown long, covering part of his face, and the rash that had emerged on his skin were visible signs of his condition. He had lost weight, and his frame looked more and more like the leper he had become. Some of the cuts and scrapes he'd accumulated were infected, and he could only hope for healing to take place. Numbness in his hands and feet had become a common visitor, which he knew would one day reside permanently. Many times he thought back to that leper on the road to Magdala—he'd now become that man. He was definitely, by all standards, a leper.

Thinking back, he wished he'd been more compassionate toward that man on the road to Magdala. He wondered just how hungry he might have been when he approached them that day. He now walked in worn sandals and understood the desperation. He probably meant no harm; he had attempted to survive another day.

Leperd finally arrived at the dump. Several beggars saw him from afar and moved along. As he started to look through the garbage, he found a few scraps of stale bread. Ants were crawling all over them, which didn't seem to matter. It wasn't much, but he ate it gladly. To his delight, he found a few more scraps, which he quickly consumed. Surely other beggars had already been there before him, and there wasn't much more to be found. He continued searching when suddenly, it seemed, someone appeared in front of him. Leperd had not seen this beggar, and by all indications, he had not been seen either.

Achan, the brash youngster, and Leperd were both startled as they confronted each other. Leperd had been so surprised that he forgot to call out his required warning.

"What are you doing here?" Achan reacted before Leperd could say a word. He spoke with a harsh, demeaning tone as he cried out after taking a step back. "This is *my* place! Go! Off with you!" he barked with renewed confidence. Leperd wondered if this might have been this beggar's first encounter with a leper. He did not recognize him at all. Could this have been his first visit to the dump? He surely did not act in line with the other beggars, as they showed their measure of respect. He showed no indication that he should have walked away from an unclean leper. He thought everyone knew that. No one had ever confronted him like this, and he did not like it.

What a strange feeling to be spoken to by a clean person in this manner. These aggressive demands, especially from such a young person, in this mean-spirited tone were unnecessary. Leperd knew this beggar dealt with the same issues he faced: loneliness, hunger, and desperation.

Though Leperd could relate to him, nothing warranted such an attitude. He understood those who considered themselves to be superior as they looked down on him because of his leprosy. He used to be such a man. But he and this beggar were nearly equal in his eyes. His annoying mistreatment would not be tolerated, and Leperd decided he would not be pushed around—not today. Anger and rage immediately started to consume him. His undeniable hunger also played a role in the part he set out to play. He stood his ground, not moving a muscle. He determined he wouldn't walk away this day.

"You're supposed to say, 'Unclean! Unclean! Unclean!'" the beggar cried out nervously, noticing this leper hadn't backed off. He couldn't believe his threats had no effect on him. Lepers were supposed to turn and walk away, and they always had in the past.

"How would *you* like to say, 'Unclean! Unclean! Unclean!'" Leperd asked as he slowly started walking toward the man.

"Stay away from me! You're unclean!" Achan said as he took a step back. Leperd stepped closer. "Stay away!" he cried again.

Leperd continued one step at a time. He could sense this man's fear, which he did not mask very well. He didn't want any contact with a leper. Surely he understood the possible consequences that would only be detrimental to him. What else would a leper have to lose? Achan's brave words had only been a transparent facade.

Leperd knew this arrogant delinquent wouldn't want to walk in his sandals. Who would? He might have been poor, but at least he was clean. Leperd decided to teach him a lesson as he moved even closer to him.

Achan didn't say another word. He turned and walked away, looking over his shoulder, before Leperd could get too close. He finally turned and ran. After running a safe distance away, his courage returned as he cried out again, "You're supposed to say, 'Unclean! Unclean! Unclean!'"

Several of the other beggars now watched from afar. "Run home to your mother!" one beggar called out as the others joined in mockery and laughter. They were delighted that this troublemaker had crossed the path of an agitated leper, and they felt he needed to be put in his place.

Achan had spoken truthfully. Even the youth understand the law, which required Leperd to give a verbal warning, but at this moment, Leperd didn't care. Who would punish him this day for breaking the law? He just wanted to eat without this man's harassment.

Leperd started cursing wildly at him. He flailed back and forth like a wild tiger trying to free himself from chains of its captor. Achan surely thought this leper had lost his sanity, which scared him all the more. When Leperd started running toward him, he ran away faster than ever without looking back. He knew the only thing worse than having contact with a leper would be having contact with an insane leper. After Achan ran off, Leperd returned to the dump. Though the remaining beggars praised him for running the delinquent off, he did not respond to them.

After finding more scraps, he headed off feeling just slightly guilty for his actions. His anger and rage had taken over as he gave no consideration to what he might have brought onto this stranger. His heart had turned cold and bitter in the heat of the moment, and he didn't care. As time grew on, he gained a reputation in that place, and the beggars especially stayed far from him.

He looked for a place to rest for the night. He'd soon begin another day looking for food and avoiding human contact. His life had developed into a routine of hopelessness. He wondered how long he'd be able to endure as each day mirrored the one before. He longed for something that might bring him a glimpse of hope. In the meantime he survived, growing increasingly weary.

CHAPTER 19

Rebekah walked toward the temple as the calmness of a new day surrounded her. With each step, she drew nearer the place where she would meet with God. Amid the quietness of the morning, her heart started to pound with uneasiness. How she longed to be running up the temple steps.

"Good morning, Rebekah. How's Justus?" asked one older woman.

"He's fine," she said unconvincingly. Distracted with so much on her heart, she hurried her pace. The typically sweet sounds of occasional birds now became almost annoying.

"Good morning, Rebekah," said a young man who had been captivated by her beauty. He started to walk beside her, which made her very uncomfortable. "Where are you going?"

Rebekah knew Philip. He had worked with Tychicus for a short time as a carpenter. She had noticed his glances before, and she knew Tychicus never cared much for him. She knew his intentions, and they were not clean.

"I'm going to the temple," she said under her breath. She stopped dead in her tracks. She looked directly into the young man's face. The stern and serious look on her face contrasted the young man's smug, flirtatious smile. "I am going to the temple to pray—for my *husband!*"

She turned to walk away as he grabbed her by the arm firmly. "Rebekah, Tychicus is dead. It's time you grabbed hold of that!"

"He might be dead to you, but he is very alive to me! And you don't have to grab hold of me!" she said directly.

"He's gone!" the man barked as his grip on Rebekah's forearm grew tighter.

"You're hurting me!" she said as she struggled to pull herself free from his grasp. "Do you think I am impressed by your strength?"

She shook her hand as if trying to shake off the discomfort he had caused.

"I'm sorry," he apologized, quickly changing his demeanor, realizing any attempt to win her attention might now be jeopardized.

"Stay away from me, Philip. I know what you want, and let me assure you, you will never have me. I am a married woman, and I will not sin against my husband!" She turned and ran toward the temple.

"You're insane! That's what you are!" he yelled in anger. "He's dead!"

The commotion caught the attention of several who watched as Rebekah stormed past them without responding to his verbal assault. No one would stand in her way. No one else would stop her. How she needed to meet with the Lord.

She ran up the temple steps and right through the main doors. She stopped to catch her breath for a moment, though each exhausted breath expressed her desperation. She knelt before the altar in reverence as she prayed. With a heavy heart, she called out to God as she panted. "Lord, God of my fathers, I continue to pray for my husband, Tychicus." She paused, finally starting to calm down. "I don't know where my beloved is or how he's doing. But I pray you'd work in his heart. Please, I plead with you, my God, draw him back to you. Create a longing in his heart for you." She started to cry as her heart ached with sincerity. How she loved him. How she missed him. She didn't understand everything Tychicus had experienced, but she knew God did—he was in control.

As she knelt, she felt someone's presence. Surely Philip had not followed her to the temple, she thought. When she looked up, she saw a familiar and unwelcome sight. She would have rather had to deal with Philip again, but instead, she found Jotham staring at her. As soon as she saw him, he walked toward her.

"Good morning, Rebekah," he said.

She knew this wasn't a polite or friendly greeting. He attempted to get closer to her, just as Philip had, and she understood both men had the same evil motives.

"I am praying," she said softly. After all, they were in the temple, a place of solace and reverence, and she had already had enough loud conversation for this day.

"Do not hinder a woman in prayer. It is a holy matter between God and her," she said, reciting his words. "Does that sound familiar? Those were your last words before my husband put you in your place. *Then you drove my husband away from God!*" She made a strong accusation, but one founded in truth.

Jotham once again saw her strength. Besides her beauty, her strength also attracted him. He remembered that day all too well.

"Your *old husband* defiled the temple, and he received what he deserved!"

Before another word could be said, Rebekah responded, "He's *still* my husband!"

"He is dead!" Jotham shouted. "When will you realize that? He's gone! You will never see him again or touch him or speak to him! He is a dead man walking!"

"For a 'man of God,' you lack faith."

"For a woman of 'faith,' you lack reality. Your husband is dead!"

Rebekah looked at Jotham. His body shook from the intensity of the moment. "Why do you mock me?" she asked. "By mocking me, you mock God!"

Rebekah, once again, could not believe Jotham's lack of warmth or compassion. She felt sad for him. What had been raging in his soul that held him back from loving people? What had caused him to build such a wall between himself and God? Surely it consisted of one small compromise after another. He now found himself in a place he never thought he would be. And he had justified it all! It was the slow fade of a man. Jotham had once been close to God. Slowly and gradually he moved farther and farther away—and it had become very obvious. How sad, she thought, when you fall, you always take someone with you. In this instance, she thought how her husband had been affected by this priest's sinfulness. She wondered how many others had fallen away.

She felt the need to share her heart with him. Even though he'd caused such pain to her and her family, she felt led to speak to him.

"Moses stood up against the impossible, and God parted the waters. Joshua marched around the walls of Jericho with faith, and God caused the mighty, powerful, indestructible walls to crumble. Joseph found himself in the depths of a dungeon when all hope seemed lost, yet God raised him up to life as a leader in the house of pharaoh. Daniel faced the lions when death seemed inevitable—but through his faithfulness God protected him and changed the heart of a mighty king. Time after time, God has proven to be in the midst of what we consider to be hopelessness. The God that performed miracles in our past is the same God I pray to today. And he's still able—and more than capable."

She stopped momentarily as she reflected on the goodness of God. Then she added, "He is able, *and more than willing!* So I will continue to pray—believing."

Jotham stood as still as a statue. A lowly woman of faith had schooled the self-proclaimed man of God. She wondered if he even heard a word she said.

She hoped he continued to listen as she added calmly, "You say my husband's dead, and to you he might seem to be. He's lost his life. His identity's gone. His community has forsaken him. He's been denied contact with his family and loved ones. But I know he's alive and breathing. Though he may be roaming aimlessly, he does so with air in his lungs and with a beating heart. With my whole being, I believe God can heal the sick. I believe God can raise the 'dead' back to life. I believe God can do whatever he pleases, whenever he pleases, however he pleases. And as long as I have breath, I will petition him to bring my husband back to me."

Her words had been direct and strong. The priest had learned not to expect anything less from her. But he didn't expect the next words at all. She looked directly into his eyes, and with compassion in her voice, she said softly, "He could even touch you, Jotham—if you'll let him."

Jotham fumed at her words as his hard heart hardened just a little more. He turned and stormed out of the room. How dare she speak such words to him—a chief priest. How dare she insinuate he needed to be touched by the hand of God. He'd denied the truth, for he did need to feel the touch of God again.

Rebekah felt anger and sadness at the same time. Her heart went out to him for just a moment. He'd caused such damage to her family, all under the guise of the priesthood. She longed for him to be the man God intended him to be. If he'd been, she thought, Tychicus might have remained in the fold. Perhaps her husband's ordeal might have been totally averted. It was all reflective speculation, of course. No one could have ever known for sure. One thing she did know for certain: Jotham needed to change. He needed what only God could provide. But until he recognized his need, all she could do was pray for him—which she did.

She knelt back down at the altar as she began to silently pray again in her heart. She prayed for Jotham. She prayed for Tychicus. She prayed for strength and understanding. The former would come soon. The latter would come in time.

CHAPTER 20

Justus knelt down beside a little lamb. He thought they were smelly, though he loved to feel their soft wool. Soon several other lambs surrounded him. He had grown to love these animals and longed for the day when he'd run them to the temple.

"Good morning, little lambs. Do you remember me?" he asked with a giggle. "Are you ready for my father to come home?"

Justus had ventured over to Demas's home nearly every day to spend time with the lambs. They'd become good friends, each one a symbol of hope. They looked at him with unsuspecting eyes. Without a care, they saw a young boy, unaware his goal was to someday sacrifice them upon the altar.

As he played with them, Demas watched with a smile. He, like many others, had dismissed any hope for Tychicus and his plight. Lepers didn't come back into the community. Once they were banished, they became faceless, nameless, homeless nonpersons. He saw this young boy as a fatherless son. In his eyes, his father had died, and he would never return. He had never witnessed a dead person coming back to life. He had been to many burials, and never once had anyone emerged from the dirt. That is how he viewed Tychicus, as most did.

By allowing Justus to play with his animals, he just might forget about his father. It could be a source of distraction. If this time brought the young boy a sense of peace, he happily obliged. But the idea that his lambs would run to the altar after Tychicus's restoration wasn't even a consideration. That would be too miraculous for him to believe.

Justus had been coming over for some time, and Demas wondered how long it would be until this whole notion of using his lambs for sacrifice would last. It had been nearly a year since

Tychicus had been exiled, and Justus still held onto hope, as did his mother.

Demas listened in as Justus continued his one-sided conversation.

"When the day comes, I'm going to run through the streets, and you're coming with me. Then we'll go to the temple, and then have a big party! It's going to be so much fun, and my father will be there. You can come to the temple, but you can't come to the party. You just can't. But that's fine. You'll like the temple."

Demas smiled as he marveled at the innocence of this child and of the lambs. Neither of them understood what life would bring. He believed, due to his immaturity, Justus had a weak grip on the truth, and he wondered how long it would take before he realized his father would never come home. He admired his young faith but knew it would eventually lead to utter disappointment. Even so, Justus continued coming over to see the lambs.

Faith was definitely being tested. If more had the faith of this child, God might have moved in mighty ways. Demas had given up faith, as had many others. Rebekah and her son were among the minority of the faithful few that prayed for God to move in Tychicus's behalf. They trusted God and believed he would work a miracle. Amon joined forces with them in praying faithfully, as did Zibeon, Tamar, and Bukkiah. But sadly, the temple priests and many in Tiberias had long forgotten the man now called Leperd.

If the truth were told, Leperd also considered his plight hopeless.

CHAPTER 21

Rebekah walked through the market toward the temple. Many gazed at her, and she knew this might always be the case. Some considered her "the carpenter's widow," while others referred to her as "the leper's wife." Though these labels weren't necessarily expressed verbally, they were expressed through continual looks and glances. She prayed this would be undone someday after her husband's restoration to full health—and to that end, she faithfully continued to pray.

She always took the same path to the temple. Every day, in the same place, she raised her eyes up toward the large, white, block building in front of her. The majestic building, with its series of gold spikes and a band of gold leaf that surrounded it in grand ornamentation, loomed before her. The white columns, adorned with gold Corinthian caps, stood majestically among many ferns leading to the temple steps. These columns were strong, and she envisioned the strength of her God—the Almighty One. She came to humbly bow at his feet in this sacred place. At the same time, though, she knew this place had been defiled.

As she walked closer, she saw the vendors who'd set up shop outside the temple. There they sold their sacrificial animals. Birds sat in their cages, curiously looking around; lambs and goats were tied up, unaware of their fate, all for sale. How convenient it had become, and almost too easy, to run over to the temple for a quick time of sacrifice.

Just one person had brought the many vendors to the temple. Jotham allowed them to assemble, exchanging his authorization for a portion of their profits. Knowing Jotham and his greedy nature made this scene appear to be even dirtier than it appeared. Wasn't this the temple, the dwelling of the Most High God? The holy of holies lay within, where God met with Amon, the high priest. In this place God accepted the sacrifices made to atone for the sins of the people. How could everyone not recognize this as a sacred place, as it had become to her?

Rebekah stopped, looking at the scene before her. It saddened her. It didn't seem right. The house of God shouldn't be a marketplace. She thought, *Someday a righteous man will surely drive these money changers out.* She didn't know how prophetic her thoughts were. She had become a woman of God, and many admired her strong faith. God honored her. Even now, the trials she faced were part of his master plan. Though she didn't understand everything, God was pleased with her faith and trust. He listened to her fervent prayers.

Just then God gave her keen insight. She looked past the sacrificial marketplace. She looked beyond the temple before her, built by human hands. At that moment, she realized God couldn't be contained in this place or in this building. Again she had a prophetic thought. God had come to this place to meet with man. To herself, she imagined the day when God would inhabit the lives of his children. She considered the Almighty God living within the very heart of his people. She smiled as she thought of those who shared her faith. To herself, she pondered this, and then quietly she said, "Our God does not live in temples made with human hands. We are the house of God, his dwelling. Under an open heaven, we live." She stopped and looked toward heaven and smiled. How she loved God.

As she continued toward the temple, she knew she could meet with God right where she stood if he desired to meet her there. Still, she found something special in having a place where she met with him.

She walked through the two large, ornamental golden doors. She enjoyed the hushed sound of this place. She knew of no other place that exuded with peacefulness and reverence. She made her way to the altar and knelt down. She started her earnest prayer. How she loved this time of her day—her intimate time with God.

In her heart, after a time of worship, she continued to pray, "O God, please do whatever it takes to bring Tychicus back to you!"

Unknown to Rebekah, Jotham watched her as he stood near the back of the temple beside a column in the shadows. The priest's impure mind filled with lustful thoughts about her.

It had been nearly one year since Tychicus's banishment, and Rebekah remained a devoted and loving wife. Most were amazed at her continual vigil on her husband's behalf, including Amon, the high priest. Sadly, most who reflected on Rebekah's efforts had sided with Jotham, believing her fervent prayers were merely offered to deaf ears. But her faith pleased the Lord, while hidden from the eyes of Tychicus. Instead of being inspired by her desire to please God, Jotham looked only at her physical form.

Slowly he walked down the main aisle, watching her with each silent step. He stopped just behind her where she knelt. She continued to pray, unaware of his presence. Finally, something disturbed her intense prayer as Jotham's hand ran through her hair. She jumped, wondering why he continued trying to seduce her in this sacred place.

"Are you still praying for that dead man?" he said with a disgusted look.

"Why do you treat me this way? I'm a married woman. You should know—"

Rebekah didn't get any further as Jotham spoke in rage, "When will you see that your prayer vigil is nothing short of wasted time? Tychicus is dead! *He is dead!* When will you finally see that? You will never see him again!" His rage calmed momentarily as a sly grin crossed his smug face. He peered around, making sure no one else could hear him. "Surely there is something better you could be doing with your time."

She knew what he insinuated, and she recognized his sinfulness. She responded to his advance with righteous anger as she cried out, "Out near the gates there sits a blind beggar. He can see more clearly than you can!"

Once again, Rebekah spoke strong words to the chief priest.

"Hear me when I say, 'As long as I have breath, I will declare to my God and to you, a demon in priestly robes, I *love* my *husband*! And until the day God causes my love for him to die, I will cry out for his healing!'"

Rebekah wondered why this scene continued over and over again. What more could she do to stop this repeated scenario? Why would God allow this to happen in his holy temple? Surely God displayed patience, though judgment would surely fall one day.

She turned to walk out, marching toward the door.

"You pray to a great, kind God," he said mockingly. "Tell me, how kind has he been to Tychicus?"

Rebekah stopped in her tracks. She turned around, looking directly into Jotham's eyes with the sternest of looks. How dare he speak such words against the Almighty God—in his holy temple! How appalling! She waited for a moment and wondered why God didn't strike him down right there on the spot.

"God's given my husband breath. Every day is a gift. I believe with my whole heart that he'll walk again in new life! Then you'll know the kindness of my God!" She rebuked him to no avail.

"Your 'husband' is dead! You are a widow, and someday you will be *mine*!" Jotham made his demands, believing his priestly authority gave his words some measure of credibility. Though he claimed to be a man of God, his actions proclaimed he had obviously become a demon in a thin disguise.

Softly Rebekah responded, "God *is* kind. So he would *not* give me over to you. That would be against his nature." She stared at him, waiting for a response that didn't come, though her feistiness intrigued him even more.

Another priest walked in at that time, unaware of what had just transpired.

Rebekah sought this opportunity to leave, heading home to Justus and Uncle Isaac. In her heart, she wept for Jotham. How she disliked him and pitied him. He had once been so close to God and had now drifted so far away.

She wondered where Tychicus might be. She wondered about his mental state. Had he cursed God? Had he made peace with his Creator? She wondered if he was still alive. She had to admit she didn't know for sure. She longed for the day when her God, a God of miracles, would start to move.

Leperd roamed. Anther typical day trudged along. He looked for food, and he wandered. The real manifestations of his leprosy were progressively getting worse. The skin on his forehead had started to harden. A reddish rash had started to spread on his skin. The numbness in his fingers had become more and more common. Several times, he woke up to find his nose bleeding, and his cloak stained with blood.

More and more each day, he started to look more like the leper he had become. With each new day, his identity as a cursed man became more and more apparent.

This day, for some reason, he decided to turn toward the sea. He headed back toward Tiberias. The following day would be an uncommon one he never could've anticipated.

CHAPTER 22

Rebekah and Justus gathered some clothes and placed them in a pouch. "Justus, please take this and give it to Uncle Isaac for the saddlebag."

Justus hurried over, grabbing the pouch. "Yes, Mother," he said with a smile. He turned and headed out toward the waiting donkey, ready for a trip to Magdala.

"I love you, Justus," she said affectionately.

"I love you too, Mother," he said with a smile.

Rebekah watched her son as he ran outside. His obedience warmed her heart, though it was filled with sadness. She reminisced about the previous year's trip to this festival. She could not believe a full year had passed since her last trip to her father's home to celebrate Pesach. She couldn't possibly count how many times she had relived the devastating details of that return trip, which had brought such change to her life.

She stared blankly across the room. She was dazed—a common state. As she closed her eyes, she could still see her husband as he fought with that enraged leper. She could still hear the desperate man's crazed scream for acceptance: "I'm a man! Help me! Touch me! Talk to me!" She could also still hear Tychicus's frustrated cries: "Get off! Get off! Get off!" She saw Tychicus twist to the right as the leper's long hair flew up behind him. Then he turned to the left as the leper held on tighter than ever. Tychicus punched behind him as blood poured out of the leper's nose. Everyone in the courtyard watched in amazement as they backed away, farther and farther from this odd scene unfolding before them. No one helped. No one offered any form of assistance. She could still feel the helplessness of that moment as she sought to shelter her son from this horrific sight. She could not do anything but protect her son, whose cries still echoed in her mind.

"Mother," Justus said.

Rebekah jumped. Her son's voice brought her back to the present. She opened her eyes and turned toward him.

"Uncle Isaac said he's ready to go when you are."

Rebekah took a deep breath and ran her hand through her hair.

"Mother, what's wrong?"

Rebekah smiled weakly. "Nothing's wrong. I'm fine." She gained her composure, realizing Justus watched her. "Yes, let's go. Tell Uncle Isaac I will be right there."

Justus smiled as he turned to run outside.

Rebekah quickly bowed her head to pray. "Lord, bring peace and healing to my husband, wherever he might be. I pray you would bring him back to yourself, then back to me." Many nights she would wake up after a dream reliving that awful day, and then she would pray this same prayer.

She finally made her way outside where she joined Uncle Isaac and Justus. As they headed toward the gate, everything seemed to come back to her in full detail.

Rebekah vividly remembered Tychicus walking in front of her with their son just a few steps away. Over the last twelve months, she often dreamed of that day. Life had been good. Life had been sweet. Then that leper appeared out of nowhere. So many times she revisited that sudden moment when everything changed.

As they left the city gates, Isaac led the donkey as Justus ran back and forth. For some reason, Justus waved at Josech, who still sat in his spot where he'd been sitting for years. He couldn't see them, though he seemed to look their way. Perhaps the sound of someone passing by caught his ear.

The festival would indeed be difficult this year. Last year, as an extended family, they shared and celebrated God's goodness. Since then Rebekah's world had been turned upside down. Her family had been torn apart. She lost her husband, and her son lost his father. She wondered what, if anything, would she be thankful for this year. She caught herself questioning God, though she knew he controlled everything she had faced and would face. Even so, she didn't have any answers to the questions she'd been asking for during the course of the last year. Why did this happen? How could this happen to them?

Justus had started to accept his lot, though he still didn't understand it. How could he at such a young age? Rebekah knew how difficult it had been for him to see his friends with their fathers. And some of the children were so cruel, teasing him about having a leper for a father. The adjustment had been especially hard for him, which raised even more questions in Rebekah's mind.

As they traveled, Rebekah looked off to her right. The Sea of Galilee could be seen, and the terrain in front of her remained still. As she looked around, she noticed a single man walking in the distance. He moved slowly, and he looked their way. Something looked familiar about him, though she didn't know what. She continued to stare as they plodded along.

Afar off, Leperd stood watching the road as he walked. He saw an old man leading a donkey. A woman sat on its back as a young boy ran around beside them. He wondered, *Could it be?* The boy occasionally picked up a rock, which he threw.

He'd lost track of time. His wandering had become a mindless, time-consuming activity. What day was it? What month was it? He didn't know. He hadn't known in such a long time. He just struggled to live every day. His hands, which were once skilled and masterful as a carpenter, were now becoming useless. He struggled to use them for the simplest of things. His hair had grown long, and it covered his face. His sandals were worn from his many miles of wandering. His body was racked with fatigue, as he'd become somewhat numb, mentally and physically. He watched people traveling the road nearly every day, but something unusual accompanied this day.

Rebekah continued to look at the man now standing there. She could barely see his features, but she wondered, *Could this man be a leper?* She really wondered if this could be *her* leper, as strange as that might sound. The more she looked, she thought her initial thoughts might be true. She just stared at him.

Leperd looked again at the woman on the back of the donkey. He looked again at the older man and the young boy that accompanied her. Could this woman be his Rebekah? He looked again, focusing harder than before. He recognized the man's walk—the man holding the reigns was Isaac. In shock, he muttered, "Uncle Isaac?" Even from that distance, the boy began to resemble his son. "Justus?" he added. He gasped in realization. Rebekah had to be the woman riding on the donkey! It just had to be her! He opened her mouth to say her name, but the emotions that overwhelmed him would not allow another sound to come out of his mouth.

He hadn't been this close to his family in a year. A tear started to stream down his dirty face. So many thoughts of the past rushed into his mind. So many good memories filled his every thought. All he had lost consumed him though a glimpse of hope started to seep in. He longed to run to their side, but he couldn't move. He knew he couldn't approach them, but he wanted to get closer. He decided to defy the law as he started to walk as fast as he could toward them.

Rebekah saw the man coming closer. She continued watching him. She had to. Could this be her beloved Tychicus? By the way he moved, she believed it might be. Her heart fluttered. She'd been praying for him so earnestly and for so long without knowing anything about what he endured. At least now she knew he was still alive, and she thanked God for that. How she also wanted to defy the laws, running into his arms. But for some reason, she couldn't move.

Leperd continued moving toward them. Isaac and Justus never looked his way as their attention was directed elsewhere. Isaac moved down the road, while Justus threw rocks. Neither of them ever noticed him. This moment had been determined for two. Leperd's eyes were fixed on the woman on the back of the donkey. The closer he walked, the more his suspicions were confirmed. This was indeed his beautiful wife, and the sight of her, even this distant glance, brought life back to him. For a brief moment, he gazed toward the boy, realizing it was his son—how he'd grown!

He stopped as his weary heart beat faster and faster. He just stood there, becoming more emotional than he'd been in so long. He knew the law. He'd been living under its authority for all these months. He knew he needed to keep his distance. There were so many words he wanted to say to her, but he knew the word "unclean" wasn't one of them.

Rebekah still looked at the man standing far away. He just stood there holding back his long hair from his face so he could see. He revealed a beard. He looked dirty. But even so it looked like Tychicus. How she wanted to scream her declaration of love, but her body seemed paralyzed. Perhaps she was in a state of shock. She didn't know. She just stared and smiled as tears slowly started to well up in her eyes.

Leperd couldn't believe it. She looked so beautiful, even from this distance. How he loved her. Justus ran around, full of energy. How he missed spending time with his son. Not a day had gone by that he hadn't thought of them. He simply stood there. Then slowly, he raised his hand and placed it on top of his head. Quietly to himself, amid tears, he muttered, "I'm this tall." He wondered if she remembered.

Rebekah watched as the man's hand rose to the top of his head. Quietly to herself, she gasped faintly, "I'm this tall." Her heart fluttered again. To herself she said, "Oh my God! It's him. It's Tychicus. You've brought him to me." Her smile broadened as she fought to look at her husband through her tears. This quick event brought her a sense of hope. It would be something she'd silently cherish in the coming days at the festival. She placed her hand over her heart, signaling her love for him.

Leperd placed his hand over his heart in response, telling her of his love.

Then he turned and walked away toward the sea. He had come so close to being with her, but the distance between them was a vast chasm that could not be crossed. He knew he'd never again hold her in his arms, barring a miracle. But he'd become so discouraged that in his thoughts, such an event would never occur. After all, he had been cursed. What good would ever come of his life? Hopelessness and discouragement consumed his mind-set, and self-pity had a firm grip on him. This short moment would become the highlight of what had become hell on earth. He wanted to remember it just as it unfolded, so he turned and walked away. Though difficult, he knew necessity demanded it.

Rebekah buried her head in her chest as quiet tears continued to fall. She experienced joy that Tychicus was alive, but once again, she mourned her loss. Still, Isaac and Justus failed to see him at all. She cherished the moment as a gift from God. She wouldn't forget seeing this form of a man so far away—knowing it was the man she loved. She prayed that one day they'd be reunited. She knew God could bring healing, and she prayed toward that end—believing.

For the longest time, she held this inside, a secret from everyone around her. It had been meant to be personal and as intimate as it could've been under the circumstances.

They continued onto the festival where her family surrounded her with love. But nothing could compare to this brief, long-distant moment.

CHAPTER 23

I decided to take a short break from telling my story as Archippus just sat there ready for more. "I can't even imagine what he must have been feeling. Why didn't she say something? How couldn't you say something?" he asked dumbfounded.

"Well, you must understand the law. Lepers are forbidden to talk to anyone unless they're giving a warning to stay away. And remember, common people are forbidden to talk to them or have any contact with them at all. Can you imagine what Jotham might have done if he knew Rebekah had communication with a leper, especially Tychicus?"

Those who lived by the letter of the law might have made more of this than they needed to. Obviously this would've been the case with Jotham, given his reputation and previous actions.

Archippus paused to think for a moment. Though he did not voice his thoughts, I could imagine what ran through his mind. Surely he pondered the same questions anyone would. How could someone be so quickly cut off from all they knew, without any form of contact? How could someone live that way?

Once again I smiled as I offered answers to questions he had not voiced. "Surely it was a difficult time. It would be for anyone living under his curse. But Leperd held on to that moment and wondered if this type of meeting would happen again. Though he often dreamed of this, they would never again see each other in this manner."

I continued.

Leperd stayed in that region for several days, hoping for a similar meeting on their return trip. He wondered what kind of effect it might have on Justus if he saw his father as a leper. He debated whether he should attempt to make contact with them. He realized Justus would probably be frightened. How would any child react seeing their father had become a monster? The manifestation of his disease had started to become more visible, and he knew it.

As he lay under the stars one night, he dreamed that he walked into his home. He sat down at their table as Rebekah and Justus walked in. He stood up, welcoming them into his open arms. When Rebekah saw him, a frightened look emerged on her face. She reacted without thinking with a gasp. Justus simply started screaming. He was horrified. They treated him like a monster. Couldn't they see who he was?

Leperd woke in a cold sweat. As a result of this dream, he chose not to do anything that might hurt his wife and son, though the loss he'd personally experience, not being able to catch a glimpse of them again, would be incredible. Still, he held on to the memory of that moment, which didn't seem like enough.

Several days later, returning home from the festival, Rebekah rode on the back of the donkey as they approached the gates of Tiberias. She looked afar off, hoping for another glimpse of her husband. Justus walked alongside, unaware of what passed through his mother's mind. Isaac, also unaware, led the way.

When they came to the gate, Rebekah looked down, seeing Josech sitting on his blanket. He sat alone, as always. He looked hungry and pitiful. As they came near, she could almost see Tychicus's face looking their way through the poor beggar's hollow eyes. Josech heard them coming and started his usual plea: "Help a poor beggar." His lifeless voice called out with no response. He'd repeated his plea so often that it had lost all feeling.

She'd just spent several days at the festival where food and drink overflowed in abundance. As she stared at him, she wondered how long it had been since he'd eaten. She imagined her husband—also alone, discouraged, and in need. She wondered just how hungry he had become. Her heart sank. She called out to God in quiet desperation. The thought of Tychicus and his suffering overwhelmed her. It took everything within her to hold back her tears.

As she entered the city gates, she looked over her shoulder once again. With one last hopeful attempt to catch a glimpse of him, she looked in vain.

Timotheus greeted them as he stood beside his cart. "Welcome home, Rebekah," he said. He meant well, but it made her think of Tychicus all the more. He didn't have a home. Where could he be? What occupied his time? So many questions ran through her mind as she became restless. Her anticipation outside the gates had turned to extreme agony that no one understood. When they arrived at home, she told Isaac she needed to head to the temple.

She ran into the temple and fell at the altar. Finally, the dam broke as she let all her emotion out. She cried out in an audible voice, "O God of my fathers! Help me! Help my husband!" She continued crying to the Lord as Jotham looked from the shadows.

Footsteps walked toward her as she buried her head in her hands. She continued crying as she fell facedown to the ground. She felt a hand on her shoulder. It startled her momentarily.

She recognized the touch.

She smiled.

She looked up into the eyes of Amon, the high priest.

"Rebekah, can I pray with you?"

Before she could respond, the high priest knelt down beside her and started praying. Truly a man of God, Rebekah had grown to love and respect him. He'd been sensitive to her needs in a practical way, unlike Jotham, who was lustfully looking at her from afar.

Leperd ended up in the hills west of the Sea of Galilee. Day after day passed without incident. He survived one day at a time, occasionally visiting the city dump to find food scraps. He still wondered why this happened to him. Answers didn't come as cursing followed.

CHAPTER 24

Leperd had been wandering in circles now for over a year. An occasional chat with Josech had been his only solace. But even their talks had become few and far between, which discouraged his blind friend. Leperd missed their conversations, but he'd become lethargic and rarely found any motivation to make the trek to the city gates. This day, however, would be an exception.

He decided to move away from Tiberias. He had been too close to Rebekah for too long, and he wondered if the distance would help him stop thinking of her so much. He waited until the sun started to set; then he moved toward the city gates to say farewell to his friend.

Josech's ears perked up as he heard familiar footsteps off to his right against the wall. "It's been a long time, my friend," he said quietly. "Where have you been?"

"Greetings, my friend," Leperd said. "I've been wandering. You know, that's what I do." He paused. What else could he say? He asked, "How are you?"

"God sent an angel to care for me. She brings me food and drink."

"Really?" he asked.

"Yes. The young woman comes to me from time to time, bringing me fresh bread, figs, and dates. And sometimes she brings grapes. She also brings me water to drink. If you were here, I'd share it all with you."

Josech had a kind soul. Even though he had so little, his initial thought demonstrated a willingness to give of what he had.

"I know she's not a real angel, but she's heaven-sent. She hasn't told me her name, so I call her my 'unseen angel.'"

Leperd smiled ever so slightly. Someone had decided to help his friend, and that made him glad. He wished someone would reach out to him in the same way, but he knew the law prohibited such an action toward those considered taboo. No one would be coming to him with such a treat. The laws wouldn't allow such a thing.

"I'm happy for you, my friend. That's good news."

By his tone, Josech could sense something unsettling in Leperd's voice. "How are you doing, really?" he asked with concern.

Leperd paused for a moment before speaking. "Well, I came to say farewell. I think it's time for me to move on." What a sad farewell this would prove to be for both of them.

"Where will you go?"

"I'm going to head north to see what I might find there. I know my father-in-law has much land there. Perhaps I could glean something from his fields."

Josech sighed. "Are you running from something?"

"Not from you." Leperd knew his friend knew him. "I just need to get away from Tiberias for a while. That's all."

Josech didn't fully understand. How could he?

"Well, I trust your journey will lead you back someday. I'll miss you. You've been a good friend."

"I'm sure our paths will cross again someday. I promise."

Leperd had accomplished what he set out to do. He said farewell, for now. He slowly but surely started to walk away. Josech sat in the silence, recalling their talks, understanding they'd be no more for some time. Once again, he'd be all alone as Leperd walked off.

Soon Leperd stopped to sleep, as the night grew dark. He woke as the sun rose, as he continued walking north. Several grasshoppers met their end as he paused to munch on them.

He stopped near a local stream to drink. As he bent over, looking down into the shallow water, he saw his reflection among the subtle ripples like looking into a mirror. He brushed the hair back from his face as he peered back into the stream. The man he saw looked different from who he remembered himself to be. A thinner man looked back at him. He wore a beard. Dirt covered his thick-looking skin, blanketed with reddish blemishes. He used to see Tychicus in the pool, but now he looked into the face of Leperd. He closed his eyes and tried to see Rebekah's and Justus's faces in his mind. It became harder and harder each day. He'd lost his own reflection, and he feared he would lose theirs as well. He had vowed he would never allow this to happen. Their memory, their image were the only things that remained of them. He considered once more how much he missed them.

As he bent down to drink, he felt as if he leaned on stubs, as his fingers were numb. He couldn't feel them. They tingled. What an awkward feeling. The frustration of the moment overtook him as he plunged into the water. He starting thrashing around, beating his hands into the water as he screamed unintelligibly. Then emerging in dramatic fashion he threw water into the air before raising a clenched fist toward heaven. "Why?" he cried in a loud, angry voice. "Why have you done this to me?" In anger, he cursed God again. Then, as he typically would do, he cursed Jotham as well.

He looked at both of his hands raised toward heaven as blood flowed from his knuckles. He'd been striking sharp rock, unaware of the fact. Blood slowly ran down his hands onto his arms. He'd injured himself, though he still felt nothing.

As he became still, he realized the hunger that gnawed at him. He didn't have any strength left as he sat in the water, now totally drenched. "Why couldn't this stream have fish in it?" he screamed to whoever might hear. Oh, to have some fish! Oh, to have any form of normal food! His diet of insects and scraps from the dump had become unappealing so long ago. He sulked for a bit, which never seemed to help. Eventually he continued on his journey north, plodding along one step at a time.

He walked along the trade route toward Magdala, keeping a safe distance from the road as the law prescribed. Several traders passed by as he went unnoticed, or so it seemed. They weren't concerned with him. He continued walking until he found himself several miles north of Magdala. He'd been here many times before, under other circumstances. He saw Zibeon's home in the distance. The workers in his fields were definitely busy as he watched them working hard. *Surely*, he thought, *when the sun starts to go down, there will be something left to glean.* Zibeon wouldn't mind if he took whatever he could find. He had a soft, kind heart.

As the day wore on, several others approached the fields. They stood together and waited. They were hopeful as they anticipated their chance to glean. According to the customs, several poor beggars received permission from the landowner to walk through the fields after the workers had finished. They were allowed to pick up anything left behind. Leperd knew he'd have to wait until they were finished. And he knew there would be little left when he walked through the field, if anything at all.

Leperd found a quiet spot and waited. He had nothing else to do but wait.

Finally, the workers left the field, heading home for another day. The poor beggars slowly walked through the fields, gathering all the barley they could find, which amounted to very little. Leperd watched, waiting his turn. When it seemed safe, he would walk toward the fields where he knew disappointment awaited him.

As he waited, he noticed someone coming down the road. He recognized the man riding a donkey. It was Abednego, Zibeon's servant. As he witnessed in the past, another donkey followed with packs across its back. He hid as best he could until Abednego rode past. He remained unseen as far as he could tell. Then from a distance, he started to follow. From the time of visiting at the festival, he wondered where he went. He remembered asking Abednego what he had in his sacks. He never did get an answer. As long as he could remain unseen, he believed, he'd soon find out.

Abednego rode west for several miles or so when he came to a clearing beside the road. Nearby to the west, he saw several caves at the foot of the mountains. Leperd noticed a large, flat stone, which resembled a small table. Abednego stopped short of this stone. He dismounted before opening the packs on the second donkey. With apparent apprehension, he quickly rushed over to the stone, placing the contents of the packs there before heading back to his donkeys. Several trips were made, and when his packs were empty, he headed back toward Zibeon's house.

What just happened? What was this place? What did he leave on the stone?

Abednego hurried off. Leperd started walking toward the road nearer to the stone. Several loaves of bread sat there accompanied by grapes and figs, enough for a number of people to feast upon. Before he could get any closer, he heard some rustling from the caves. One by one, several men appeared. He looked again. In a way, they all looked similar to one another. They all walked with the same posture and a similar limp. *Could it be?* he wondered. His initial suspicion had been confirmed. He had stumbled upon a leper colony.

Apparently, Zibeon had been regularly delivering food to this colony, feeding those who lived there. Leperd thought back to the days of festival he'd spent at Zibeon's home and the full packs on the donkey's backs leaving with Abednego. The abundance of God's goodness had been shared during those times of celebration. Zibeon had been blessed with much, and his generosity had been exhibited in more ways than most knew.

Leperd stood in amazement. Zibeon had never spoke about this act of charity—though such a gesture consistently characterized his father-in-law's humble nature. While these thoughts filtered through his brain, he noticed the lepers looked up as they brushed the long hair from in front of their eyes. They instinctively started to say, "Unclean!" when they noticed Leperd. The first repetition never crossed their lips as they realized he was also, quite obviously, a leper.

"Who are you?" one of the lepers asked. "What do you want?" The leper's hoarse voice muttered faintly as if he had a touch of laryngitis.

Leperd stood still for a second. Someone actually spoke to him? Other than Josech, he hadn't talked with anyone in so long.

"My name is Leperd," he said confidently.

"What do you want? Go away! Now!" the leper barked back as best he could.

"Stop, Zebediah," said another leper who now emerged from one of the caves. By the careful way he took his steps, it appeared his eyesight had gone dim. Blindness had accompanied the other traits of an older leper. He looked like everyone else, though a little worse off. From his tone, he obviously had some form of authority in the camp. You could tell by the confidence he displayed and by how the others responded to him.

Zebediah immediately stepped back. "My name is Jazer," said the older leper. "What brings you here, my friend?" His very hoarse voice showed even more evidence of his advanced leprosy. Several fingers on both hands and most of his toes on one foot were missing. Varying degrees of this scenario could be seen with some of the others. He walked slowly with a grossly deformed frame. His exposed arms were covered with a red rash.

"I followed the man with the packs," Leperd said.

The other lepers huddled together behind Jazer as he spoke.

"Will you join us, my friend? We don't have much, but you're welcome to eat." Jazer held his hand out, pointing to the stone. Although several fingers were missing, Leperd noticed the ring he wore on his right hand. He wondered what significance it held for him, if any.

Zebediah looked more than a little disgruntled at this invitation, as did a few of the others. They all headed for the stone as they began eating. Leperd enjoyed the little he fought to get. He hadn't eaten food like this in such a long time. Josech had been privy to this type of food when visited by his unseen angel. Leperd never expected such a treat.

Soon it became dark, and most of the lepers headed back into the caves for the night. Leperd lay down under the night sky, looking up at the stars. He was thankful for Jazer's kindness, though he felt tension with some of the others, especially Zebediah.

All in all, it had been an interesting day indeed. He wondered what the next day might hold. He stared at the stars until he fell asleep.

CHAPTER 25

Rebekah walked into the temple as one of the priests welcomed her.

"Good morning, Rebekah. How are you?"

"Good morning, Laban. I am doing well. Do you know if Amon is here? I was told he wanted to meet with me this morning."

"Let me get him for you," Laban said before walking away.

Rebekah looked around, glad that Jotham could not be seen. How she loved coming to the temple, though she felt as if she had to be on guard to be sure Jotham wouldn't be watching her. She just wanted to spend time alone with God in that place. She continued to cry out to God for her husband. The love in her heart for Tychicus hadn't diminished as many told her it would as time passed by. Instead, she continued to pray fervently for him. She could only imagine what he dealt with on a daily basis.

At times, she wondered if he was still alive. Her doubts were short-lived as she remembered that day she saw him from a distance. She knew he was alive. He possessed such a strong will, and she truly believed in her heart that God would answer her prayer for restoration. Tychicus needed to turn back to God, and for that, she prayed earnestly, asking God to do whatever it would take. Could leprosy be part of his divine plan? Though very little made sense to her, she continued to put her trust in God.

Amon greeted Rebekah with a smile as he walked into the room. "Good morning," he said kindly. "How are Isaac and Justus?"

"They're doing well. Thank you. Your kindness has been much appreciated. I don't know what we'd do without your thoughtfulness."

Amon lifted a basket he had been holding near his side. "This is for you, Justus, and Isaac. If we can ever help, in any way, please let me know." The basket contained bread, figs, dates, and grapes among other items—all provided through the generosity of Amon and the temple.

"Thank you, Amon. We see this as God's provision, for which we are very thankful."

"Jehovah Jireh, my Provider," Amon said with a smile. "He will always provide for his own. Sometimes through friends and family. Other times through your friends here at the temple." Amon, unlike Jotham, found practical ways to meet the physical and spiritual needs of those under his care.

Rebekah gave Amon a gentle hug. Amon felt a special attachment with Rebekah and cared for her like a daughter.

As she stepped away from him, his expression became somber. His smile faded into an earnest seriousness. "Rebekah, I'd like to talk to you about Tychicus. As your high priest, I want to share some concerns." Amon spoke from a kind and loving heart, and Rebekah had found that to be true.

"What would you like to say?" she asked, looking downward. She wondered if she would be confronted with the same lecture many others had given her before. It seemed to be the consensus that she should forget about Tychicus and start a new life. Many men had shown interest in her. Her beauty surely attracted other men who saw her as the widow she appeared to be. But in her mind, even the thought of another man would be an act of betrayal toward her husband. But she had learned to respect Amon and instantly decided to lend her ears to his words.

"Rebekah, it's been a long time since Tychicus's banishment from the city. It's been well over one year now. I'm sure you know that."

Rebekah nodded in agreement.

"I know you have spent much time here in the temple praying for your husband." Amon stopped for just a brief moment. "My child, what has God said to you?" Rebekah looked up. She wasn't expecting this at all. Amon spoke again. "I know you're a woman of prayer. What has God been saying to you? Has he been speaking to you?"

Rebekah looked into the eyes of the high priest. There she found compassion. There she found sympathy. "I believe God will restore Tychicus. I pray that he'll come back to God and be a man of faith once again. I've prayed that God would give me a peace about letting him go if that's what he wanted. But I haven't received that peace. I believe God will perform a miracle in his life. I can't let my husband go. I just can't. I won't."

Amon looked at Rebekah. His eyes started to well up as he smiled again. Her faith amazed him. "My child, let's pray to Jehovah and ask him to do wonderful and amazing things that will only lead us to give him praise!" Amon broke out into a song of praise, which reminded Rebekah of her father, Zibeon, during the days of festival.

Now, convinced more than ever that God would do great things in her husband's life, she prayed—believing, though she wondered when that day might come. She decided she would wait on the Lord—however long it might take.

CHAPTER 26

Leperd woke as the sun rose in the east. Some of the other lepers were already awake. They sat together talking about him as if he couldn't hear. Zebediah, still obviously disgruntled, led the conversation. "We don't need another mouth feeding off the little we have. I think we should send him off. Who does he think he is?"

The small colony consisted of seven men and two women. They all sat together except for Jazer and one of the women, Athalia. From what he heard, they all seemed to agree with Zebediah, who obviously wanted to rise and become their leader.

As he complained, a hoarse voice called out from the caves, "Stop, Zebediah!" The colony heard this familiar phrase regularly. Jazer slowly emerged from the cave, sternly scolding Zebediah. They constantly battled back and forth, which Leperd understood by the tone of their voices.

"Why don't you just go off and die, old man!" Zebediah shouted in anger as he walked away from the camp in a huff.

"My day's coming, but not yet! I have a few more days left in me," Jazer shouted back as he displayed his authority in the colony.

Leperd walked up to them. They could all see he had become aware of the colony's day-to-day exploits. It didn't take long for Leperd to develop contempt for Zebediah.

"Don't let him bother you, my friend," Jazer said. "He's always like this."

The other lepers agreed as Leperd discovered their respect for Jazer. Though they agreed with Zebediah about the food situation, they agreed with Jazer about Zebediah's attitude. They seemed to agree with whoever spoke. What a pitiful lot they were.

"I don't want to cause any trouble. Maybe I should just move on," Leperd said as he noticed blood coming from Jazer's nose.

"Your nose is bleeding," he said. Lepers commonly suffered nosebleeds. Athalia, who had apparently paired off with Jazer, helped him as Leperd stood nearby.

"Stay, my friend. As long as I'm here, you're welcome. You're my guest, my friend." It became quiet for some time as the others respected him, even though they disagreed with what he proposed.

After a while, Zebediah came back to the camp and gave Leperd a disgruntled look. He imagined this to be the same face Jotham had seen all those years when he looked at him following the first incident at the temple. It wasn't a kind look, and he wondered if he really looked as disgusted as this leper did. What an ugly look, which came from an ugly heart.

Those in this group seemed to share and share alike for the most part. The other woman had paired off with Zebediah and another man, who continually grumbled quietly most of the time. Apparently they shared her. This group of individuals were an odd lot—without any children or adolescents around. Leperd knew lepers couldn't produce children as the males with this degree of leprosy became infertile. Of course, children from before the time of banishment were not allowed near them. The pairing of these men and women were more for companionship than anything else, though surely some form of sexual connection drew them together. He understood loneliness and the need for companionship. He thought of Rebekah and knew he'd never share her with anyone, under any circumstance.

The day passed slowly as they hoped "the donkey man" would come with more food. They relied on him, waiting for him at the same time every day. Some days he came; on rare occasions, he did not. When they saw him afar off, they would enter the caves. Then after he dropped off the food, they would come out to eat. From a way off, the man always looked back, seeing they'd received the generosity his master had him deliver. Their lives depended on him, and they wondered what might stop his visits. They just hoped he'd continue his deliveries.

About that time, they headed into their respective places in the caves. Jazer motioned for Leperd to join him with Athalia in their cave. They sat back in the dark, waiting for the sound of the donkeys they had come to know.

"Is he always like that?" Leperd asked.

"What do you mean, my friend?"

"It sounds like Zebediah wants you to die."

Jazer chuckled slightly. "When lepers get to the end of their life, they know it. It's the thirst, my friend. When that day comes for me, I'll leave the colony to go off to die. I just think he's ready for me to find that day. It's coming."

Leperd had heard that unquenchable thirst indicated a leper's life was drawing to an end. He understood this. What he didn't understand was why this old man constantly called him "my friend." After a while, he discovered this term was used with everyone in the colony, except for the women and Zebediah, almost like a nervous tick.

"How long have you been in the colony?" Leperd asked.

"It's been a long time. I don't know for sure. But my days are numbered. I'm getting weak, and the signs of my final days are drawing near. I can feel it, my friend. It's been a long road, and I'm coming to the end."

Leperd remembered seeing the golden ring on Jazer's finger before. Its ornate engraving particularly intrigued him. His curiosity piqued as he asked, "Where did you get your ring?"

"My best friend gave it to me. We grew up together north of Magdala. We went different directions at one point. He became very successful while I wasted many years. He had pity on me, though, and allowed me to work in his fields. Eventually I managed some of his workers. He was always so good to them, very patient and kind. What a good man, what a good friend! He gave me this ring the day of my exile, so long ago, as a promise that he'd take care of me, of us. It's the only possession I treasure from my former life."

Leperd knew Abednego, the donkey man, was one of Zibeon's servants. Could this "best friend" be his father-in-law?

"What was your friend's name?" Leperd asked.

"His name was Zibeon."

Leperd couldn't believe it. Jazer had worked for his father-in-law! Surely he knew Rebekah. He acted naive as he said, "Tell me about this man Zibeon."

"He feared God and was well respected by all who knew him. He married a godly woman named Tamar. What a kind, beautiful woman! They had several boys who grew to be good men like their father. Mattaniah, Shubael, and Bukkiah. They were all hard workers."

He knew the answer to the next question but asked it anyway. "Did they have any daughters?"

"Just one. Her name was Rebekah."

Leperd's heart fluttered. Just the sound of her name reminded him of the love he had for her. How he missed her!

Jazer continued, "The girl was the youngest child and a very beautiful little girl who grew to be a beautiful young woman. Also very pretty too. Do you know what I mean, my friend? Her beauty on the outside was only second to the beauty of her heart."

Leperd nodded, indicating he understood, though no one saw him.

Sitting in the dark, Jazer thought back so many years. "We used to talk about her in the fields. Her brothers were so proud of her. They spoiled her. I'm not sure she ever realized that. They really loved their little sister, especially Bukkiah. We all knew some young man would be fortunate to win her heart someday. My exile came during her teen years. You could tell even then that she would make someone a wonderful wife. What a beautiful young woman."

"Whatever happened to her?" Leperd asked, trying to hold back his emotions.

"I have no idea. I don't talk with Zibeon anymore, of course. It's forbidden, you know. I've been here for a long time, my friend. I hope she's well. She probably married and has children and is doing well. At least that's what I hope for her. I think of her from time to time. What a precious girl, hard to forget. Have you ever known someone like that?"

Again Leperd nodded. He hadn't forgotten about Rebekah. He thought of her every day. To say she was precious was a gross understatement.

Jazer chuckled. "She couldn't say my name as a little girl. I tried to teach her, but she couldn't say it. She called me JJ, that's how it came from her lips, and she even called me by that name as she grew to be a young lady. It became my name to her. I don't think she even remembered my real name. If she did, she never used it."

Leperd flashed back to their last trip to Zibeon's home. Rebekah mentioned this man in passing, and for some reason, he remembered it now. Jazer and JJ were one and the same. Rebekah had been privy to his kindness in her earlier years, and now he had benefited from his kindness in his time of need. This realization overwhelmed Leperd. He didn't know what to say.

Leperd imagined Rebekah as a little girl. He wished he could've seen her then. She had indeed grown into an incredible woman, and how he missed her now more than ever.

Jazer interrupted his thoughts. "I wonder whatever happened to her. Surely I'll never see her again, though I'd like to. I wish I could see Zibeon again. But I fear my days are numbered."

Leperd thought, *I'd like to see her again too.*

Athalia didn't like Jazer talking about "last days" as she scolded him. "Just sit quiet. I think the donkey man is coming."

They all stopped to listen. Sure enough, they heard the clomping of donkey hooves getting closer. Then they stopped. They heard the man scuffling around, bringing the food to the stone table. Then they heard the hooves again. The donkeys rode away, and the time to eat had come once more. The lepers considered this the highlight of their day, though Leperd treasured the moments talking about his wife.

As they walked out of the cave, some of the others had already begun eating, especially Zebediah, who wanted to get his portion before this newcomer might take what belonged to him.

Leperd waited for Jazer as they slowly made their way out of the cave. They walked up to the stone and ate while Zebediah glared all the more at Leperd. This whole scene would take place many times over the next few weeks. Then it would suddenly end.

CHAPTER 27

Leperd woke as he heard the other lepers talking about him. It had become a common, early-morning scenario. Zebediah led the conversation as he complained in his usual dark tone. Though some of his grumblings were somewhat unintelligible from where Leperd lay, his pointing, his glaring eyes aimed in his direction, and his occasional outright verbal tirades left no question as to whom he directed his distaste. Leperd lay in the dirt with his eyes closed, waiting for Jazer to emerge from the cave, telling Zebediah to "stop," a very common start to the day—one he had come to enjoy. He enjoyed hearing his friend rebuke the colony's bad apple. Even more, he enjoyed watching Zebediah cower as he huffed off like a defeated misfit.

Leperd waited and listened for several minutes. Perhaps Jazer had not yet awakened, he thought. He waited several more minutes, but Jazer never appeared—a very uncommon start to the day.

He sat up and rubbed the sleep from his eyes as Zebediah noticed he had awakened. He'd been waiting for this moment, for this day, for some time. He wasted no time as he started yelling in Leperd's direction. "You must leave now, *my friend*!" he demanded as he mocked Jazer's typical greeting. His tone reminded him of an arrogant beggar he once confronted in the city dump of Tiberias. Since Jazer had not come out of the cave to defend him, Leperd stood alone as Zebediah attacked with full force.

Leperd looked around. He still didn't see Jazer. Where could he be? He saw Athalia off by herself, curled up in a ball as if in mourning. He could tell something wasn't right as soon as he saw her. The two of them were seldom seen separately. He jumped up and ran over to her.

"Athalia. What's wrong?" Leperd asked.

He could tell she'd been crying for some time. Her tears were spent, and she now sat quietly staring off into the distance, in a daze.

"I said you must leave *now!*" Zebediah demanded again as he took a step closer to him.

Leperd crouched down beside Athalia, ignoring Zebediah's remarks. "What happened? Where's Jazer?"

Athalia looked into his eyes coldly. "He's gone," she said without feeling.

"What do you mean 'he's gone'?" he asked.

"I knew this day was coming. I just didn't know it would be this soon. He told me his time had come. I thought he'd leave today, but he left during the night. He's gone. I would've gone with him. I should've gone with him." Again she stared off into the distance as she repeated her lament over and over: "He's gone. He's gone. He's gone."

Jazer had left to die. His time had come, just as he said it would. He'd shown no signs of his final days. The thirst had come sometime ago, yet he didn't speak of it. He disguised his pain and suffering as best he could. He didn't want to concern anyone; his considerate character would not permit it. He also knew this day would bring Zebediah much joy, which he didn't want to encourage. He just struggled alone, and now the struggle would end quietly, though Athalia knew she'd begin living with a new sort of loneliness.

She said one final sentence. "I'm ready to die too." With that, she looked into Leperd's eyes with a strange emptiness. Her inner being, the part of her that brought meaning to her existence, had already gone, and her body was all that remained. Her spirit had died, but her body hadn't realized it yet.

Before Leperd could fully comprehend this, Zebediah called out again, "Did you hear me? I said you must leave! *Now!*" All the other lepers sat quietly in fear of Zebediah, who ruled like a tyrannical dictator. He longed for the day when he'd become the colony's leader, and apparently his day had come. Now Leperd, a certain threat, had to be extinguished.

Instantly Leperd's concern turned to rage. "What did you do?" he demanded. He believed Athalia, though part of him wondered if Zebediah had a hand in this. Had he finally driven Jazer off? After all, he wanted to eliminate Jazer from the colony. He said he wanted him to die. Zebediah's venomous temper already indicated what kind of havoc he could inflict, and there was no telling what he might have done.

"I did what I should've done when you first came here. I told you to leave!"

Leperd took a step toward him as Zebediah picked up the biggest rock he could handle. He hurled it as Leperd dodged at the last moment. His natural reflex was to move toward safety, which he would immediately regret. He had temporarily forgotten that Athalia lay on the ground behind him. The rock struck her in the temple, and he heard the crack of her skull. She slumped down as her body went limp. She moaned. But her pain wouldn't be for long. She too would soon find release from her infirmities.

Leperd looked toward her, wondering if he could help her. The blood ran down the side of her face. Her eyes were open but lifeless. She'd surely passed on. As he knelt down in front of her, another rock hit him in the shoulder. Then another struck him in the back. He turned to see the other lepers had now joined in as several rocks headed his way. They decided to participate, less they become a target themselves.

Leperd had but one choice. He quickly picked up Athalia's body and ran away from the colony. He felt the pain in his shoulder and in his back. Surely the rocks had caused some major damage. When he thought he had moved beyond danger, he looked back over his shoulder. Rocks still came his way, but they fell far shy of him. Zebediah stood boldly in front of the others as he gave his last order. "If you ever come back, I'll kill you!"

Leperd stood looking at him from a distance. Perhaps Zebediah didn't understand—he was already dead.

Leperd carried Athalia as pain raced through his body with each step. Though she was small, her weight seemed almost more than he could bear. But he had to press on, for Athalia, for Jazer. He moaned as he slowly and steadily moved beyond the sight of the leper colony. He laid her down tenderly. He breathed heavily, gasping for air. He remembered when such an exercise would have been welcomed with little to no effort at all. His young strapping body had been reduced to that of a weak old man. Even as he panted, his exhausted body racked with pain. His back and shoulder ached from the rocks that had hit him. Surely several bones had been fractured or broken. He wasn't the man he used to be, and he knew he would probably never be.

As he sat in the dirt, he glanced over toward her for a little while. What a sad life she lived, at least toward the end. What a pitiful existence she had endured in the colony. What a terrible way for it all to end! The only solace he found was in knowing she now rested in peace. He knew the nightmare had come to an end, though it reminded her that his was still developing.

Reflecting on this caused him to consider Jazer, who also rested, though the location of his body remained a mystery.

He started gathering rocks to cover her body. One by one he carried them toward her, enduring the excruciating pain, which shot through his shoulder and back. He had to complete this task no matter how hard, how painful, and he had to do it now. Slowly her body disappeared beneath a mound of rocks. He covered her until she could not be seen and then added more to the stack. Animals would not feast on her ravaged remains as long as he had something to say about that.

He completed his task as the sun started to set. It had been a long, tiring day. Though Athalia had lived a life absent of respect, he would honor her in death. He knew this would please his friend, Jazer. After he finished, he stood and looked at the mound before him. Softly and reverently, he said, "Rest, Athalia, rest." Leperd felt sad, and he was now more exhausted than ever. He soon fell asleep in the dirt.

The following morning, Leperd gathered his strength and roamed back toward the hills west of Tiberias. Again he faced the day on his own.

Meanwhile, Rebekah could be found in a familiar place, in the temple praying at the altar. Careful eyes watched her from a distance, though this day they were not the evil eyes of Jotham. Amon, the high priest, watched her from the back of temple. A smile of admiration emerged from this familiar sight, though what he saw this day amazed him. A tear of joy rolled down his weathered cheek. Beside Rebekah another one knelt in prayer. Her six-year-old son, Justus, had learned the importance of prayer, and he couldn't have had a better example to follow than his loving mother. Amon knew confidently; Justus would grow to become a man of God, by reflecting Rebekah's heart.

Amon loved watching her living faith, as she continued her prayer vigil for Tychicus's restoration. Softly, to himself, he whispered, "Oh, that more people in Tiberias had her faith." He smiled and then said a prayer for Rebekah and Justus. Then he prayed for Tychicus.

CHAPTER 28

Leperd headed back toward the hills west of Tiberias. After living in the caves with Jazer and the other lepers, he wondered if he might find a cave there. It would be a place to call home, a place where he'd someday lay his head down to die. It would be his eventual resting place.

His disease had started to progress even more, and each day the symptoms became more unmistakable. Some of his fingers were damaged from his rant in the stream. Walking became more strenuous as his feet and toes had started to become numb. His hands and fingers followed suit, as feeling was mostly absent. He wondered if his whole body would someday lose feeling, with his heart finally completing the process, finishing its final beat.

He held his love for Rebekah in his heart, and he couldn't imagine a time when it would lack the capacity to do so. He still thought of her every day. How he missed holding her in his arms. He still cherished the last time he saw her with his own eyes on the road outside of Tiberias. It seemed so long ago, much longer than it actually had been. How he longed to see her again, but he didn't want her to see him in his current condition, and he knew it would just get worse. Trying to catch another glimpse of her seemed like such a selfish endeavor. So he continued on, leaving those hopes behind, clinging to every memory.

Leperd's back and shoulder still ached. The rocks hurled by Zebediah had done much damage. The blow to his shoulder had fractured a bone while the blow to his back left a deep bruise. Even if healing would take place, Leperd knew it would take much time. He'd learned to live with discomfort, and this would be just one more ailment to add to his many burdens. Perhaps, he thought, soon his shoulder and back would also become numb, and he wouldn't feel the pain. But such convenience wouldn't be.

He wandered somewhat aimlessly, paying little attention to where his steps were taking him. He believed he headed south, but his steps actually led him straight toward the northern trade route to Syria. As he walked, he ventured toward the road. For some reason, he decided to walk down the path without a second thought. Usually he stayed away from any road. Some form of traffic would surely appear.

He walked with his head down. His long, unkempt hair covered his face. He simply continued to roam, heading nowhere in particular. His mind wandered as many random thoughts filled his head. The fact that Justus faced life alone without a father continually entered his mind. How he longed to have another opportunity to be the father he should have been!

The sound of a caravan coming down the road brought him back to reality. He wondered why he didn't hear them sooner. They were approaching quickly, leaving little time to turn and run away. He turned and headed from the road as he yelled, "Unclean! Unclean! Unclean!"

The caravan slowed to a stop. Time stood still as they waited for the unclean leper to disappear. After a few minutes, they proceeded on their way. They peered back at the cursed man with disdain. How dare such a contemptible wanderer occupy their road.

Leperd stood now afar off, breathing heavily as their glaring eyes followed him. His body ached as he heaved. He sat down in the dirt to catch his breath. He hated having to say those ungodly words: "Unclean! Unclean! Unclean!" They echoed in his head. How he wished he'd never have to speak them again. He also hated being judged over this dilemma for which he had no control. He did not choose to be overcome by this disease. Then he recalled how he looked at lepers not that long ago. He had been numbered in the lot of those who judged him, and who he now judged.

How could this day be any worse than it had already been? What else could possibly be added to it? He continued toward the hills west of Tiberias, where he found the answer to this rhetorical question. From a distance he saw something ahead of him. It looked like something lying in a heap, but it did not look familiar. His curiosity drew him closer as he watched something flapping in the wind. As he walked near, his heart sank. The heap was still. He watched for any sign of movement beneath the draped piece of cloth, but he watched in vain.

Even from a distance, he understood what lay before him. From beneath the cloth, a deformed foot protruded out. From where he stood, he could tell several toes were missing. He had stumbled upon a body lying out in the hot sun. It looked like an overlooked island in the middle of a vast ocean, lost and forgotten.

As he neared the body, he walked around to the far side. He shuddered as a hand lay visible. The fears that started to well up in his stomach were now realized. Several fingers were missing on the body's right hand. But on one finger, he saw a gold ring encircled with ornate engraving. He recognized the ring and now recognized the man.

Leperd stood there for some time, staring at the body of Jazer, his friend. His body never looked more deformed and thin. He had been reduced to very little. His long hair blew in the subtle breeze as it blanketed most of his face. His body reflected the torment it once endured, though Leperd knew Jazer had found peace. He was now at rest.

"Will this be me someday?" Leperd wondered. He knew the probability of such an outcome would be more likely than not. Eventually he'd come to the end of his days, and then he'd die alone without anyone to mourn for him. No one would know or care. Then he would rot away or be eaten by some wild creature. His fate had never been more real to him than it had become at that moment. How he dreaded the days to come!

"Oh, Jazer, my friend," he said softly to himself. No one heard his voice but God. He wanted to say his friend's name, just so someone would acknowledge him in death.

Someone knew, and someone cared.

He knew, and he cared.

In a moment of silent contemplation, Leperd searched for answers as he did so often. Why should a man like this—a kind and compassionate man—have to suffer and die in this manner? He didn't understand. This did not make sense. It was illogical and wrong. He found himself in this very quandary many times, though this time, anger and rage did not follow as it commonly would. Sadness and hopelessness covered him like an oversized cloak. He just wondered why.

First, the weight of Athalia's death burdened him. Now, the realization of Jazer's death heaped more grief onto his already-heavy soul. Before he could stop mourning the one, he mourned the other.

Leperd spent the next day and a half finding stones, which he carried over to Jazer's body. His back and shoulder still ached from the injuries caused by Zebediah's stones. After taking Jazer's ring from his finger, he buried him beneath a mound of rocks. Jazer's remains would be safe from scavengers, and his ring would become a constant reminder of his life. Leperd looked at the large mound of rocks before him. It looked all too familiar. He felt the need to say something in memoriam.

"Jazer." He paused. "Thank you for being my friend. You were kind to me. Thank you. Rest in peace." Then to mirror Jazer one last time, he added, "Thank you, Jazer, *my friend.*"

Gathering the stones had been another arduous task, and Leperd's body had become more exhausted than ever. He said farewell to his friend and knew he had to leave. He headed off once more. After walking awhile, he found a place to lie down for the night and fell into an uncharacteristically deep sleep.

The next morning as he started to wake, he heard something odd but couldn't place the sound. It was a scuffling, rustling kind of sound. He lay there quietly with his eyes shut. Still half-asleep, he wondered if he was dreaming, or was this sound part of the reality of a new day. He listened intently, realizing the noise appeared to be very close. What could it be? He opened his eyes, looking up into sky. He could still hear something stirring as he lay rather still.

He peered down toward his feet. As his eyes focused, he realized a rat had been chewing on his foot. He immediately reacted, pulling his foot back. This scared the rat, which scampered off, but not before causing much damage. Leperd hadn't felt a thing as a portion of two of his toes had been chewed away. A small pool of blood remained where Leperd's foot had been just moments before.

The rat ran off as Leperd's mind filled with unbelief. He screamed at the top of his lungs in anguish. Instant bitterness met with fury as he once again raised his fist toward heaven. "What are you doing to me? What did I ever do to you? Why don't you leave me alone? Haven't you done enough? Why don't you just let me die?" Several more screams of frustration and cursing toward God followed. More curses aimed toward Jotham were added, as the hatred for the evil chief priest grew deeper than ever.

Another day had dawned. It would be just another one to endure—just another day to loathe.

CHAPTER 29

I could tell by the expectant look in his eyes and the careful attention he gave to every detail that Archippus found my story very fascinating to this point. But one fact troubled him. I could sense it. How could I know so much about this man who lived so much of his life in isolation? His curiosity could wait no longer as he confirmed my suspicions with the following question. "Simon," he asked, "how could you know so much about Leperd? Would not he alone know all the intimate details of this story?"

Archippus looked directly into my eyes. "Unless, you were…" He paused before adding, "But that would be impossible! You couldn't be Leperd…" He looked down toward my sandal as I could tell he counted my toes. No evidence of rats chewing on either of my feet was evident as I slightly pulled up my cloak and wiggled my toes.

Archippus looked up at me again. He knew I understood what he was doing.

I couldn't help but smile. Such an inquisitive young man. "You are from Cairo, my friend. Many people here in Tiberias know the story of Leperd," I chuckled. "It has been told many, many times over the years. It has been passed down by those who heard it so long ago. Surely most anyone here could tell you this same story." I looked into his eyes and could tell this answer did not satisfy him.

Archippus started asking questions that could no longer remain unanswered: "But whom did he originally tell his story to? How did it get passed along if the law forbid him to talk to anyone? There was no way he could share it with the masses. And since lepers lived a relatively short life, he must have died so long ago. Someone had to hear it for the first time, but who might that be?" I could tell he had pondered over this dilemma. He wanted resolution to these questions as if to give my story credibility. Before I could remark, he spoke again.

"It would seem the only one who had insight into his story, besides Leperd, would have to be Josech, the blind beggar. Did he start the retelling of this story? Perhaps Laban and Massa had something to do with it?"

I smiled once again. "I am sure Josech heard this story himself from the very mouth of Leperd. You know, he was an integral part of the story as it unfolded. Other than Leperd himself, no one else had the insight Josech had. He and Leperd spent much time talking over the years during their late-night visits. And who knows what he might have said to almost anyone in town, including the temple priests."

Archippus looked bewildered though a little more satisfied. "How else could this story have been passed on if it wasn't Josech's doing? Leperd, a leper, had no other way to pass it on to anyone else. Josech *had* to be the originator of this tale! But the story was told which such detail. Could Leperd have shared such intimate details with him? And could this story be relayed all these years with such great accuracy?" I could read his mind. Others before him had posed the same questions many times before.

"The only one Leperd could talk to was Josech. Surely he confided everything to him."

"Surely the story has been embellished over the years. Perhaps much of this is just folklore, a story that has grown over time," Archippus suggested. "After all, you are quite a storyteller."

"Well, some have speculated about that in the past, but let me assure you, this tale is true, in every detail, as far as I know it. Even Leperd could not have known Rebekah's thoughts completely, so some license may well have been used in the retelling of this tale," I said confidently.

Archippus seemed to be satisfied, enough for now at least. He had become more at ease and comfortable with me during the telling of the story, much more than when he first questioned my ability to offer him help earlier in the day. "Please go on," he said with anticipation.

Happy to oblige, I continued.

Leperd never felt so low. Days of existing turned to weeks and months of meaningless time. It had been nearly a year since he saw Rebekah on the road to Magdala, and the remembrance of that moment came to the forefront of his mind nearly every day. Some days he regretted not running to her, at least not running closer to her. Other days he wished the encounter never happened. Then at least this reoccurring memory wouldn't continually remind him of his loss. The depression that had descended upon him had never been so oppressive. The thoughts entering his head were foreign to him, until now. His ability to think rationally had been challenged.

As he walked, he looked west toward the Plain of Gennesaret. Looking into the distance, he stopped dead in his tracks. *That was it!* he thought. He knew where this would end. Why hadn't he thought of this before?

Mount Arbel loomed into the sky some 1,300 feet above the sea. He recalled stories of how the steep cliffs had once been used by the Assyrians, who forced many off the mountain to their deaths on the rocks below in the Valley of the Doves. He considered this an obvious solution, a sure way to end his misery.

His will to survive and his drive to endure had plummeted after seeing Jazer's body. He hadn't been able to get that image out of his head. He also remembered the sight of Athalia slumped on the ground with blood running down her face. How sad. He knew if he didn't do something to end this impending fate, he would surely find his end to be the same. He didn't think he would be able to live through the long, grueling process of deterioration.

He knew this disease wouldn't allow him to live a long life. So what would be so wrong in just speeding up the inevitable? The loneliness his exile had brought on had become nearly unbearable, and he knew it would always be this way. Why should he subject himself to such a horrible fate? He couldn't imagine living the rest of his days this way, only to die in this manner.

He had quite a hike to reach the top of Mount Arbel, and nothing but time to walk. As he walked, his mind processed the pros and cons concerning his predicament. He started contemplating all he'd lost.

First and foremost, he thought of his wife. He knew she wouldn't approve of the thoughts running through his brain. She had such a love and respect for life. But surely she could never understand what his life had become. How could she ever know what he endured each day? He did not believe she wanted him to live such an existence, would she? He knew he'd never be close enough to hold her again. It wouldn't be so bad if he could just stop thinking about her. But his mind wouldn't stop. Why couldn't she just leave his mind? Why couldn't he just disappear without a trace? Most likely no one would ever find his body—not that anyone would be looking. The best-case scenario would find him with a handful of years of misery and suffering as his body and mind degenerated. Why not just end it all now? It seemed like a logical option that he kept revisiting as discouragement hindered his thinking.

Again, his mind wandered as he walked. He realized he'd lost his focus as he tried to concentrate. He thought about his son, Justus, and Rebekah, during her pregnancy with him. Even while she carried their child, she radiated with beauty, perhaps more than ever. The physical changes she went through did not detract or mar her beauty. She anticipated becoming a mother, and she radiated with joy. He remembered the day of Justus's birth as one of the happiest days of his life. A boy! Rebekah had bore them a son! They were both so proud. And as Justus grew, his pride for his son grew as well. He had great memories of the times he spent with him.

Just then one phrase came to mind, from the day they headed to Magdala for the festival. He could still see the dusty road and the donkey with Rebekah riding on its back. Justus had a confused look on his face as he asked, "What is a hard heart?" As he placed his hand on his chest, he added, "Is my heart hard?" And then he recalled the final question that he couldn't shake. "Father, is *your* heart hard?"

Had his heart become hard toward God? Had he become like the pharaoh standing before Moses? He remembered Rebekah's refusal to look directly at him. He knew the truth. His heart had turned to stone, opposed to God, the culmination of much time of resentment and bitterness. It had become a condition he could not overcome. The roots of his anger had grown deep and strong.

He stopped in his tracks. He placed his hand inside his cloak. His hand had turned numb, and he could not feel his heartbeat. He remembered the relief Justus had when he discovered his heart was not hard. But even at that moment he could not feel his heart, which had become hard.

His son's question haunted him: "Father, is *your* heart hard?"

He tried to forget that moment as he thought through the last moment they spent together. They were walking side by side in the courtyard just inside the gates of Tiberias. He glanced over at his son and smiled. He didn't say a word. But he remembered his exact thought. His simply thought, "I love you, son. I'm so proud of you." He now regretted not verbalizing those thoughts. He and Rebekah had talked about having more children, and the sight of his firstborn at that moment thrilled his heart with the thought of sons and daughters to come. Someday, he knew, he'd look at many children walking beside him, with Justus, the oldest, leading the way.

Just then the attack occurred. Life changed at that moment. Now the dreams they once had were gone. The future they planned would never be.

He'd never see his son become a man. He wouldn't be the one to teach him so many things a growing boy should learn from his father. Just that thought discouraged him even more. Why didn't he take better advantage of the time he had with him while he had it? Why, instead, did he work so much? He wondered what kind of memories Justus had of him even now. Did he believe he had been a good father? He would never know.

He'd also lost his home, his social status, his identity, the privilege of being a part of a community, and now his health slowly slipped away. He'd lost so much. He'd lost everything! He felt like Job, though God had forgotten the end of his story.

He stopped to think of the positive side of life. He wanted to consider all that life offered him—a reason to live. He didn't know where to start. Not one thought came to mind. He'd lost everything, and the future promised nothing more than pain and agony. This made him consider ending his life even more. What did he have to live for? He did have his friendship with Josech, but that was it.

Once again his mind went back to Jazer. He couldn't get the sight of his forsaken body out of his mind. Then he thought something that had never occurred to him. He'd seen many lepers. Each of them had been affected with the same disease he had—with all its destructive characteristics. And in each case life became something to cherish. He'd never seen a leper commit suicide. Maybe he'd just never seen one. Surely some had ended their life. There had to be some, but he couldn't recall hearing of one. He considered their overwhelming desire to live—even those whose leprosy exceeded what he dealt with. What hope did they strive for? Why did they long to live? Did they not understand no cure would ever restore them to health? He almost felt guilty for even thinking about killing himself. He just didn't know what he had to live for.

He walked as his mind considered all these things over and over again. He battled his own thoughts. He grappled with deep turmoil that he did not know how to overcome.

He continued walking until nightfall. He lay under the stars and watched them for some time. This might be the last chance he would have to marvel at them. The sky looked so large, and the number of the stars was so vast. In comparison, he was just a speck—a meaningless speck. God had made all in his view. God had made him. He wondered why he had become so insignificant, so worthless. He struggled with this question until, finally, he fell asleep.

He woke the following morning, feeling the usual morning stiffness. With renewed vigor, he set out to complete the hike before him.

Finally, he approached the peak of Mount Arbel. It had been a long and arduous climb. He walked up to the edge and peered over. He looked way down to the ravine far below. He sat down to rest for a moment. His tired feet enjoyed this time of relief. He stopped for a moment though the sweat continued to run down his face. The warm sun overhead steadily covered him as he wished for shade. An occasional breeze brushed past him, cooling him off. During this brief moment, the task at hand temporarily left his thoughts. He just relaxed.

But soon he came back to his senses. He had been driven to this place for a specific task. He knew he had to jump.

He stood up, looking over the edge once again. Slowly he leaned over. Should he jump headfirst? Should he just jump? How should he do it? As he contemplated this, his foot slipped, and he started to fall. He reached out to save himself from the plunge. As he hung on with his feet dangling over the edge, he looked behind him as a rock fell into the ravine so far below. It bounced off one rock after another on its way to the bottom. He'd come here to die, and he now found himself halfway over the edge of the cliff. He would plunge to his death as soon as he released his grip. He would follow that rock down to the bottom. He wanted to let go, but something within him held on. If he really wanted to die, he wouldn't have instinctively reached out to save himself, would he? Didn't he want to die? He realized that he wanted to live—just not like this.

With all his strength, he pulled himself back to safety. He sat there for a moment, breathing heavily. His anger started to build, and soon his rage emerged from him as he clenched his fist and raised it toward heaven. "Why have you done this to me? What did I do to deserve this? What did I do to you?" His scream echoed in the ravine as he reached deep within to let it all out. He simply screamed in torment. His agony poured from him. He yelled loud and long, until no more strength remained. It became quiet, still. He lowered his head and started to sob. He'd longed for answers that hadn't come. He felt that God had forgotten him, and he didn't know where to turn.

He stayed there for several days, numb to his predicament. His heart continued to harden toward God as the reason for his circumstances remained a mystery.

CHAPTER 30

The night had once again fallen on Tiberias. It had been a normal day for Josech, and now loneliness was again his companion. He had begged for food, receiving a typical, timid response, which left him hungry—a common feeling. His daylong quest for food had left him exhausted. He would soon retreat to unconsciousness—his only refuge from the reality he lived with day in and day out, before waking to endure it all again. His eyes became heavy as he lay down on his blanket. Nearly asleep, a sound off to his right startled him. He sat up and listened intently.

"Who's there?"

"It's me," a quiet voice said.

"Leperd? Is that you?" Josech always welcomed his visits.

"Yes. How are you, my friend?" Leperd said softly.

Josech smiled. "How do you think I am? I'm a blind beggar—things couldn't be better!"

"Well, it's good to see you," Leperd said, immediately regretting his choice of words.

"Well, I wish I could see you, but I'm a *blind* beggar!" Josech responded with a chuckle. Remarkably, for someone in his position, he had an incredible sense of humor.

Leperd smiled, indeed a rare occurrence. Before this trial, he'd seen Josech sitting in his place for so many years, never taking time to see the man inside the beggar. He had discovered a good man. He found Josech to be a kind man. He wished he'd taken the time to help him earlier when he had the ability to do so—all the years of friendship they could've shared. And how he and Rebekah could have ministered to him. Why didn't they? He felt remorse for that.

"It's been awhile. Where have you been?" Josech asked.

"You know… just wandering. It's my life."

"I'm sorry," Josech said to Leperd's surprise. "You know, I remember the day you were banished. You've lost so much."

"What do you mean?" he asked.

"I listen. Since I don't have my sight, my sense of hearing has become very keen. It's all I have. So I listen to everything." He stopped as if reflecting. "You told me you didn't have a family. I never believed that. You had such a sense of loss in your voice. I knew you were missing someone."

Leperd remembered that day. He felt forsaken when no one reached out to him after his banishment. Under the circumstances, he felt abandoned—he'd lost his family.

Josech continued, "You were being escorted to the gates as the priests declared you were unclean. Then your wife ran to you. She told you how she loved you, and you told her you loved her. Then they sent you away. There was something familiar about your voice when I first heard it. I placed it eventually. When we talked the first time, I couldn't place you, but eventually I did. You are the leper, called 'Leperd.' That is why you roam and why I only hear from you from time to time."

Josech paused before saying the most remarkable thing. "My friend, I'm sorry for your loss." His sincerity was genuine, and Leperd knew it.

This poor man had practically spent his entire life in isolation. He'd been exiled from anything normal, and his family had abandoned him. And he was sorry for *his* loss? What a selfless statement. Leperd was humbled and amazed at his friend's heart. Seeing this act of compassion could only be described as incredible.

"Josech," he started. His emotions overwhelmed him as he became choked up, having to pause before continuing. "I'm sorry. For years I walked right past you and didn't offer you any help. I even stopped and talked to you for a brief moment just once, then walked away. I'm so sorry." Leperd felt deep remorse again. He took a deep breath and swallowed the lump in his throat. He pleaded, "Will you forgive me?"

It took a lot to bring Leperd to this point. He'd been so self-consumed that he hadn't looked beyond himself. His friend had suffered for so much longer than he, and he now saw his selflessness, and it humbled him.

"Thank you, my friend," Josech said softly. He didn't verbalize his forgiveness, but by the tone of his voice, Leperd could sense it.

They talked for some time. Toward the end of their conversation, Josech said, "What a sad lot we are. A leper and a blind beggar." He smiled. What a strange pairing indeed. But neither of them had anyone else, and they needed each other.

Leperd changed this lighthearted moment as he asked, "Have you ever felt like giving up?"

"Have *you* ever felt that way?" Josech asked in return, not giving an answer to this rhetorical question.

"Just once," Leperd said. "Just once."

He thought back several days to his time at the peak of Mount Arbel. He still felt as if God had forgotten him. He still wondered why he should continue living through the struggle of each day trying to find any form of purpose in it all. He still struggled with the lack of answers for so many questions.

It became quiet for quite some time. Finally, Leperd spoke. "Don't give up." His words were offered to Josech, though they were also meant for him.

Quietly Josech whispered back, "Don't *you* give up." They were in agreement, and now they shared a measure of accountability.

Leperd promised to return soon. Then he headed off, disappearing into the night.

CHAPTER 31

Days turned to weeks, which became months and years. Leperd's disease grew increasingly worse as time slowly wore on. Infection had taken several of his fingers and a few of his toes. He barely recognized his old self when he peered into a stream, which he purposely avoided looking into most of the time. His skin had become very thick and covered with a rash that had grown out of control. His malformed frame brought constant discomfort, and his hair had grown long over his face. He had become quite a hideous sight to behold. He'd indeed become like the poor soul he shunned from the road to Magdala so many years before. His leprosy had become full. Every part of his body reflected the contamination and symptoms of his disease. Every day he waited for the shadow of unquenchable thirst to find him.

He returned to the city gates regularly, where Josech remained—his only true connection with the human race. How he cherished his kindness and faithfulness. Over the last few years, they'd grown as close as they could under the odd circumstances that defined their lives.

Leperd understood his time was growing increasingly short. He could not deny the fact. He remembered Jazer telling him he'd know when his time drew near, and that brought daily fear. He never wanted to die a leper, but he knew his days were numbered. He didn't know how much time he had left, but surely he couldn't go on much longer.

During all these years, Rebekah faithfully called out to God for her husband's restoration. She refused the advances of many men and endured the frequent ridicule from Jotham and others in town, who thought her vigil had become ridiculously excessive; she continued her pleas at the temple altar—praying that God would heal her husband's heart and bring him back to himself.

Her love for Tychicus never dwindled, not one bit, though everyone told her it would. She became the recipient of much scorn from those who thought she must be insane to continue holding onto a hopeless delusion.

Justus also prayed for his father's return, experiencing the same ridicule that his mother faced, as he believed his return could be any day. From time to time, he continued visiting Demas and the lambs. Demas believed he'd grow out of this false expectation and awaited that day. Justus had grown strong in his faith though at a high price. He simply learned to live with it all. He had faith like his mother, and he believed God was still God—able to perform miracles.

Amon stood by their side, understanding their desire for God to answer their many prayers. He also believed God could not be limited by any timetable. He could move whenever he saw fit. Many days, Amon stood alone by their side, but he didn't mind. He consistently encouraged them with his prayers and through his position at the temple, which supplied them with food and other basic needs.

Many years had passed.

Many prayers had been offered.

Many lonely days had been endured.

Leperd came to terms with his circumstances. He never received the answers he sought. He still had many questions without answers. So it had been, and so it would be.

CHAPTER 32

Leperd sat at the Sea of Galilee. He'd been watching the waves. It had become a common occurrence. Over the last few years, he found this to be a mindless, hypnotic way to pass time, which he had plenty of. It had now been nearly seven years since his banishment, though he was unable to track the time. As he watched the waves this late morning, one thought consumed his mind. This thought had crossed his mind before—many times. He had simply learned to suppress it. But today, he made a decision. He would not only entertain these thoughts, but he'd also follow through and act on them. He knew what he had been led to do. Due to his stubbornness, he stalled in the past. He realized the time had come to follow through, and he would hesitate no longer, though for a brief moment he continued watching the late-morning waves.

Then suddenly he stood to his feet. He turned his awkward frame around, facing the mountains off in the distance. He'd seen this sight so many times over the years. But today he glanced at them while seeing them in a different light. Slowly, he started to walk. He looked west toward the Plain of Gennesaret. Looking into the distance, he stopped dead in his tracks. *That was it!* he thought. That would be where it would end—and this time he would find resolution.

He walked and walked. He climbed with determination. He knew he had to go to the top of Mount Arbel. It had been nearly five years since he first hiked to this peak, where he intended to end his life. He didn't follow through that day. This day his mind determined to complete the mission he set before himself. His objective had never been clearer. This would be the day when he'd accomplish the task at hand—he had to!

He started to walk, looking at the mountains in the distance. With each slow step, they drew nearer. He knew his pace, though slow but steady would take him back to the peak. With each step, he remembered his last attempt to find resolution there. He recalled every emotion associated with that endeavor. They rose once again in his chest. On one hand, he knew the necessity of the moments ahead. On the other hand, he understood the difficulty of what lay before him.

As the sun beat down on his head, he tired. The heat of the day poured down upon him. He stopped for a moment to rest. He pulled his shredded garment over his head for shade. He welcomed any kind of relief from the hot sun. As he sat, he stared. He looked at the top of the mountain and the distance he still had to climb. This journey would surely take longer than it had before. But he had nothing but time, so he plodded along.

As the sun started to set, he rested beneath a tree. He watched the full moon in the sky as it hung above the mountain peak. It looked so large, so close. Just a little rest and he would continue his trek when the hot sun would once again rise into the sky.

The morning came sooner than he expected. He woke as the sun shone in his face. Time had come to walk once again. He plodded along step by step. Occasionally his mind would drift as he stepped on a rock that would transfix the arch of his foot. His sandals had worn down long ago, and his feet had become calloused. Sometimes the pain would cause him to fall to his knees. He panted during those moments, gathered his strength, before standing back up to continue his journey.

As he saw grasshoppers or other insects, he reached down to catch them. He never acquired a taste for any of them, but survival demanded he try to fill his belly. Most times he did this without a thought. It had become common for Leperd to wake from a moment of temporary daydreaming to find himself chewing on something that squirmed in his mouth. He merely maintained an existence as he walked.

Finally, the peak of the mountain drew near. He could nearly see it before him. From inside, he summoned some unseen strength as he fought to take the final steps he needed. His faithful plodding had finally brought him to his destination.

He sat down to rest. Then, on his hands and knees, he edged the last few feet toward the edge of the cliff and looked over once again. Far below he saw the Valley of the Doves. More cautious this time, he shifted his weight to avoid slipping, as he'd done before. He tossed a rock over the edge and watched it fall down to the valley below. It bounced several times on its way to the bottom. If he'd taken the plunge so long ago, he wouldn't have had to endure the last few years. There were many days he didn't want to face his lot. But today he knew he must. He had made the journey, and the time had come.

He stood there for some time. Again he stalled, and he didn't know why. He looked down into the valley, then out over the Sea of Galilee. His body was badly deformed and filled with exhaustion. He reflected again as so many thoughts he'd thought before raced through his mind. He thought of Rebekah and Justus. He thought of the last few years and all he'd endured. He thought about Jazer and Athalia. He thought about his friendship with Josech, and all he'd suffered and still suffered. He considered his life in its entirety. Was it worth living? Time for consideration became complete. A decision must be made—and the time had come! His thoughts were complete as his mind stopped circling through all the roads he'd traveled. He became numb. Nothing consumed him any longer. He had emptied himself of his burden and now found himself simply staring off into the distance.

He had not found understanding concerning his predicament. He had come to the realization that he would probably never know the answers to most of his questions. But one thing had become perfectly clear, after all this time—*it was time.*

Leperd fell with his face to the ground. He started to sob uncontrollably. He'd been bitter for so long. His anger and rage had consumed him so many times. His heart had become as hard as the mountain he found himself upon. Again, his thoughts brought him back to the temple and how Jotham had lusted after his wife and how this priest's ungodliness had turned him from God.

His bitterness started there.

His anger started there.

His heart started to harden there.

Most of his rage had been initially aimed toward Jotham, but somehow it had turned toward God. But had God wronged him? He'd cursed God so many times with a clenched fist toward heaven. He'd cursed God in anger more times than he could ever count. He had blamed God for all his infirmities.

He thought back to that trip to Magdala for the festival. They were talking about the story of Moses. He recalled his own words that he spoke to his son, who marveled at God and his mighty hand. He voiced his own words: "God can do whatever he wants." He stopped to ponder the truth he had shared with his son, truth he had not fully accepted for himself. It was truth.

How could he question God? In that moment, he felt so small and so insignificant. He felt completely dirty inside and outside. His heart had become dark and cynical, and he knew it. Once again, he heard the words of his son as he asked, "Father, is your heart hard?" He confessed it had surely become hard.

He thought of his beautiful wife, who had such a passionate love for God. He could not deny that. She had peace in her heart. Even during the trials she also faced these last few years, he knew she had true, inner peace. She might not have understood it all, but he knew she trusted God nonetheless. She had been praying for him all this time. He knew it! He could feel it! The culmination of all those faithful prayers had softened his heart.

He knew God could have taken his full vengeance out on him at any time. But he hadn't. Yes, God had allowed this disease to consume him, but even so, he had supplied breath each day. Life itself had been a deeply challenging gift, which he now embraced for the first time in such a long time.

The sky grew dark as a storm grew strong above him. It started to rain. Thick drops rapidly became more intense. Thunder boomed nearby as lightning lit up the mountaintop for brief, sporadic moments. Soon his cloak became heavy on his shoulders and back, drenched with rain. He parted his long, wet hair as he looked up toward heaven. As raindrops hit his face, he raised his hand.

A clenched fist had gone as he raised an open hand, a gesture of need. He had become more than desperate. He stared into the sky for a moment before bowing his head. Then loudly and confidently, he started to pray above the loudness of the storm. "O God of my fathers, I've come back here to meet with you. I don't want to fight anymore. I can't do it on my own. I know I've sinned against you. Please forgive me. Soften my heart of stone. I want to have the peace Rebekah has. I want your peace. I don't want to be bitter or angry anymore. Change me. Break me. Teach me to praise you in this storm. Bring back the faith I once had. Restore me, O God. Please take me back."

Leperd now bent down low, with his face to the ground. He'd humbled himself as he sent his pride away. He earnestly repeated his words several times, "Please take me back. Please take me back. O God, please take me back."

For a moment, he felt numb, and it had nothing to do with leprosy. Why had it taken so long for him to come to this place? Why did he ever think he knew better than God? He waited for his response.

Suddenly he noticed the rain had stopped. The sun emerged from behind the clouds. The storm had calmed. He raised his head as a white butterfly fluttered toward him. It had appeared from nowhere, it seemed. It hovered in front of him for just a moment. He raised his hand again as the butterfly found a resting place on his finger. It was obviously a sign from God. It was breathtaking. And finally, after all his days of struggling, he felt inner peace. God heard his cry as mercy and forgiveness were released. And now God had given him a sign—new life.

Leperd's spirit had been restored. He'd given his life back to God. Even though he still felt somewhat like a dead man physically, he knew his spirit had new wings—just like the butterfly still perched on his finger, slowly flapping it's wings. Whatever remained of his shattered life, he now offered back to his Maker.

He smiled as he looked at the butterfly again. Then, just as quickly as it had come, it flew away. Again, he looked toward heaven and prayed out loud, "Even though you may not heal my body, thank you for healing my heart." Then Leperd started to laugh with a laugh of joy. He had been released, and he never felt happier.

God had indeed answered his prayer.

He had also answered Rebekah's prayer that God would do whatever it would take to bring her husband back to him. God had answered, though at a great price. He had been patient, and he had been kind. He chose to reward her faithfulness, even though she didn't know it yet. The day of her enlightenment would come soon.

Leperd stood up. A smile covered his face for the first time in so long. The joy of the Lord filled his spirit as the warm sun shone over him. He took a deep breath. Even the air seemed fresh. He knew he could face whatever might cross his path—and he finally found himself at peace.

"Thank you, my God," he said with a smile. Then he headed down the mountain. He set his sights for the city dump, where he'd ask its inhabitants for forgiveness. Leperd's heart had truly been changed.

CHAPTER 33

Rebekah knelt at the altar as fervent, faithful prayers were lifted to the heavens. Though she hadn't had any contact with Tychicus in many years, she still believed he was alive and that God would bring healing. Somehow she just knew it.

Amon talked with Rebekah several times over the years, always concerned about where God had been leading her. She hadn't lost her passion for prayer, and her love for her husband hadn't diminished in the least.

Jotham's predatory behavior continued though Rebekah kept him at arm's length, in great part due to Amon's help. Jotham's anger boiled as his advances had no effect on her. Yet he still vowed to have his way with her someday.

Amon helped Rebekah with food and spiritual guidance, as he had with other "widows." There were a select few who'd also stepped up to help them. Uncle Isaac's friends Demas and Epaphras and their families met many of their needs and became close friends.

After all these years, she found herself at the temple again, praying. But this day something appeared to be different. Something special had happened, and she couldn't deny it. She felt the presence of God, and she knew he was at work. An overwhelming peace flooded her soul as if a heavy burden had finally been lifted from her back. She broke the silence in the temple as she breathed a deep breath, sighing loudly. Then she started singing at the top of her lungs. She danced before the altar, praising God unashamed.

Through tears of joy, she glanced around. Several watched her as she danced. Jotham stood afar off. He'd been watching her with evil in his heart. Several others who'd also been praying looked at Rebekah with a bewildered look as she caused a disturbance in this typically quiet, reverent place. Some wondered if she'd gone mad. Had she finally lost her sanity after all these years? What could've possibly caused this sudden outburst? She'd been seen praying here countless times, and such a scene had never accompanied her visits.

Laban ran into the room to find what had caused this commotion. Massa soon followed. Rebekah made quite a stir. The only one now standing in the room with a wide smile on his face, besides Rebekah, was Amon, the high priest. He knew why she rejoiced with such passion; it could only be one thing, and it brought such joy to his heart.

Rebekah ran to him as they embraced in a hug of celebration. Amon laughed as they started dancing together—singing praises to God. They didn't need to verbalize their thoughts or explain their actions. They both knew God had answered her prayer. They didn't know how exactly, but they praised God for his goodness without regard for what anyone else might think.

As Rebekah praised God, Leperd prepared to deal with a very difficult situation.

Josech sat at the gate as the sun set. It had been some time since he heard the footsteps that brought joy to his heart. Recently they'd been altered as Leperd's steps had slowed. His pace had deteriorated over time. They were no longer steady as they had been in the past. Even so, Josech recognized them as they came near.

"My friend, you've returned," he said quietly. "I've been worried about you."

Leperd smiled. "It's good to see you." His voice sounded hoarse and tired. His body ached from fatigue. He'd recently spent time at the city dump, where he asked forgiveness from all who lived there. Leperd now looked forward to talking with his friend, though he feared it might be their last conversation.

Josech immediately sensed something wrong. "Tell me, Leperd. How are you? You sound so tired."

"I'm tired and thirsty." Leperd became quiet for a moment. He knew this would be hard, and he wanted to say the right words. They talked for a while before it came time for him to deliver the message that encouraged this visit.

"Josech, you've been a great friend. You've inspired me like no other. You've been my best friend." This seemed unusual since Leperd really didn't have any other friends. "The only other person I'd call a friend since my exile was an older man named Jazer. I met him at the leper colony. His disease had progressed far along when we met, and I only knew him for about a month. He told me he'd know when his time had come. Then he'd head off..."

He meant to say, "Then he'd head off to die," but he couldn't get the rest of the words to come out.

"I've said farewell to you before. But I'm afraid this is my final farewell. My time has come. It's time for me to head off."

Sadness filled Josech as he received this unwelcome news. He always knew Leperd's disease wouldn't give him a long life. When there were long gaps between visits, he started to wonder where his friend might be. He wondered if air still passed through his lungs. He wondered if his heart still beat in his chest. He wondered if the struggle of every day continued. Josech understood he could sit as a blind man for a long time, but the outlook for a leper wasn't as promising.

"I just wanted to tell you something before I go." Leperd became emotional. He would truly miss his friend, and he knew he'd also feel the loss. "I've made peace with my God. I'm ready to go rest in his arms. So please, don't worry about me."

Josech could not speak. He became quiet. He also had something to say and didn't know how to say it. "Would you like me to tell your wife anything?"

Leperd's eyes opened wide as shock enveloped him. How could Josech talk to Rebekah? After all this time, how could this be?

"I need to tell you something." He paused. Leperd anxiously awaited Josech's words. "I believe the woman who's been bringing me food, my unseen angel, is your wife."

Leperd could not believe what he heard. He could imagine this type of generosity coming from Rebekah's heart. But why had Josech kept this secret from him all these years? This made no sense at all. How could this have happened?

Josech continued, "I know my angel's voice. It always sounded so familiar, but I couldn't place it. It always frustrated me. She always came to me with whisperings at night, unlike when I heard her screaming, when you were banished. Then recently I heard her talking to one of the vendors at the gate. Suddenly I knew. After all this time, I recognized her voice. I recognized her, and I was sure of it. After she left, the vendor said something about her husband—the leper. He said he couldn't believe she still actively prayed for him after all these years—that God would bring restoration."

Leperd's eyes welled up with tears. Rebekah had been praying for him all this time. This evidence of her love overwhelmed him. Josech didn't know that quiet tears streamed down his cheeks as he continued.

"I wondered if she was talking about you. He mentioned a name: Tychicus."

Leperd hadn't heard that name in years. It almost seemed foreign to him as if he was talking about someone else.

Josech asked, "Are you… Tychicus?"

It became quiet for some time. Josech waited.

Finally, Leperd said, "I used to be a man named Tychicus—so long ago. I haven't heard that name since my banishment."

Josech didn't know if Leperd would be angry that he hadn't been able to tell him earlier. The opportunity to directly communicate with his wife had been so available all this time, yet he didn't know it. Rebekah didn't know it either. Life could've been sweeter and much more bearable.

Leperd thought for a moment. At one time he would have become angry, and his rage might have manifested in an ugly manner. But now, with inner peace, he tried to understand. He knew his friend wouldn't have done anything to intentionally hurt him. He would have been more than happy to mediate between him and his wife, if he could.

Josech felt remorse as he pleaded, "Please forgive me. I'm so sorry. I'm so sorry. I'm so sorry." Josech understood how life would have been radically better for his friend, and he understood the isolation he'd endured.

Leperd could only imagine how difficult this must have been for Josech. "My friend, you didn't know. Please don't say another word."

Then Leperd thought for a moment. "If you talk with my Rebekah, please pass this on to her: I've come back to God. I have inner peace. I'll be fine."

It had been so long since he communicated with his wife. What could he say to sum up everything he felt? He imagined talking to her so many times over the years. What would he say if he had one more chance to speak to her? He'd rehearsed this moment so many times in his head, and he couldn't believe the time to relay his message had finally arrived. With great emotion, in his voice he said, "Please tell her I love her. I've always loved her—and I always will." He'd spoke his heart. Then he added one more thing. "And tell my son I love him too."

It became silent for some time. Josech had been touched by his words. He couldn't imagine having a wife and a son, then losing them, yet thinking of them for so many years.

"I will." Josech could say no more.

"Farewell, my friend." Leperd held his hair back in order to take one last, long look at his friend. Josech turned toward him. His eyes were empty—lifeless. He had already started to mourn his loss. What a wonderful man, Leperd thought. What a faithful friend. He would miss him.

"Thank you, my friend—Tychicus." Josech recognized him as the man he was and not the leper he'd become. He added his final word, "Farewell."

They both shed tears. They shared sadness at the impending loss. They also shared joy for the time they'd shared. What a bittersweet moment.

Leperd walked away. He'd find a place to sleep, before heading to the burial site of his friend Jazer. There he would die.

Josech remained near the gate. He looked forward to the next time his angel would visit him. He'd relay Leperd's message as soon as the opportunity became available. But she'd never again visit him outside the gate.

CHAPTER 34

The sun had come up several hours earlier, starting another day. Leperd saw it as another day to endure, one more day to add to the seemingly endless collection of days that all blended together. He wondered if this day would be his last. He prayed it would be. How he longed to rest.

It had been nearly eight years since leprosy started to consume him, and not one day went by that he understood why. He'd finally come to a place where he didn't need to know anymore. Since that day on top of Mount Arbel, where he met with God, he'd given the remainder of his days to him to do what he pleased. He lived with peace.

He dreamed of just one more day to spend with his son. One more day to spend time with his wife and hold her in his arms. One more day to look them both in the eyes, at close range, and tell them he loved them. He knew it was an unattainable dream. He believed that someday heaven would bring a joyful reunion.

He'd thought of them each night as he closed his eyes. He had trouble remembering what they looked like at times. It had been so long. He could barely remember Rebekah's voice, and surely his son's voice would be unrecognizable to him. He wondered if he'd recognize Justus if he saw him. He had to be nearly twelve years old now. During this long, lonely journey, his biggest regret had been the loss of time with his son, never to be recovered.

His heart had softened. His anger had gone, and total reliance had taken its place. And though each day seemed to be more difficult now than ever, he experienced his days with peace, which made each day a little easier to accept. The completion of his journey would come soon. He knew his time had come, and he wasn't afraid.

He actually looked forward to the release death would bring. He knew his whole body would soon go numb, and then he'd come to the end of his suffering. He longed to feel the touch of another—finally resting in the arms of God. To this end, he started to pray. "God of my fathers. I pray you'd end this suffering and accept me into your presence—"

Leperd's prayer had just begun when a voice far off interrupted him. He pulled the hair away from his eyes the best he could as he tried to stand up, though his grotesque and deformed frame wouldn't fully allow it. His bones ached, and his joints were stiff. He focused on someone running with determination far in the distance. He saw just a speck of a person at first, who periodically yelled something that he could not understand.

Leperd turned and started to walk away at a slow but rushed pace. If he could just get out of sight, he thought, he wouldn't have to stop and raise his voice with the one-word warning he'd come to despise so intensely. Each time he yelled "unclean," it reminded him of his sad lot. Each passing moment was a constant reminder of that fact without having to hear the cursed declaration coming from his own mouth once again in triplicate. His thirst could not be quenched, and the exertion he'd have to put forth to give this warning would make him even more thirsty. So he labored on.

The man drew closer and closer, and as hard as Leperd tried to move away from him, he realized he would not be able to escape. He knew his options had been reduced to the one he despised so much. He had been forced to do this far too many times. He turned around toward the man who now approached him several hundred yards away. He fell to his knees, putting his head in his numb hands. He thought the man approaching him would have to be blind not to see him.

He then sat up the best he could. Hoping it would be the last time, he yelled at the top of his lungs, "Unclean! Unclean! Unclean!"

He'd grown accustomed to hearing feet scatter in the opposite direction after he made his pronouncement. Slumped in despair, he waited for the man to turn and run as everyone always did. Everyone treated him like the plague—for that he was.

Instead, something happened that Leperd never anticipated. The man stopped dead in his tracks, now less than one hundred yards away. He just stood there. Then he started walking *straight toward him.* With each step, the man drew closer and closer.

He took another deep breath before declaring again, "Unclean! Unclean! Unclean!" He screamed in desperation as he sought to warn this man approaching him. But even with the undeniable warning, the man did not respond. Didn't he know that the law forbid him to come near? How could he not know the law? Didn't he know what it meant to be in the presence of someone identified as unclean?

But the man kept walking. Leperd again yelled his warning, Unclean! Unclean! Unclean!"

The man walked within twenty yards of him.

Leperd couldn't remember the last time a clean person willingly came so close to him. He sensed the closeness as the man breathed heavily. He'd run some distance from the city, and he panted as if he hadn't run like that in a long, long time.

Leperd knew he could give his warning from where he knelt, without having to scream at the top of his parched lungs. Hadn't he given enough warning already? Surely this man must've heard his repeated cries. But one last time he said with a wavering, coarse voice, "Unclean! Unclean! Unclean! Can't you see—I'm unclean?"

As the man tried to catch his breath, he said clearly and softly, "I'm looking for Leperd."

Leperd heard him but didn't believe his own ears. What did he say?

The man spoke again. "Are you... Leperd?"

"What did you say?" he asked in shock. He brushed his hair aside again, though the bright morning sun still filled his eyes.

Did this man just purposely speak directly to him, from such close proximity? Did this man say his name? He thought he must have been imagining it all. Surely his mind was playing tricks on him. Jazer didn't tell him hallucinations would be part of the near-death experience.

Leperd looked again. As he squinted to see despite the sun, a healthy man stood upright before him. For a second, he wondered, *Am I dead?* He thought perhaps he'd passed on and just didn't realize it yet.

He looked again. Could it be? He asked, "Jazer, is that you?" Could this be his friend from the leper colony? How could this be? Could this be heaven?

Leperd touched himself in the chest. He brushed his hand across his face. He was still alive. His hands and feet were numb. His skin had been overtaken with a reddish rash. The aftermath of a recent nosebleed had dried on his cloak. His body felt the exhaustion, which had become a constant companion. And more than ever, his parched throat longed for a drink to quench his thirst. Undoubtedly he had come to the very end of his life. Had his imagination taken control in this moment? Had an angel come to take him away? Had his time finally come?

"Is it time?" he asked as he tried to focus beyond the bright sun again. He could faintly make out the silhouette of the man standing before him. The man spoke again. "Leperd? Is that you... my friend?"

What did he say? Did he just call me friend? Leperd thought. "I don't have any friends, except..." He brought his head up, trying to focus on this stranger again. He looked directly into the eyes of the man who now blocked the sun.

Could it be? No.

As he slowly stood to his feet, he looked again in disbelief. He stared and focused with all he had. He now recognized the man standing before him, though he'd never seen him like this before. He looked directly into his eyes. They were bright and full of life.

They nearly twinkled though the sun was behind him. This just couldn't be. This man had *run* from the city gates looking for *him*? Impossible! Surely he was hallucinating. That would make sense of all of this.

"Leperd?" he asked once more with a wide smile on his face. "I recognize your voice," he said. "I know it's you! Leperd!" He now had his arms outstretched as if he acknowledged his presence.

Leperd stood in disbelief. He had never been delusional, until now. He looked at and heard something logically impossible. He shook his head and rubbed his eyes. No one in their right mind would talk to a leper. Or seek one out. Or welcome one with open arms. Especially the man he thought he saw. He knew him. But this couldn't be.

He looked again. The man still stood before him, though he had now moved a few steps closer. The man walked the last few remaining steps. He now stood just a few feet away—close enough to touch, though he didn't lay his hands on him. Not yet.

The man simply said three words that caught Leperd's attention. "What did you say?" he asked. Although he didn't believe it, he never could have imagined what would unfold in the next few moments.

CHAPTER 35

Once again I paused from telling my story as I looked eye-to-eye with Archippus, who was now more intrigued than ever. Another man wearing a blue sash joined us to listen to the rest of my story.

"Good morning, my friend," the newcomer said with a joyous tone.

"Greetings in the name of the Lord!" I replied as I rose to my feet.

We embraced each other with a brotherly hug.

"Are you telling stories again? I love to hear you tell a good tale. Is this the story of that leper?"

I chuckled and simply smiled in affirmation. "That's quite a nice, blue sash you're wearing," I remarked before realizing this man's intrusion bothered Archippus who longed for the story to continue.

"Well, you know I enjoy the brighter colors."

Archippus saw this man's interruption as rude. This unexpected delay was surely untimely. How dare this stranger walk right into the story during such a dramatic scene. Unwilling to wait even one more moment, Archippus snapped impatiently, "The man standing before Leperd, who was he? What did he say?"

I exchanged a smile with the newcomer before looking off into the distance. I chuckled softly to myself, just once. The man in the blue sash echoed my smile. How he loved hearing this story in particular—which he'd heard many times before. Silently we both relished in the scenes to come.

Impatiently again, Archippus asked, "Tell me the identity of this man! Who was he? What did he say?"

I looked back down into Archippus's eyes as my story continued.

Leperd was confused as to what unfolded before his eyes. How could this be? "What did you say?" he asked.

"Don't give up," the man said again. He became aggravated that he had not been recognized. Surely his identity was obvious by now! Emphatically the man called out, "It's me! It's me!"

Leperd now recognized his voice. He knew his identity. It was shocking to him, though undeniable.

"It's me—Josech!" the man said boldly as his eyes were filling with tears of joy.

Leperd stood still for just a moment. He stared at the man standing before him. "This can't be," Leperd said. "You're blind. You've been blind for so long. But your eyes... how could you run...?"

Right before him stood his only friend, Josech, a man defined by his blindness, but now with the full ability to see. For the first time in Leperd's memory, Josech was somewhere other than on a dirty blanket outside the city gates. He stood upright before him, with open eyes, looking directly at him! How could this be? *He could see!*

"Come with me!" Josech said with excitement in his voice. "You have to see the man who opened my eyes. He just touched my eyes, and now I can see. He's the Christ! The Messiah! I know it! He can help you—"

Leperd stopped him in midsentence, falling to the ground in despair. "I can't go... *in the town*. It's forbidden!" What he'd accepted for so many years had just emerged from him without a thought. He knew all too well the restrictions his curse demanded. He'd been living under the restraints of them for so long, and deviating from them in any fashion had never been a consideration. How could he oppose the laws and standards set down for him—a leper? Filled with sudden grief, he said in his rough voice, "Can't you see? I'm unclean! Unclean! Unclean! I'm a leper!"

It became silent for just a second. Leperd fell down on his hands and knees nearly facedown on the ground as he started to sob. Eventually he looked up slowly, peering through the hair that covered his face. Tears streamed down his cheeks, carving lines down his dirty face.

Josech continued looking at him, unwilling to leave without him.

Leperd finally looked into Josech's new eyes. He saw hope. He saw confidence. He saw evidence of a second chance. As a result, for the first time, he considered: maybe God had heard his prayer. After all this time, had his time come? Would God possibly give him the hope of a second chance?

He picked himself up slowly and looked off into the distance. The city sat afar off, but he could see it. He glanced back at his friend. A smile once more emerged on Josech's face as he sensed a change of heart. He raised his eyebrows as if to ask the question, "Are you ready?"

Leperd just looked at Josech. A new man stood before him. God had surely touched him, and the evidence of the fact overwhelmed him. How humbling that Josech's first reaction to becoming whole had been to find him and offer him the same hope—if only he had enough faith.

Leperd looked down at his withered feet. Two toes were missing from his left foot, and the rest of them were curled under. His other foot looked similar. He stared at them for just a second—first, the right; then the left. Then without looking up, he said, "Let's go... for a walk—into town!" He started taking one slow step after another until his pace accelerated. His strides were slow by most standards, but with a new sense of determination, he pressed on. For the first time in a long time, he had purpose.

Josech walked right by his friend's side. More than ever, he wanted to help his faithful friend as they slowly neared the city gates of Tiberias.

"Mother. Are you coming?" Justus called out to Rebekah. "The teacher they've been talking about has come into the city. Are you coming?"

Isaac joined in as he saw his nephew's desperation. "Rebekah. It's time to go, my child."

Rebekah wanted to see and hear this man whom some thought could be the long-awaited Messiah. Rumors had been spreading, and she wanted to make her own determination. Soon Justus and Rebekah, accompanied by Uncle Isaac and Epaphras, joined the crowd gathered in the courtyard. Her heart filled with amazement at this man named Jesus. He spoke with the authority of someone who had been sent directly from God himself. Such wisdom, such insight—there was no denying the fact: this man was special indeed.

Suddenly Rebekah started walking away from the crowd. Justus followed after her. "Mother, where are you going?" He didn't understand.

"Son, please stay with your uncle. Please."

Justus returned to Isaac's side as Rebekah headed to the temple. Before long, her walking turned to running. She ran through the streets looking up, seeing the temple drawing near. She climbed the steps and headed toward the doors. She walked in and headed straight for the altar. She fell down on her face and started to pray. "O God of my fathers, I feel you've summoned me here at this time. Please hear the cries of your humble servant. I feel the need to pray for my husband. Oh, how I still love him. I plead of you, my God, on his behalf. Work in his life this day."

Her earnest prayer continued as, unbeknown to her, Leperd and Josech approached the city gates at that very moment.

Even from the road outside the gates, they both noticed the unusual quietness surrounding the area. Where had everyone gone? It seemed the normal activity of the gateway had ceased. Something was happening, but what?

They'd soon find out.

CHAPTER 36

As Josech and Leperd stood outside the city gate, Josech picked up his old blanket, which still lay in the dirt where he once sat. He shook it, rolled it up, and then put it under his arm.

Looking through the gates, they saw a large crowd assembled inside the city. As they stepped between the gates, several fruit carts seemed abandoned as wicker baskets full of fruit sat unattended. Flowers in vases, carpets, blankets, and other goods surrounded several carts, yet no one supervised them. These vendors, like the courtyard shopkeepers and their patrons, were all compelled to join the crowd that gathered to listen to the Teacher.

As they stopped to catch their breath, Leperd's mind flashed back to that courtyard. He had walked through it so many times so many years ago. He recalled his last few memories of this place: that desperate leper attacked him here. He last held his wife in this place—and heard her wailing, which haunted him all these years. In this very location, his life turned toward the nightmare he'd been living through the past eight years. Would this be the same place he'd find restoration? He could only hope so.

At the same time, Josech stared at the place where he'd sat for so many years. He couldn't believe he could see it. He couldn't believe he had the ability to be somewhere else other than there. His heart filled with great emotion. He just had to bring Leperd to the place of restoration, which came through healing. What a great place to be! Josech was so thankful.

The time had come. Josech turned and looked at Leperd. "Here. Cover yourself. Don't let anyone see you." He handed him his old, dirty blanket. They both knew what kind of reaction they'd anticipate should a leper walk openly into a crowd, especially *in town*.

Leperd struggled to slip the blanket over his back. He pulled it up over his head and hid the best he could, allowing just enough room to see in front of him. As he peeked out, he looked into the face of Josech, who said, "Let's go!" His eager smile indicated what he believed to be just ahead of them: restoration.

Josech led the way as Leperd followed close behind him, holding onto his cloak. As they neared the back of the crowd, they stopped. Josech stood straight up and looked beyond them. No one noticed either of them *yet.*

Josech took a moment to look at the one who gave him the ability to do so. What a beautiful sight. He listened for just a moment. The Teacher's words were powerful and authoritative. Coupled with the fact that the miracle Jesus had performed in his own life was still fresh, his wisdom again reinforced his thought. *Truly, this man is the Messiah!*

Again, he looked back at his friend, smiled, and said, "Let's go!" Leperd was ready.

Josech put his head down as he started pushing his way through the crowd as he cleared a way for his friend to follow behind him. The people in the crowd were so enthralled with Jesus's teaching that by the time they noticed someone pushing through, Josech and Leperd had already passed by.

They moved all the way toward the front of the crowd when Josech turned around and looked into Leperd's eyes. "It's time," he said. Without any further warning, he grabbed the blanket and pulled hard. Such a sudden revelation caught everyone in the crowd by surprise. In fact, it even startled Leperd as the blanket flew from his back. It all happened so quickly.

Leperd fell to the ground for just a moment before dramatically rising to his feet.

Almost instantly, someone realized what happened and shouted, "Unclean! Unclean! Unclean!" Others joined him, while some simply gasped as panic ensued. The crowd scattered. Even the Teacher's disciples started to run a safe distance away. Leperd stood alone in the courtyard with the one who had given Josech sight. As he peered through his long hair, he glimpsed into the Teacher's eyes. Unlike the fear he'd just witnessed in so many others, in this man's eyes, he found peace. Jesus had been waiting for him.

Calmly Josech continued to take slow steps back toward the retreating crowd, allowing Leperd to enjoy this private encounter with the Master. As he stepped back, his smile continued. He stared at Jesus, seeing compassion in his face. He heard a few people gasp as they started to murmur, "Isn't that the blind beggar?" Josech heard them but didn't respond. His eyes focused on Jesus and his friend, and everything else at that moment did not matter.

The time had come. Leperd fell to the ground with his face in the dirt. Over and over and over again, he started to plead, "Lord, if you are willing, you can make me clean! If you are willing, you can make me clean! If you are willing, you can make me clean!"

As he lay in that humble, dependent, and desperate position, this outcast felt what he hadn't felt in years. It had to have come as a shock. He pondered what just happened as he thought, *Could this be? Surely that is not the pressure of a hand, the touch of a clean person.* And it had not been a light hand; this man had firmly grabbed his shoulder. He'd taken hold of him. It almost startled him. *I haven't been touched like that in years*, he thought to himself. *Oh, thank you for touching me!* He had expressed his thankfulness in silence, though somehow he knew this man heard it.

Leperd looked up as he brought himself to his knees. He peered out, realizing the Teacher had bent low and was now also on his knee. He had come right beside him, down to his level. The Master's hand still grasped his shoulder, and he could feel his strength.

"What's your name?" Jesus asked with quiet compassion. He did not ask for the sake of the crowd, who now stood afar off. He intended this to be a private and intimate moment between the two of them. By the tone in his voice, Leperd sensed his genuine spirit of kindness and concern.

He couldn't believe this man of such prominence would touch him, much less speak to him. He lowered his head as his hair once again draped over his face. Quietly he said, "Lord, my name... is Leperd."

They were accompanied by silence for just a moment. Slowly Leperd raised his head as he peered through his hair as best he could. Jesus still focused his gaze on him. His eyes were unwavering as a smile emerged across his face.

"Is not your name... Tychicus?"

Did he say "Tychicus"? Leperd thought and fell to the ground once more. Who might this man be that he would call him by his given name? How could he know that, unless he had been sent from God? In that moment, he knew this man was the Messiah, just as Josech claimed.

Instantly he felt unworthy to be in this man's presence, being a dirty, malformed, cursed outcast. His unworthiness covered him like Josech's blanket had moments before, and he knew it. He was *unclean, unclean, unclean.*

Then the most amazing thing happened. In a quiet yet strong voice, Jesus said, "I am willing."

Leperd fell back into the reality of the curse he'd lived with for so many years. All the restrictions, laws, and limitations flooded back into his mind. They'd been the standards that his whole existence revolved around. The fact that this man would speak directly to him, in and of itself, brought disbelief. He thought, *Did he just speak to me? Does he know he's not allowed to talk to me? Did he just speak?* Was *that compassion, married to power, that I heard in his voice? Did he just say, 'I am willing'? I'm willing? No, no, maybe you don't understand.*

Filled with emotion, Leperd began to shake. "But, Lord, I'm dirty."

Again Jesus said, "I am willing."

"No, but I'm declared unclean."

"I am willing."

"No, but I'm rejected. No one wants me."

"I am willing."

"But I'm *so* lonely."

"Yes, I know. And I'm *so* willing."

"But I'm undeserving."

"I know. I'm willing."

"Can't you see me? I'm hideous!"

"I see you, and I'm willing."

"But no one else will take me."

"I will. I am willing."

Leperd understood, as did Josech, Jesus had spoken with sincerity. When he said, "I am willing," he understood there wasn't an ounce of unwillingness in his being. He was completely and unreservedly willing. He could not be more willing!

Jesus tightened his grip on Leperd's shoulder as he said, "I am willing. Be clean. And let me be the first to say, welcome back to community."

Jesus stood up taking his hand off Leperd's shoulder.

"Wait, what's happening?" Leperd asked under his breath. "I feel the surge of new life flooding my veins. Fingers are growing out of my stumps, I mean, toes are growing out of the scar tissue. I feel like color is returning to me. My skin is smooth. I think, I think I might be clean. I think I'm clean. I don't know, but I think I'm clean. Yes, I'm clean. *Yes, I'm clean!* Wait, my voice isn't hoarse anymore. I'm clean! Clean! Clean!"

The people in the courtyard gasped. They'd just witnessed a miraculous healing right in front of their own eyes.

Some of them started walking slowly toward Leperd, who'd already started jumping for joy. He ran back and forth, proclaiming his cleanness over and over again.

Most in the crowd still didn't understand the identity of this man who had been healed. His long hair still covered his face.

His clothes were overly torn and dirty. But undoubtedly, this man had been leprous, and he had been made wonderfully whole. He was clean.

As Tychicus ran, he brushed his hair back, looking into the faces of some he hadn't seen in so long. He recognized them, though they were puzzled as to his identity. They'd considered him dead for all these years.

As Tychicus looked into the face of one man, he said, "Timotheus! Praise God! I'm clean!"

The man's jaw dropped. He asked in disbelief, "Tychicus?"

Another old man beside him nearly went into shock. "Timotheus, what did you say?"

He smiled in wonder and amazement before declaring, "I think... it's Tychicus!"

The old man couldn't believe his ears. He looked at his dear friend, Epaphras, who'd also come to hear the Teacher. He also wore a look of disbelief. The old man turned to his nephew, who stood beside him, still unaware of what had really just happened. "God be praised!" he chuckled. It had indeed come to pass. They received God's work, and it was amazing in their sight.

"Come! Let's get the lambs!" he exclaimed.

"The lambs?" the boy said in a surprised tone. He knew what that meant.

They headed off rejoicing.

Tychicus suddenly stopped dead in his tracks. He'd stirred up the crowd, and now they were all making such a noise. He turned and looked through them. His eyes met with the eyes of the Master. For just a brief second, they looked at each other. For a brief moment, it seemed like the crowd became silent. Once again, the two of them were set apart from everyone else in the courtyard.

Jesus smiled.

Then a most interesting thing happened. As if perfectly timed, a white butterfly appeared in front of Tychicus. It fluttered before him for a few seconds. He lifted his hand as the butterfly flew over and landed on his finger. It sat there just a moment, spreading its wings, as if satisfied that it had been noticed. To Tychicus, it symbolized the fulfillment of a promise. He understood this to be a symbol of new life—a pure and fresh beginning. Then slowly and quietly the butterfly fluttered off.

Tychicus dramatically ran across the courtyard, pushing people out of his way. He just had to get to Jesus! He fell at his feet and grabbed his garment, exclaiming, "My Lord and my God!" Overwhelmed with joy, he began to sob uncontrollably.

Once again, Jesus placed his firm hand on Tychicus's shoulder. He held it there as the crowd started to gather around once again. Slowly the crowd started to cheer even louder. They rejoiced with this healed leper, and they cheered for the miracle worker.

Finally, Jesus spoke, "Stand, my friend."

Tychicus stood to his feet and looked directly into the eyes of Jesus again as the crowd hushed.

"Tychicus," Jesus said, addressing him.

Many in the crowd gasped. The identity of this man had been revealed to their amazement. A man they'd considered dead had been brought back to life, and it was astonishing!

Jesus continued. His words were unexpected as he gave him an order. "Don't tell anyone, but go, show yourself to the priest and offer the sacrifices that Moses commanded for your cleansing as a testimony to them."

Tychicus looked back at Jesus with disbelief. He couldn't believe what he just heard. He simply asked, "What?" How could he not tell *everyone* what had just happened? What kind of a joke could this be? As he looked into Jesus's face, Tychicus knew he meant what he had said. So he decided to do exactly as he had been told.

One last time, he looked into Jesus's eyes and said, "Thank you, Lord."

Jesus smiled again before saying, "Now go."

Tychicus immediately turned, intending to head for the temple. The first person in his way was Josech, whose eager smile had turned into one of extreme joy. The two men embraced. Then they laughed. Then Tychicus ran all the way to the temple, not letting anyone stand in his way.

CHAPTER 37

"Wait!" Archippus said. "How could that be?"

I couldn't help but smile. "That's how it happened."

"I'm not questioning your story, but Jesus told him not to tell *anyone?* How could you not tell *everyone?* I mean, wasn't he already telling people in the courtyard? He had been a leper for all those years. Then he was miraculously healed. Then he told no one? How could anyone keep that to themselves? And why would Jesus even ask such a thing?"

"Well, I'm not sure why Jesus made such a statement at that time. We may never know, though I do have several ideas."

Archippus couldn't wait to hear my insight.

"I think Jesus might have been saying, 'Please don't spread this and make a big scene about who I am. Let me do that.' Jesus also knew the law required a person healed of leprosy would have to offer certain sacrifices to make up for all the sacrifices they couldn't offer while they were exiled. And then they would go through an eight-day cleansing restoration ritual that included a seven-day party thrown in their honor by the community. Jesus was saying, 'I want the priest to know that I'm not opposed to the law, so go and obey the law and go through the ceremonial process.' He wanted it to be known he did not stand opposed to the law. He didn't disregard the law. But he wanted the community that rejected him to confirm his healing and celebrate his restoration. He set the stage for letting the community confirm and celebrate what he'd done. But we'll never really know why Jesus said that."

Just then a pretty young girl walked up to us. "Excuse me, Grandfather. We'll be leaving soon for the festival. Grandmother wanted me to remind you. We're going up along the sea, right?"

Once again I smiled with delight. How I loved my granddaughter. "Yes. I'll be home shortly, my dear," I said as she returned my smile and walked away. "That's my daughter's girl," I said with pride. I looked away again reminiscing. "We named our daughter Zoe. That means 'life.' Oh, precious new life," I said. "She's beautiful—just like her mother."

Archippus sat impatiently, waiting for the story to continue, and I sensed this. "Well, my friend, let me tell you my favorite part of this story. I think there could have possibly been another reason Jesus wanted him to go directly to the temple."

I continued.

Tychicus ran up the temple steps with a smile crossing his face. He was clean! Such freedom! Such joy! God was so good! How he wanted to sing God's praise with all his might. He didn't slow down as he pushed through the doors, making a rather emphatic entrance. He had arrived exactly where God wanted him at that moment, and he vowed he would never again stray from his walk with him. His obedience had been demonstrated, and it was time for his reward.

He'd entered the temple unashamed as everyone became aware of his presence, especially one woman who'd been earnestly kneeling at the altar in prayer.

Tychicus stopped dead in his tracks. He stared. He couldn't believe it. There she was, right before him.

She turned around, looking over her shoulder, still on her knees. She stood to her feet slowly and faced him. She also stared before tears started filling her eyes. The day she'd prayed for had finally come.

Step by step, they started to walk toward each other. Each step escalated as they ran into each other's arms.

Tychicus embraced his wife, which he hadn't done in nearly eight years. Rebekah's tears now turned into a fountain of joy, streaming down her cheeks as she clung on to her husband with all her might. He felt strong, just like she remembered. How she'd longed for this moment and prayed for it to come to pass.

The last time someone held onto Tychicus with such passion, it led down a road of misery and tribulation. He'd come full circle, and he'd now be the one holding on with all he had. He would never let Rebekah go.

They both fell to their knees. Rebekah held back Tychicus's long hair. She looked into his eyes. She couldn't believe he had come back to her, and he had been made whole.

"Praise be to God!" she said tenderly.

Tychicus smiled as he responded with joy, "Praise be to God!"

They declared their love for each other as Rebekah thanked God for answering her prayers. She had prayed for God to do whatever it would take to bring her husband back to himself. She understood now that Tychicus needed to go through this trial to break him and bring him back to God. God had done more than she ever dreamed, and she declared God's excellencies.

Laban and Massa, who had been in the courtyard, entered the temple. They knew something unusual was taking place in this solemn and reverent place. They'd seen Rebekah regularly praying for all these years, and now she embraced a dirty man with ragged clothing right in the aisle of the temple. Could it be? Before they could start rejoicing, another priest stepped forward.

"What are you doing, acting this way in this holy place?" Jotham demanded. He understood Rebekah was one of the participants, and he didn't yet understand who she held in her arms. He had not gone to see the Teacher and had no idea what had just happened. Partially out of jealousy, his unjust anger raged.

"God has performed a miracle!" Laban proclaimed in awe with his hands raised toward heaven.

"Blessed be the name of the Lord our God!" added Massa.

Amon, who now joined them, stood with his hands raised to heaven, rejoicing in God's goodness.

Tychicus stood to his feet with a smile crossing his face as he approached Jotham.

"Guards!" he called out instinctively. He recalled the incident when Tychicus was declared unclean and how he attempted to attack him. The guards rushed over, though stood from a distance to see what might happen.

Tychicus and Jotham now stood face-to-face, looking into each other's eyes. Jotham stood overtaken with shock. He never expected to see Tychicus standing before him. The tension broke as Tychicus said, "The Lord instructed me to come and show myself to you. God has made me whole!" A smile emerged on his face as the rage inside the priest became even more intense.

Just then, the doors opened again as a young boy ran in with several lambs. "Father!" he cried. "I brought the sacrificial lambs."

Tychicus turned around. His son stood in his sight for the first time in so many years. How he'd grown! He'd become a young man. He looked strong. He'd learned to be in his father's absence. Again, tears started welling up in his eyes. Emotion flooded into his whole being. Such joy! Tychicus had so much he wanted to say, but he could not find one word. He slowly placed his hand on the top of his head.

Justus responded, placing his hand on his own head. Amid tears and with great emotion, he said, "Father, I'm this tall!"

Tychicus and Justus ran into each other's arms. The moment both of them had dreamed of had come to be. Tychicus wasted no more time. He said what he wished he'd said the last time he saw his son, eight years ago in the courtyard. "I'm so proud of you, my son. I love you!" Again, he embraced his son and held him tight.

Rebekah wrapped her arms around her husband and her son as the whole family had come together again. What a miraculous event! Uncle Isaac watched with a wide smile as he finally made it to the temple, out of breath. Such joy! Such reunion! Much praise was offered to God.

In the midst of this time of jubilation, Tychicus told Rebekah and Justus he had something he had to do. He walked away from them, heading toward the altar once more. He walked up a few steps and once again faced Jotham, the chief priest, who had caused him and his family such heartache.

He simply smiled and softly said, "Jotham, I forgive you."

Once again, Jotham stood in shock. These were the last words he ever thought he'd hear from this man who had hated him so deeply.

Tychicus had never been in a better place. He had truly been forgiven, and as a result, he was forgiving.

This joyous occasion would be hindered by only one man whose evil heart refused to see or accept all God had done. From a selfish, unrepentant heart, the temple was filled with a loud, horrific cry of disenchantment: "Noooo!" Jotham's long, agonizing scream bore witness to the fact that he realized his hopes of attaining Rebekah were forever dashed. His cry of selfishness turned to anguish as everyone now stared at him. It became oddly and unusually quiet.

Rebekah joined her husband at the altar, holding his arm. She looked into the evil eyes of the chief priest speaking the last word, which seemed to echo throughout the temple. She reminded him of his own words, "When you sin against God, there will be a reckoning."

Instantly Jotham's skin started to break out in a severe rash. The curse he'd so willingly welcomed into Tychicus's life would now embrace every aspect of his. He wouldn't, however, ever experience restoration.

Tychicus gathered his family and the sacrificial lambs as Laban led them to the place of sacrifice. Massa set off to start preparations for the eight days of the cleansing restoration ritual.

Amon, the high priest, along with the temple guards, escorted Jotham to the infirmary.

CHAPTER 38

Archippus sat on the temple steps wanting more. The story surely hadn't ended, had it? I paused as Archippus said, "This surely isn't the end of the story. There must be more. Isn't it just the beginning for Tychicus?"

"A good question," I replied with a smile, "but let me ask you something more important. Isn't it just the beginning for *you*, Archippus?"

Archippus thought about the predicament that led him to the temple this day. He had temporarily forgotten about his own drama. Instantly all his concerns rushed back to his mind.

Before he could say another word, I continued, "Archippus, there's a reason I told you this story. You see, we're all spiritual lepers in need of cleansing. We can all identify with Tychicus, can't we? Because isn't he really just us, and aren't we really just him?"

Archippus hadn't considered that but now realized how true my words really were. I placed my hand on Archippus's shoulder, looked directly into his eyes, and continued, "In Scripture, leprosy is a living illustration of the incurable disease called 'sin' and its all-contaminating effects. Archippus, you're a spiritual leper, as we all are. We all suffer from this disease that attacks the nerves—not of the skin—of the heart, causing us to lose feeling and become numb. And before we know it, we eventually stop noticing that we are doing harm and slowly killing ourselves. We're socially exiled, standing on the outskirts of true community, not meaningfully a part of God's people—God's family. We hide our identity, our unkempt souls behind overgrown facades. We're spiritually condemned, because after all, we've all sinned and fallen short of the glory of God. We're all covered in filthy rags anytime we try and make up for what we lack because of this disease by doing 'good things' for God. We, as lepers, are all sentenced to death, even though we live, for the wages of sin is death. We're all dead in our sins and trespasses in which we live. We're all, indeed, dead men walking."

Archippus sat and listened more intently than ever. I could sense he realized I had spoken with seasoned wisdom, I had spoken the truth. He could now relate personally with the story of Tychicus. For the first time, he realized his problem had actually been a spiritual one.

I continued, "We've had this condition for years. Every part of our life has been affected by this disease. And if we could see through spiritual eyes, the sight of our sin would be so repulsive, so disturbing that we'd look at a literal leper and think him beautiful. So repulsive is the condition our sin has left us in. We're all unclean...unclean...unclean."

Archippus sat in comtemplation, looking back into his mind's eye. Surely he must have imagined Leperd in his most hideous condition, perhaps envisioning his hopelessness and his uselessness. He could vividly imagine his grotesque frame. He considered all of his uncleanness, which had gotten worse and worse over the years. Nothing visually pleasing could be seen in him. He imagined the leper in all his wretchedness, and no one would ever choose the word "beautiful" to describe him. It really helped him understand just how ugly his sin was in God's eyes. His sin was far more repulsive than all of that! His thoughts were interrupted once again.

"You see, Archippus, a spiritual leper is anyone who's been contaminated by sin and its effects. Anyone who suffers from this condition can only be healed at the feet of Jesus. We're all spiritual lepers in need of cleaning." I smiled offering hope. Then tenderly and lovingly, I added, "And Jesus still cleans spiritual lepers. Lepers like me and lepers like you! He made me whole, and he can do the same for you!"

Archippus felt conviction. He knew his sin was great. He'd been trying to handle his burden alone, a weight no man can carry. He fell before me and confessed, "I need to be cleansed. I'm a spiritual leper. Please tell me what I must do."

Nothing brought more joy to my heart than sharing the gospel, which I had done countless times after telling this story.

"Archippus, we've all sinned and fallen short of the glory of God. While many people tell us they love us, God showed us his love. God demonstrated his own love for us by this: while we were still sinners—with a fist clenched toward heaven—Jesus Christ, God's Son, died for us."

Archippus looked up in amazement. "This man, the Teacher, died for us?"

"Yes. He was God's Son, the promised Messiah, and he gave his life to shed his blood to cover our sins—the perfect sacrifice, once and for all. This happened just about forty years ago, and I remember it like it happened yesterday. They crucified him. They watched him die. They buried him in a rich man's tomb. Then he rose from the grave to show God had accepted his sacrifice for our atonement! I saw him—he was alive! I'll never forget him." He looked off into the distance, with a wide smile.

I had been changed and a joy and hope could be seen in my countenance. Archippus longed for God to work in his life as he asked, "So what must I do to be saved?"

"If we confess our sins, he is faithful and just and will forgive us our sins and cleanse us from all unrighteousness. The spiritual leper can be cleansed! Archippus, the wages of sin is death, but the gift of God is eternal life in Christ Jesus our Lord. If you confess with your mouth, 'Jesus is Lord,' and believe in your heart that God raised him from the dead, you will be saved."

I paused. The story had come to an end, and now it was time for Archippus to respond. I looked at him, saying one last line, "I urge you to be reconciled to God."

Archippus smiled. He'd found what he had been searching for—hope. He cried out, "Lord Jesus, forgive me, a sinner—a spiritual leper. Forgive me for trying to live by my own strength.

Forgive me for all the wrong in me. I need you. Thank you for dying in my place, shedding your blood to cover my sins. Thank you for rising from the dead. Please save me! Please cleanse me! Be my Lord. Be my King. Amen."

Smiling, I proclaimed, "Archippus, you're clean! And let me be the first to welcome you to community. You're now my brother in the Lord." I gave Archippus a fatherly hug.

Archippus felt new. The weight he'd been carrying had finally been lifted. He had become a new creature. He was forgiven! He was clean!

The man who'd been sitting next to us, wearing a blue sash, put his hand on Archippus's shoulder, saying, "My brother, welcome to the family of God." He smiled, sharing my enthusiasm.

I addressed him, "Well, my friend, it's time for me to meet up with Rebekah, Justus, and Zoe. We're off to the festival! May God be praised!"

The man wearing the blue sash spoke up. "Tell Tamar I send my greetings. I know she's well up in years. And give Rebekah, *my unseen angel*, a hug and a kiss for me."

"I sure will, Josech, my friend." One last time I smiled at him and at Archippus before turning to walk away.

"Wait," Archippus said. He looked at the man who'd been sitting beside him. "Your name is…Josech?"

He just smiled before saying, "I was blind, but now I see—praise God!"

Archippus then turned to look at me as I started to walk away. I paused for a moment before turning around, looking directly into his eyes. I smiled. I knew my work had been completed. Aloud I prayed, "Thank you, Lord, for allowing me to offer hope to the hopeless, as you brought hope to me."

As I turned to walk away, I heard Archippus ask Josech, "Who is that old man? He said his name was Simon, but who is he?"

"He told you his name was *Simon*?" Josech chuckled as he placed his hand once again on Archippus's shoulder. "He does tell people from time to time to call him Simon. But that is not his real name. You see, the name 'Simon' is the Greek form of the Hebrew name 'Shim'on,' which means 'he has heard.' And I can testify that he, God, has heard the prayers of my dear friend. He has heard an abundance of prayers offered by his lovely wife too. There are few prayer warriors that can compare to her!"

For the first time, Archippus really understood the storyteller's true identity. A wide smile started to emerge across his face upon this realization. I heard him say, "So this old man is..." He didn't finish his sentence as I saw awe on his smiling face.

I smiled back as I heard Josech continue, "I used to call him Leperd, but Jesus gave him his life back. Jesus gave him everything back and more. I choose to call him by his given name. To me, he will forevermore be Tychicus—to the glory of God!"

— A SUMMATION —

JESUS IS IN THE
BUSINESS OF CLEANING SPIRITUAL LEPERS

The sermon that inspired this novel "A Leper Like Me" concluded with the following challenge:

> This story is a vivid reminder that there is hope for lepers like me. There is also a reminder, if you really think about it, that Jesus will not just heal any leper. *He doesn't heal every leper.* He only heals the one who comes and asks him in desperate dependence.
>
> He will not heal the cute and self-conscious leper. Because this is a person who says, "I would go to him, but what would people think? I don't know that I have the big words or that I look the part." Hear me out! You are not desperate enough. You are still concerned about what people will think, and you will get *nothing* from him.
>
> If you are worried about being cute and being well thought of and obeying cultural norms because they are still too important to you, you will get *nothing* from him. If you are thinking, "What happens if I'm so stirred to fall on my face in his presence, or to shout out his name in his presence, and people look at me with condemning thoughts? Ooh, that's too risky. I don't know if it's worth getting to Jesus if that's the cost," you're not going to get *anything* from him. You haven't gotten to the place where you say, "I don't care. I've got to get to Jesus—excuse me."
>
> How desperate are you to feel his touch and to hear the words "be clean"? You can't be cute and get the cleansing that you so desperately need.
>
> Jesus is not going to cleanse the mildly contaminated leper. This is a person who says, "You know, I only have

a little bit of leprosy. It's not really bad leprosy like that homosexual person or like that adulterous person. My leprosy is a little milder than that. Me? I'm just a little blotchy on the arms. But you know, I guess I might as well go to Jesus to get this stain off my theological suit. You know we all have a few 'issues.' It couldn't hurt to go to church once a week and get a touch-up from Jesus." You, my friend, will get *nothing* from him because your sin is not sinful enough in your own eyes. Your dirt is not dirty enough.

If you have come to Jesus because you have "issues," he won't clean you. If you only have a couple of blotches on your skin, he won't restore you. If all you need is a slight touch-up, he won't touch you. *Jesus Christ does not give religious manicures—he gives spiritual overhauls!* And you've got to really need it—not just kind of with issues.

How needy are you to feel his touch and to hear the words "be clean"?

It is sad. Our reputation in the community, Christ's Covenant Church, I've heard it many times. We have a church of "clean people." Just mildly contaminated. Our leprosy isn't too bad. "Those people are okay. They seem to have things together. Have you heard how they talk and see how they dress?"

I'm saying, "If we are mildly contaminated, *get me out of here!*" Because it means Jesus Christ will not be walking up and down the aisles touching people who really need him. I don't want to be around mildly contaminated people. I don't want to be *mildly contaminated*. I want to come to him and say, "I am completely full of leprosy, and only your touch can restore me!"

Interestingly, Jesus won't heal or clean the overly sinful. This is the person who says, "No, you don't know how bad my sin is. I've sinned for so long, and I've done so many bad things. It's too bad for him to deal with. I'm just too sinful." I ask you, my friend, "Where are you going to go? Where *else* are you going to go?" Because if he can't do it, no one can. If he won't do it, no one will. You've underestimated his compassionate grace and you will get *nothing* from him because you are not dependent enough.

And especially to you that might be in that situation, feeling overly sinful. Friend, he came to seek and save the lost. There is a reason Luke tells us this guy was *full* of leprosy. There wasn't an ounce of him that wasn't affected by leprosy. And do you remember what Jesus did? He touched him and said, "Be clean."

There is no sin too great that Jesus cannot cleanse it. Don't let the feeling of incredible sinfulness keep you away from him. God made him who knew no leprosy or isolation or rejection or separation from community or the feeling of filth to become all those things for us so that in him we might become clean—the righteousness of God.

I don't know in which situation you are in. Maybe you're self-conscious. Even now you are saying, "I *need* to encounter Jesus Christ and deal with my sin. But what will people think? I've been going to church for years. What would people think if I did that?" I urge you, humble yourself, fall on your face, and ask him to clean you. *He will!* There is not an ounce of him that will be unwilling to clean you.

Maybe you might be thinking, "You know, I've done well most of my life. I haven't really rebelled majorly, and even right now the thing that I struggle with are regular things. Nothing really overly contaminating." I plead with you. Come to him and confess that your sin is utterly sinful, and only he will cleanse you. *And he will!* In the moment you ask him, he will do it.

Maybe you are feeling over sinful. You've just done so much. You've messed up your marriage. You've messed up your life. And you just cannot fathom how Jesus Christ could possibly still touch you. Please hear me say, "He will make you clean. Just ask him."

I don't know what your condition is or where you are. But I would encourage you, don't put off dealing with him. You know how it gets. We get into the street, we get to lunch, we have a conversation, we watch a game, and the next time we think about it, it's gone. I urge you. Deal with him now.

Lord, I ask that by your Spirit, you would move in the hearts of each one of us, that we might stand humbly before you, and deal with you regarding the leprosy of our hearts. I plead with you, Jesus, touch life after life today, making people clean, that they would sense the fresh air of sins forgiven, restored to you, and restored to community. Give courage to anyone who knows they must meet with you. Do your amazing work, please, transforming lives for your glory. In Jesus's name, we pray. Amen.

As a spiritual leper, there's hope for you. Jesus still heals those who come to him in desperate dependence. Consider these verses:

- For all have sinned and fall short of the glory of God.

  —Romans 3:23

- But God demonstrates his own love for us by this: while we were still sinners, Christ died for us.

  —Romans 5:8

- If we confess our sins, he is faithful and just and will forgive us our sins and cleanse us from all unrighteousness.

  —1 John 1:9

- For the wages of sin is death, but the gift of God is eternal life in Christ Jesus our Lord.

  —Romans 6:23

- If you confess with your mouth, "Jesus is Lord," and believe in your heart that God raised him from the dead, you will be saved.

  —Romans 10:9

I urge you to be reconciled to God! Call upon the name of the Lord Jesus Christ and be cleansed today! Confess "Jesus is Lord" and believe that God raised him from the dead. Then start living the abundant life God intended you to live—and be welcomed back to community!

It's important to find a good church that can help you grow in your faith. Find other Christians who can encourage you and whom you can be accountable to. Read God's Word, the Bible, and pray. Then tell someone what God has done for you!

ABOUT THE AUTHOR

Marc Thomas Eckel was born and raised in Madison Heights, Michigan, a northern suburb of Detroit. He is the Creative Director for Blue Spaghetti, LLC, a creative arts company. He has been a performance artist with Splat Experience, a Christian Performance Art Ministry, since 2002. He currently resides in the small country town of Claypool, Indiana with his wife Juli. Together they have three sons: Beau Nicholas, Tyler Matthew and Andrew John Thomas.